Praise for ***England is Mine***

'Gripping, intelligent, streetwise and absolutely contemporary, *England is Mine* is a stunning first novel. It's a piercing depiction of online radicalisation that I sped through with appalled delight. Hard to think how it could be any more timely'
Toby Litt, author of *Exhibitionism*

'A truly thrilling and innovative writer. His portrayal of radicalisation, of the strangeness and loneliness of a life lived on the internet, is subtle, entirely believable, fresh and compelling. A brilliant, original book'
Rachel Connolly, author of *Lazy City*

England Is Mine

NICOLAS PADAMSEE

First published in Great Britain in 2024 by Serpent's Tail,
an imprint of PROFILE BOOKS LTD
29 Cloth Fair
London
EC1A 7JQ
www.serpentstail.com

10 9 8 7 6 5 4 3 2 1

Typeset in Freight Text by MacGuru Ltd
Designed by Barneby Ltd
Printed and bound in Great Britain by Clays Ltd, Elcograf S.p.A.

A CIP record for this book can be obtained from the British Library

ISBN: 978 1 80081 951 1
eISBN: 978 1 80081 952 8

FSC
www.fsc.org
MIX
Paper | Supporting responsible forestry
FSC® C018072

For Kabir

‘It was not you who ate the idea, but the idea that ate you.’

– Dostoevsky, *Demons*

I

David

THE PRE-SHOW MUSIC STOPS. Darkness. A plastic cup whizzes over David, showering him with beer. He laughs and runs a hand through his hair. Brixton Academy, Karl Williams, a gig he's looked forward to for eight months. He's wearing two T-shirts: the one he came in plus a new exclusive one from the merch stall with tonight's tour date. The girl in front screams, starts to video, wrists wrapped in red and black barbed-wire gummy bracelets. He's tall enough to see over her phone and all the other phones. Zoe, his stepsister, not so. Fans jostle to get closer. In shards of smoke and sherbet light, Karl walks on, swigging a bottle of wine, and salutes the crowd. 'Good evening, London.' The crush worsens, helping David and Zoe slide into the pit.

Karl opens with 'Sleeping Pills' – a song by his former band, Salomé. Guitar jangles, spiky and blue. David closes his eyes to savour the moment and finds himself tumbling left in a sway. Zoe grabs hold of him and tumbles too. Karl yanks the collar of his shirt and claps and points and punches the air. 'I'll return empty-handed,' David sings. 'But with you.' Before the next song, Zoe untoggles her chunky chain necklace and pockets it. 'No way that was staying on.'

David falls on the sticky, beer-soaked floor again and again but each time is pulled up. There is no menace in the crowd. Everyone is on the same team. He manages to take a couple of photos.

The sways are too intense for him to aim the camera. He's thankful for his Dr Martens.

Behind Karl and his touring musicians, large screens play fast-moving black-and-white videos of bleak empty streets, interspersed with images of Germaine Greer, Ralph Ellison, Emily Dickinson. Floodlights spray vibrant colours over the stage and out on to the crowd. Karl says little between songs. It's a slick, professional performance. When he returns for the encore, he mumbles something about England: 'Unrecognisable. Isn't it?' Cheers. Karl smirks, shrugs and motions to his musicians to play the final song. David wonders what Karl meant, then puts it out of his mind. 'Black Glass' is a favourite, an early solo one. 'You'll pay a price,' he sings.

Outside, he can't stop shivering. The steady slash of winter air. Yet he's seen Karl and it was even better than he thought it would be. His eyes rest on the entrance, which glows neon green and whose battered old billboards are slotted with black letters that read 'Karl Williams Sold Out'. His eyeliner has run. His ears ring. His hair is frizzy, swamped with beer. His jeans no longer seem super skinny. The plastic cap on a lace has split open, leaving a thready mess. Sharing a cigarette with Zoe, he examines his photos and posts the least blurry one on Instagram with a simple comment: 'Best night of my life. #karlwilliams #salome #brixtonacademy.'

'HOW WAS IT?' MUM ASKS, leaning against the radiator, legs crossed. She has on a yellow shirt, black trousers and gold lace earrings, and looks ready to leave. David is hung-over.

'Great,' he says. 'Just sent you the *Guardian* review.'

'Positive?'

'Five stars.'

Stephen joins them in the kitchen. 'Have fun last night?'

'Yeah.' David is now willing to engage with him, but not in a meaningful way. However much Mum might want it, they will never be pally. His loyalties will always lie with Dad.

They divorced three years ago. Mum started seeing Stephen six months later and married him last summer. They knew each other from Action Aid, where she still works (Stephen has moved on to Amnesty International). David has no reason to believe that Mum cheated on Dad with Stephen or that Stephen was in any way connected to the divorce. But David blames him nonetheless.

'It was at Brixton Academy, right?'

'Yeah.'

Stephen tells him again that he saw U2 and The Cure there. 'Great venue.'

'Yeah.'

'Good crowd?'

'Yeah.'

Stephen checks his Apple Watch. 'I'll see whether Zoe is awake.'

They are supposed to be having brunch in Broadway Market. David and Zoe went to a pub after the gig. He stuck with beers. She shifted to double G&Ts, a decision she might be regretting. She hasn't tweeted anything this morning. She hasn't even retweeted or 'liked' anything.

At twelve they finally make it to The Oaktree. Its tables have flyers for a sister company, Creative Block. The windowsills are decorated with cactuses. The curtains are frilly. Scandi-pop foams out from ceiling speakers. At a nearby table, someone tinkers with a PowerPoint presentation on a rose-gold MacBook. Home for David is Newbury Park, where Dad lives, and the cafés there are not like this. He has now been vegan for six months and, scanning the menu, is taken aback by the number of options. Knowing that Mum or Stephen will pay, he orders scrambled tofu with sun-dried tomatoes, a freshly squeezed orange juice and an oat flat white, a change from his normal breakfast: Rice Krispies, instant coffee.

'There used to be a place in Broadway Market called Hey Sugar,' Mum says. 'They had *poolaki.* I've never seen it anywhere else in the UK. It's an Iranian candy that looks like a coin, and is made from sugar, water, vinegar, saffron, coconut, cocoa powder. Baba would bring it back from his trips to Isfahan.' Zoe reveals that it has moved to Deptford. They discuss rent prices for businesses. David has zero interest in the conversation. He is itching to watch YouTube videos from the gig and read more reviews on the Karl Williams subreddit. But whenever Mum takes him to a café or a restaurant and he starts using his phone she has a go at him. 'How's university?' she asks Zoe.

The compulsory Shakespeare module is dull. A Hollywood cinema one starts soon, though, and that should be fun. She is also organising a protest as part of the Ally Club society.

'We put a petition up and three thousand people signed it in twenty-four hours,' Zoe says. 'Yet they're still going to go ahead and let Rachel Vine speak on campus. Just because they're scared the government will send them a strongly worded letter for going against their guidance. It's cowardly. They're giving a platform to someone who spreads hate, who has made a career solely out of spreading hate.'

Zoe once revealed to him that from twelve – when she lost her mum, Stephen's first wife, to cancer – through to sixteen she was such a wreck that she couldn't communicate offline. This still surprises him: her, a wreck. Since starting at Queen Mary, she's learned to speak with confidence, authority. Her words come fast, in full sentences and from the centre of her mouth, not from the corners, as with David.

The Ally Club will picket the event. They won't stop Rachel Vine from speaking or use violence, but they will make their feelings known. Stephen offers his support. 'You can be sure the right will claim the Ally Club interfered with Rachel Vine's freedom of speech,' he says, topping up their water glasses. 'They have no idea what freedom of speech means. It means no one should face violence, intimidation or imprisonment for what they say. That's it. Nothing less. Nothing more.'

'Exactly.'

'What do you think, David?' Stephen asks.

He shrugs. In his autobiography Karl wrote that he is a free-speech absolutist, and quoted Voltaire: 'I disapprove of what you say but I'll defend to the death your right to say it,' or something like that. David has read it twice and agrees: he's happy for anyone to say anything. But he doesn't want to argue. He's impressed Zoe managed to style her blue-black hair today. He must look like shit.

'We're peacefully letting the university know that they made a mistake in inviting her to speak,' Zoe continues. 'People talk about "healthy disagreement" as if saying transphobic things were totally harmless. That's ridiculous. Because speech isn't harmless. It has consequences. If it had no consequences, what would be the point of protecting it in the first place?'

David takes out his phone. He might not be able to get away with watching or reading something, but he will get away with quickly checking how many 'likes' his gig photo has got.

No more. It has stalled on five.

A waiter brings their food, which he hopes will ease his tentacling headache.

'I think it is a tricky subject, free speech,' Mum says. 'I remember . . . Near the end of the Shah's regime, Baba, my father, went to ten evenings of poetry at the Goethe Institute, and each evening people recited anti-Shah poems. And for the next two weeks I would wake up every night at three or four a.m. and go to my parents' room to check whether he was still there. I was scared that the secret police, the SAVAK, would come and take him away. Everyone was scared of the SAVAK. And then, of course, with the new regime, he spent a week in prison for his painting of a man with his hand on a woman's body. So much changed from the time of the Shah to the time of the Islamic Republic, but one thing that stayed the same was a yearning for free speech. It seemed obviously dreamy, free speech . . .'

'I can't imagine how scary that must have been,' Zoe says. 'What you and your family experienced in Iran. That's a real freedom-of-speech crisis, unlike the manufactured one here.'

Mum nods and sinks her fork into her egg yolk.

BACK IN NEWBURY PARK, David pops into Gnanam Food & Wine, picks up supplies – baked beans, bread, hummus, toothpaste – and walks home. He hates taking the underpasses because they're connected by a large bleak square in which someone from college, Mo, likes to hang out with his mates. But he has too much pride to take the other route, which is ten minutes longer.

Approaching the first underpass, he hears hip-hop beats. They will be there. Just half the lights work and even those that do fuzz, flicker. Graffiti tags loop in and out of shadow, and Coke cans and McDonald's paper bags and the carcass of a shopping trolley. He curses his way through a puddle and on into the square. Sure enough, perched on the back of a bench: Mo and a mate.

Mo looks up. 'Oi oi. Ibrahim.' There's a Bluetooth speaker between his feet.

'Yeah?' Ibrahim says, spinning a hi-vis football.

'Recognise him?'

'Erm.'

'Pussy from my college.'

'Ah. Course. Yeah. Makeup Boy.'

Mo makes the wanker gesture.

Ibrahim laughs. 'Look how scared he is. Look.'

He passes them, focusing on the second underpass: close, close, close. As he enters it, the square hardens with the slap of trainers on concrete, making him jittery, but he resists the temptation to turn. 'Watch this,' Ibrahim shouts. 'CR7!' Following a thump and a swoosh, David experiences a shock on his back, and tumbles over, backpack clanging. The ball bounces away.

'Ohhhhh. Ibrahim, man.'

'Siuuuuuuu!'

Jeans torn, palms sore, he picks himself up. The music romps on. There is an unmistakable smell in this underpass – piss. He rubs a mushy cigarette butt from his knee.

'That was some Champions League shit.'

'Siuuuuuuuuuuu!'

'You need to bring that curl to our five-a-sides, man. That was . . . Oh, man.'

Without looking back, David continues home.

He stares out of his bedroom window. Smoke pours from a chimney opposite. In the garden the frizzled black stems of a creeper plant cling to the back wall and rustle over on to the roof behind. After a series of complaints from the neighbours – the previous owners made sure to prune it every summer – Dad killed it, but he never bothered to remove the cut stems. On the paving stones, a watering can lies sideways. The sound of children's laughter from somewhere. He wonders how college ended up being so bad, worse than secondary school.

There is no PE. There is no maths. There is no dress code. And still . . .

Fucking Mo. Since the incident in the common room six weeks ago he has been making David's life hell. It is partly David's fault – he should never have brought it with him; he should only have used it at home – but he suspects Mo is such a prick that he would have found a reason to bully him anyway. David was naive to think he might make friends, might be popular in college.

Because he was so self-conscious about his skin – the oiliness, the spots, the redness – he decided to give Active Duty Makeup for Men a go in the summer. Having got nowhere with any of the girls at secondary school, he was determined to get somewhere with one in college. He ordered the essentials kit, which included a primer, a concealer pen, a compact with anti-shine powder, a face sponge and a remover. From September to November he sensibly left everything at home. Then he grew paranoid that for it to have the effect he wanted he would have to keep reapplying it throughout the day, so he took a makeup bag with him to college and spent his free periods in toilet cubicles. One afternoon in December, he left his backpack on the customary heap in the common room and went to read a book. The next thing he knew Mo was hysterically waving the compact in front of him and shouting: 'What the fuck?' They had similar ASOS backpacks and Mo had accidentally ended up rummaging around in his. David muttered, 'Give it back,' and attempted to grab it, but Mo swaggered away, over to a group of girls, and paraded it, motioning towards David. They pissed themselves, apart from Selina, who asked how 'fucking insecure' Mo was about his sexuality. 'Just leave him alone. And, besides, have you looked in a mirror? Trust me, you could do with some makeup.' She rolled her eyes, grabbed the compact and returned it to David. There was whispering among the other girls. At the time, this appeared to faze Mo – he dabbed his cheeks – but he soon doubled down and started calling David a faggot. The cool guys in their year followed his lead, and Selina was ostracised by Jennifer and Alice for her intervention. David became Makeup Boy.

Having Karl at Brixton Academy on the horizon made life bearable. He could spend his walks to class scouring Instagram for new tour content, his lunch breaks weighing up outfit options, his evenings refreshing setlist.fm to see which songs were being played. What now?

The sky is slate grey. A small white feather has got itself gummed to the drainpipe. He opens his notebook, re-reads his lyrics. 'There's a boy wrapped in chains / Lies by the river Thames / There's a boy wrapped in chains / Dead or alive no prize / You were his only flame / Till you changed / He couldn't play your game / He's just a child / Born without a name / You wrapped him in chains / And fed him sinners' shame.' He is pleased with them. But not sure whether he can sing them. He has only a limited understanding of melody, and that might not be enough to emulate Karl. He can't tell whether something is in or out of tune. It all sounds the same to him.

The snap of the front door. He heads downstairs.

'Ah. You're home?' Dad says, wearing his camouflage cap with the R+ logo of the German metal band Rammstein. A gym buddy gave it to him ages ago, when he used to regularly go to the gym. It is unlikely that he has ever looked up the band, let alone listened to them.

'Yeah,' David says. 'Got back at three.'

'How was the concert?'

'Great.' He wants to say more, to tell Dad how it felt hearing his favourite songs live; being caught in the welcoming tides of a crowd and tumbling left, right, left, right; spontaneously, euphorically, hugging strangers who shared his love for Karl and therefore, surely, feelings of self-doubt and unlovability. But he stops there. He finds it hard talking to Dad about music or books, much harder than to Mum, which bugs him, but is the way it is and probably always will be.

'Been working?'

'Seven Kings. Girl moving into a flat she bought. Only twenty-three. Can you believe that? Only twenty-three. You should have seen her TV. Basically a cinema screen.'

David asks what she needed help with. Dad methodically lists everything: the wall mount, the flat-pack wardrobe, the furniture in the kitchen, the treadmill in the spare room, the sink.

'All right then?'

'It was fine.'

As a teenager, Dad joined the British Army and served as an electrician in the Royal Engineers. After leaving, he expected to find a job easily. However, as the army hadn't provided him with an AM2 assessment, companies didn't consider him fully qualified, in spite of all his knowledge and experience. According to Mum, he could have undertaken the assessment without much trouble, but he was too stubborn to do so and instead decided to strike out on his own. He started civilian life as a self-employed electrician. He is now a general handyman hirable on TaskRabbit. Throughout David's life, he has been falling: falling, falling, falling. David worries that he will keep falling.

From his Reebok sweatshirt, the slop of belly.

'Want to watch an episode of *Only Fools and Horses*?' David asks.

'When?'

'Nine?'

'That works. Eight would too.'

A shimmer of need in Dad's eyes – or is he imagining it? That Dad once had the self-confidence to buy Mum a drink at a Rolling Stones concert is difficult to believe.

He apparently only knew 'Gimme Shelter' but was at Wembley Stadium with two army colleagues, who loved them. She had gone on her own. She hadn't yet made any friends in London but as a child had dreamt about one day seeing them and didn't want to miss the opportunity. She ended up sharing the experience with Dad and they went on their first date soon afterwards. Having learned that her father was a famous painter, he turned to *Time Out* for inspiration, and took her to the Tate. She found him charming and funny and kind – kinder than any of the other men she had met in Britain – as well as attractive. He confessed to not being the artiest of men, but made an effort, researching films, exhibitions, theatre shows they could see together. He kept this up for some time. But as his fortunes changed the effort became too much to muster and the research fizzled out.

'Sure,' David says. 'Sweet. Looking forward to it.'

David inserts the DVD and returns to the sofa. He sits on the right side, Dad on the left, a large bowl of ready-salted crisps between them. 'Which episode?'

'How about the one with the chemical corporation?' Dad says.

David selects it. They have seen each episode countless times. He has suggested other series they could try – *The Office*, *Peep Show*, *Seinfeld* – but Dad wants to stick with *Only Fools and Horses*. They have the *Complete Collection* box set. It has all seven series, plus fifteen Christmas specials.

Watching this, David feels close to Dad, certainly closer than at any other time. Although they aren't talking, they are laughing together. And that is surely something.

ON MONDAY MORNING, DAVID has a history class on the origins of the Cold War. The subject is interesting, but Mr Davies sets too much homework, and David is falling behind. In the afternoon, a German class on weak masculine nouns. Grammar is mind-numbing. Tuesday: English.

'So,' Mr Knowles says. 'Has everyone read *The Crucible*?' A scattering of nods. 'Good. Well, I want to start with the character of Abigail Williams. What did you make of her? Did you see her as a straight-out villain? Did you sympathise with her at all? I want to hear your thoughts.'

David has plenty he could say, but he hates speaking in class; whenever he contemplates raising his hand he feels his throat constrict.

'Come on,' Mr Knowles continues, sweeping his eyes over the cramped, airless room. 'Okay. How about I kick things off by sharing one possible response to Abigail?' He coughs. A West Ham pin badge glints out from his navy-blue blazer. The fans in the class are convinced he wears it only to curry favour with them and each Monday interrogate him about that weekend's game to try to catch him out. 'She is a villain through and through. The least complex character in the play. She lies. She manipulates. She's responsible for the deaths of nineteen innocent people. And her motivations are transparent – envy plus a thirst for revenge on Elizabeth Proctor. Do we think that's a fair response?'

'Bang on, sir,' Freddy says. 'Class over?'

'Very funny,' Mr Knowles says. 'Anyone else?'

'She's a bit of a hoe,' Kalila says.

'Ohhhhhhh.'

'Shiiiiiii.'

'What you mean?'

'You know what I mean,' Kalila continues. 'It's like Sir was saying. She's only in it for revenge on Liz. And she cast a spell on Liz and everything because she wanted Liz's man. She saw him and she was, like, "Oh my God, I want a bit of that. He mine."'

'Kalila's right,' Jennifer says, raising her hands over the hooting. 'Abi's in it for one thing and one thing only. She's a hoe with no morals. Allow her.'

'Okay,' Mr Knowles says. 'That is a possible interpretation. Any others?'

A wobbly silence. 'Nah,' Doug says. 'Jury's verdict is hoe.'

After sliding his fingers through his short, tidily cropped hair, Mr Knowles encourages the class to think about the mores of the time, about Abigail's background.

'She embodies the repressed desires of Puritan women,' Selina says exhaustedly. 'But unlike the other right-on Puritan women in the village, like Elizabeth, Abigail doesn't suppress her desires or repent for them. She gives herself up to them and goes all in for what she wants.'

'Good,' Mr Knowles says. 'And how about her methods?'

'You're right. She lies. She manipulates. She's ruthless. How else can she go about things in a Puritan age though? Besides, she's never had any guidance from anyone on how to act in society. She's an orphan who had a shitty childhood. Right? She's used to solving problems alone in her own way. She's a villain, sure, but she's also independent and strong and free-thinking. Between Elizabeth and Abigail, I know who I'd rather be.'

'Uhh. That's such a *you* thing to say,' Jennifer says. 'It's obvious—'

'Jennifer,' Mr Knowles says. 'Let's stay on track. Selina has made an intelligent contribution. She raises valuable points. I would like us to consider and expand on those points.'

Selina sits back, unmoved by Jennifer's snarky comment or Mr Knowles's praise. David wonders how she always manages to look so effortlessly cool. Today, the jangle of necklaces, the Grimes hoodie, the washed-black jeans with the rips at the knees, the rocky black boots. He senses that in her head she has already left college behind. Her Instagram stories show how comfortably she fits in at literary events in London, performing slam poetry, knocking back boxed wine. She must be counting down the days until university. Like him, she doesn't have any friends here. Unlike him, she doesn't seem to care. Last Friday he saw Jennifer and Alice confront her at the lockers. Jennifer asked whether her skirt could be any shorter. Selina regarded her with distaste but neglected to respond. Alice followed up by asking why Selina wore nose rings. 'If you want to get the boys' attention, babe, I would take them out. Not looking like a hobo tends to help. Just saying.' Selina turned to Alice and said: 'How about I wear what I wear and you wear what you wear. We can't all be basic bitches.' Then she slammed her locker shut and strolled away, giving them the finger.

'Okay,' Mr Knowles says. 'Let's talk about the history of Puritanism. Does anyone know where the Puritan faith originated and what it was a response to?'

David read the Wikipedia entry for Puritanism last night. The Puritan faith originated in England. The Puritans sought to purify the Church of England of Roman Catholic practices. He could say this. If he starts speaking more, it's possible Selina will see him as more than an object of pity.

'Anyone?'

Feeling his throat constrict, he looks away.

In the afternoon, another history class on the origins of the Cold War. Mr Davies gets them to discuss the launch of the Marshall Plan. The last chapter David properly read was on tensions at Yalta.

AFTER HIS PARENTS SPLIT UP, they sold the family house in Goodmayes; Dad moved to Newbury Park, Mum to Stratford. Unable to agree on custody arrangements, they went to court, where the judge sided with Mum, ordering David to spend seventy per cent of his time with her. He endured this for three years. But when he turned sixteen, and Mum had swapped Stratford for Haggerston with Stephen, he exercised his legal right to choose and reversed the ratio. She had wanted the divorce; she could suffer the consequences. Sometimes he even spent a whole week with Dad.

Then her father died and her despair grew and he agreed to a new schedule: Mondays, Tuesdays, Fridays, Sundays in Newbury Park; Wednesdays, Thursdays, Saturdays in Haggerston.

This Wednesday Stephen has to work late, so he lounges with her in the living room. Bob Dylan records crackle away. The music is boring, but he enjoys lowering and raising the needle.

The following evening Stephen is around and asks Mum whether she has seen the video of Zoe's protest. It shows a knot of students outside the entrance to the building where Rachel Vine was scheduled to speak, holding HATE REWARDED HERE banners and shouting.

David felt uneasy watching it. He's become friends with Zoe – somehow. They bonded over anger. As a widower, Stephen had promised her that he would never remarry, and she had believed him. For weeks after David and Zoe were introduced, they shared links to famous horror-movie scenes on WhatsApp with comments like 'wouldn't mind this happening at the wedding lol' and eyes emojis. Then he found out she liked Salomé. He had never met someone who liked Salomé. They started chatting about music and the messages continued even after the anger subsided.

He now considers her his closest friend – well, his only friend. But what would Karl make of her protest?

'Yeah,' Mum says. 'I finally had the chance on the bus home. Work was so busy. Who knew you can receive sixty emails in one day?'

'No lunchbreak?'

'None.'

'Damn,' Stephen says. 'At least it's over now. I walked past Chris watching it on the *Guardian* and had to point Zoe out. A small claim to fame, I know, but . . .'

Mum assembles ingredients for dinner. 'David, we were thinking of making *sangok*. You can have it with vegan cheese or hummus. Does that sound okay?'

'Sure.'

He is snacking, idly listening and scrolling on Instagram. A new selfie from Selina. Black choker necklace. Sleeveless white Metallica top. The subtle red highlights in her long black hair. The fullness of her cheeks. The plumpness of her lips. Those lips. God, she's hot. The selfie has fifty-one 'likes'. He has never had that many 'likes'. Someone even commented with a fire emoji.

'I thought I used to get UK politics,' Mum says. 'But watching the video of Zoe's protest . . . I admire her activism. And I have so much sympathy for vulnerable students who feel . . . But it's strange how the left's attitude towards freedom of speech has changed. It's hard to get my head round it, to square it with life in Iran.'

David looks up. She is rubbing the bump on the bridge of her nose. It annoys him each time she performs this reflex, as it reminds him of the bump on the bridge of his nose. The one facial feature he inherited from her. Not the symmetry, with the narrow forehead, the strong cheekbones, the small, pointed chin. Not the striking eyes, rounded eyebrows. Just this bump.

'I know what you mean,' Stephen says. 'Things aren't the way they were when I was Zoe's age. I was convinced that freedom of speech was absolute. And with your experiences in Iran . . .' He pauses, gathering his words. 'I guess we just need to remember that freedom of speech is now being exploited to maintain the status quo far more than it is being used to challenge it. And the status quo still needs work. Really, Zoe and her generation are fighting for the same things that we were – equality, dignity, respect. They're just doing it in a different way.'

'Mm,' Mum says. 'I suppose so.'

DAVID STARTS HIS ENGLISH HOMEWORK. In spite of himself, he enjoys studying in his room here: a view of a leafy street from the glass desk, a HomePod, a functioning lamp.

The walls are white, except for a whale over the bed, where a cot had apparently once been. As a child, he liked whales, so, predictably, Mum left it there for him. The built-in wardrobe: empty. The built-in bookshelves: empty. Even the Persian picture frame on the bedside table: empty. Since moving here in autumn, Mum and Stephen have repeatedly tried to convince him to bring more of his things over and personalise the room. But he wants it to remain as it is: hotel-like.

For his homework he has to write a thousand words in answer to the question 'Discuss John Proctor, the protagonist, and Abigail Williams, the antagonist, in Arthur Miller's *The Crucible*'. Within twenty minutes, he has five hundred. Keying his thoughts into Google Docs is manageable.

A knock. 'Can I come in?' Mum asks.

'Yeah.'

'Busy?'

'English.'

She tilts her head to see the book on the desk. 'You've started *The Crucible*?'

'Yeah, I like it. Definitely the best book we've done so far this year.'

She read it in Iran. It was the first literary book she read from start to finish in English. 'I still remember buying it. A street called Ghandi Avenue, where people would sell black-market Western books and cassettes. When I came home with it – that might have been the proudest I ever made Baba. He read it two or three times after me. Then we had to burn it, of course.' Until her father died, she rarely spoke about her past. Now she can't stop.

'Right.'

She sits on the bed, adjusts her tortoiseshell glasses. 'Sayeeda finally sent his things.'

'Your father's things?'

A box with notebooks, photographs, sketches, diaries. 'Hopefully it will make it to London. I'd like to show you. It breaks my heart that you never had the opportunity to meet him.'

'I spoke to him on the phone.'

'It's not the same. You would have loved him. Everyone who met him did. He was a free spirit, an artist. I'd like you to know more about him.'

'Okay.'

She misses speaking Farsi too. David suggests that she return to Tehran for a holiday sometime. It wouldn't be safe, she insists. Her father was known to the authorities. She would be flagged by the system. Besides, with him gone, and her mother long gone, there is nothing left for her there. He mentions her cousin Sayeeda. Mum says she barely knew her, to be honest. Everyone in Iran she was close to has now died or emigrated to America. Her school friends are in California.

'But . . . I do want you to know your heritage. I want you to know your grandfather. So, when the box arrives, it would mean a lot to me if—'

'Yeah, no worries.'

'Thank you.' A press of the bed with her palms. 'How's the mattress, by the way?'

'Fine.'

'Better than the previous one?'

'Yeah.'

She fidgets. A tingle from her vintage bracelet. 'The reason I came was actually to speak to you about college. How is it going? Are things getting better?'

'Yeah.'

'Honestly?'

'Mm.'

'You're so quiet these days. I know you don't like talking about college. But I need to ask.'

He swivels in his chair, concentrates on his laptop. 'It's fine.'

'You've made friends then?'

'Mm.'

'Just promise that you will tell me if you're ever unhappy again there, and know that you can always talk to me about anything. Or Stephen. Or Zoe.'

'Or Dad.'

'Can you talk to him?'

He closes his eyes. 'I want to finish my homework.'

THE NEXT MORNING DAVID CHECKS Twitter on his phone and sees that Karl Williams is trending.

Is Karl's new single out? Are there rumours of a Salomé reunion?

Seven forty. Grim outside. David will be late for history class unless he gets in the shower now. But he needs to find out why Karl is trending. What if it really is a Salomé reunion?

He opens the top tweets. @coolist: 'Dinosaur turns out to be Islamophobe. big surprise lol.' @oracleTM: 'so Karl Williams is cancelled then.' @GuruBanks: 'bye bye Mr Williams.' A string of users are sharing an *Independent* story with the headline 'Karl Williams sparks walkout at Leeds show after Islamophobic comments' – including one of Zoe's friends.

'Fuck,' he mutters, before loading the story. During his show in Leeds, Karl said: 'We passed Farfield primary school on our way to the arena this afternoon. Last Monday twenty Muslim children were withdrawn from the school in protest against its LGBTQ lessons, twenty. Quite a lot. No? Could it be that maybe, maybe, Islam isn't a hundred per cent compatible with Western values? Could it? You tell me.'

The story includes the accounts of a few fans who walked out. 'Everyone booed his comments, and a large percentage of people left. Where I was sitting, in section K, dozens did.' 'I couldn't stay after hearing him say something like that. He's become racist. I wouldn't have enjoyed the rest of the show.' 'It hurt leaving, but there was no choice really. Sad on so many levels.'

He closes the story. A shiver in his spine. Will there be a backlash? Will people stop listening to Karl? Will the release of his new single be postponed? Will UK festival bookers pull him from their plans? Will Zoe's Queen Mary friends start calling David out for wearing Karl and Salomé tops?

This could happen. And it terrifies him.

On the bus, a message from Zoe: 'Omg. Did you see? I can't believe Karl Williams has moved to the far right. wtf is happening?' He wants to respond: What? So one controversial comment has wiped out all his LGBTQ and environmental activism? He's been vegan for a decade. And the far right? Really? Instead, he responds: 'Damn. Disappointing. Still, looking forward to the new single.'

By the evening, every media outlet in the UK has picked up on the controversy. It is the top entertainment news story on the BBC and the subject of opinion pieces in the *Guardian*, the *New Statesman* and the *Quietus*. 'Why I'm done with Karl Williams' and 'What happened, Karl Williams?' are only two of the many headlines David considers unbelievable.

His blasé message to Zoe didn't go down well. She responded: 'Really? Did you read his comments? He's a racist.' David ignored this. Another message followed: 'I know Karl is your hero. But he's also a racist. We didn't know that before. Now we do.' He ignored this too.

In the garden, raindrops fill an empty plant pot, fizz against a heap of loose bricks. The pigeon perched on the TV aerial of the house opposite looks soaked. He flicks on the light switch, giving the cobwebs on the windowsill a gentle glow and his Coke can a shadow with trembly edges. The more he chews things over, the more unreasonable and hypocritical the outrage appears. Karl made one controversial comment and he is being cancelled; the R&B star Giselle Gomez wore trainers custom-made from crocodile, snake, ostrich, and stingray skins and everyone still worships her as 'The Queen'. How can a comment be worse than that?

He wants to tweet something, something intelligent, eye-opening, in support of Karl. But it's risky. Zoe's friends could block him, and she could stop inviting him out. Then who would he hang out with? He's been looking forward to drinks at her flat tomorrow.

A cowardly string of curses. There's no choice. He has to keep his mouth shut.

OVER TINS OF RED STRIPE, David chats with Zoe and her friends Rory and Eleanor. A Spotify playlist frisks about in the background. He has recognised a few tracks, one by Bowie, one by Sharon Van Etten, one by FKA twigs, but most are too positive, too uplifting, for him.

Rolling a cigarette, Zoe asks Rory how he found this week's reading for their Shakespeare module. Her black nails gleam as she distributes tobacco. She is wearing a white shirt with a black ribbon around the collar and a dark silver raveny necklace.

'Boring as fuck,' Rory says. 'How much Frank Knight can someone take?'

'I know, right?'

'Studying Shakey is one thing. I'm on board with that, of course. Frank Knight on Shakey though?' He raps his knuckles on the red-and-black Marvel Comics cycling helmet sitting beside him on the sofa. 'Are we still in the eighties? Is cock-rock back?'

Dua Lipa's 'New Rules' comes on to whoops.

David contemplates the living room. He's still unclear whether the Soviet Union workers poster was put up ironically or not. It's red and strawy, featuring a burly man and a busty woman, both in overalls, together holding a hammer and sickle, and Cyrillic script. Zoe and her flatmates are obviously not right wing. Yet they are not so left wing either as to want to see the Soviet Union resurrected. So why did they put it up? He is on edge, clearly. Zoe invited him round once before, and it didn't bother him then. The other one in the room is easier to interpret: a monochrome image of Maya Angelou, with the phrase 'The Future is Female' written in white on pink blocks.

'What's English like at school?' Eleanor asks.

‘For me?’ He squeezes his Red Stripe. Every twenty minutes or so, either Zoe, Rory or Eleanor has been making an effort to involve him in the conversation. But he has nothing interesting to contribute. ‘Yeah, fine. We’re reading *The Crucible* at the moment. Arthur Miller.’

‘I wish we’d studied that at school,’ Eleanor says. ‘We had *Atonement* and *Tess of the d’Urbervilles*. McEwan and Hardy.’ She sticks her index finger into her mouth and makes a retching motion.

‘I’m surprised you stuck with English after being tortured like that,’ Zoe says.

Rory asks David what his plans are: English at university? Ash flops to the floor. David has noticed that Rory spends more time holding his cigarettes than smoking them. ‘Yeah, maybe.’

‘Your A levels are English, history and . . .’

‘German. Erm. Yeah, I looked at the entry requirements for English at some of the London unis a while ago. I think I should be able to apply with those A levels.’

‘Definitely,’ Zoe says. ‘Don’t worry. You’ll be fine.’

‘Check out Goldsmiths,’ Rory says. ‘I’ve heard good things about the course there. They seem to be making a real effort to shake things up. If I’d known Queen Mary was still wanking Frank Knight off I would have taken Goldsmiths’ offer instead.’

Having promised that he will, David slugs beer: a signal for them to return to speaking among themselves. They seem to take it. As Kendrick Lamar’s ‘King Kunta’ comes on, Eleanor launches into an anecdote about someone she is messaging on Bumble.

He slips back into his thoughts. For a while, he did seriously consider university. He even read personal statement samples. But now he is set against it. The average student ends up with fifty thousand pounds of debt, according to the BBC. The thought of five hundred pounds of debt unnerves him, let alone fifty thousand – *fifty thousand*. And for what? All the articles about university claim it is a unique chance to meet ‘inspiring’ and ‘like-minded’ people and make ‘lifelong’ friends. Having spent several hours with Rory and Eleanor tonight, he is sceptical of that. It may be that he isn’t meant to have friends, which is probably for the best.

Dad needs someone to watch *Only Fools and Horses* with, after all. The articles also emphasise employability. But he has zero interest in becoming a teacher – he has no intention of spending a second more than necessary in the classroom – and English doesn't seem to lead to other jobs. Dad suggested law. That would mean memorising thousands of cases though. If he isn't going to read novels and poems all day, he may as well get a job. Then he will at least have the money to go to gigs. And he can continue writing song lyrics regardless. At some point he will tell everyone this. At some point.

Kendrick Lamar melts into – Salomé. He recognises 'The Forest' instantly.

The haunting piano intro gives him the same tingling sensation it always gives him. He glances over to Zoe, who is speaking animatedly about Bumble and doesn't seem to have noticed the track yet. He wonders how she will react, whether she will react. He didn't reply to her last two messages about Karl and was hoping the subject wouldn't come up tonight. As the vocals jab in, she turns towards the speaker and groans. He tenses up.

'Who is this?' Rory asks.

'Salomé,' Zoe says. 'You're closest to the MacBook. Press skip.'

'This is Karl Williams?' Rory holds up a palm. 'Hang on.'

David watches him closely.

Rory listens for ten seconds before saying: 'You like this?'

'I liked it,' Zoe says. 'Just skip it already.'

'Even if he weren't racist,' Rory says, 'I would—'

'Fine,' Zoe says. 'I'll skip it.'

A spark of rage. David has sat through hours of shitty music – hours. Can Zoe not let 'The Forest' play out? And then it's over, skipped.

'Ohhh,' Eleanor says, as the next song starts. 'Solange.'

He tugs at the neck of his T-shirt. The room is thick with cigarette smoke. As much as he romanticised the idea of smoking indoors, he is finding the reality of it uncomfortable. He would like to open a window, but it's icy. Just half an hour ago, Eleanor asked Zoe to turn up the heating. Even though he doesn't need one, he decides to go for a piss to get a few minutes alone. He leans forwards—

'Sorry, man,' Rory says. 'Just remembered. You were into Karl Williams too. Right?'

David nods.

'Fair play. Just never been my thing. You see him at Brixton with Zoe?'

'Yeah.'

'Good you caught him once at least.'

David cannot comprehend the way they are speaking about Karl – as though he has committed suicide. 'He's still rumoured for All Points East. If that happens, I'll buy a ticket.'

'You would still see him?' Eleanor asks.

'Sure. I love him.'

'Don't say things like that,' Zoe says.

'Why?'

'Because.' Her tone of voice: condescending, patronising.

As well as feeling dizzy from all the smoke around him he is starting to feel drunk. Red Stripe number four, and it's darting to his head. 'You think . . . You think everyone should stop listening to Karl?' He imagined saying this many times. Yet never really expected to.

'You can't separate the art from the artist,' Zoe says.

'Maybe. Maybe not.' His hands are blotchy. 'But come on. Karl isn't exactly R. Kelly. He's not a monster. It's important to have some perspective, right?'

'He's Islamophobic.'

'Is he?' David says, riding a wave of recklessness.

'He thinks Islam and the West are incompatible. So. Yes. He's Islamophobic.'

'But he said what he said because he cares about LGBTQ rights.'

Zoe sighs. 'Don't let the far right get you too.'

David's eyes widen. 'What?'

'Karl Williams cares about LGBTQ+ rights,' Zoe continues, 'but, as strange as this might sound, it's possible to care about LGBTQ+ rights without being Islamophobic. The parents at that school don't represent Islam. They're bigots. But they don't represent Islam. We're talking about forty, fifty people. There are more than three million Muslims in the UK. The Leeds school is being blown out of proportion by racists to push the agenda that Islam and the West are incompatible.'

'He only said Islam and the West might—'

'And saying that is ignorant as fuck. Muslims are stigmatised enough in society without people like Karl Williams weaponising homophobia to smear them further.'

Is Karl being ignorant or are you being ignorant? David thinks. But he knows that saying this would be taking things a step too far. Even in his current state, he knows that. The back of his neck is slicked with sweat. Head swimming. A thorny hush. Eleanor asks him whether he has heard of Radio Free. 'Cool. Guitary. Indie. But politically progressive.'

'Don't know them.'

'Their most famous song is "Earthquake" I think. You might have heard that?'

'No.'

'I'll put it on in a minute,' Zoe says.

David gazes at his Red Stripe. He wants to go home. It was a mistake coming.

IN HIS ROOM ON SUNDAY MORNING, David searches on Twitter for the hashtag #farfieldschool.

A patchy, uncomfortable sleep on Zoe's sofa has left him irritable, confrontational. His head is sloshy. He rubs his temple, trying to remember how many Red Stripes he ended up having: six, seven, eight? For an hour after waking up, he was unable to move. Just lay on the sofa, shivering and shaking, right arm crooked in front of his eyes, shielding them from the sunlight the curtains were cruelly letting pass. The journey back was excruciating too. A jolt or wobble on the Central Line, and he would feel nauseous. The entire rest of the carriage seemed to be having a wholesome weekend; a woman with a pram kept looking over. Using his phone is still taxing: screen tap after screen tap reverberates in his head. On the mattress lies a smattering of Subway vouchers handed to him outside Newbury Park station. He hasn't had the stomach to check what they entitle him to. The mere thought of sweet-onion sauce . . .

The top #farfieldschool tweet reads: 'All the Muslims I have met in the UK have been liberal, tolerant, funny people supportive of LGBTQ+ issues and lifestyles. This #farfieldschool story is being blown out of all proportion by the right-wing media #LGBTQ+together.' The next reads: 'My thoughts are with the Muslims affected by the #farfieldschool fallout. I've been hearing v worrying reports of a rise in Islamophobic hate crimes this past week. It's vital to stand in solidarity with UK Muslims & keep working to fight homophobia without feeding Islamophobia.'

He scrolls on. A user with the handle @Macca_0160 posted a thirty-second video of a Muslim protester outside the school. Retweeted fifty-five times. He clicks 'play'. 'Don't teach our children that gay is okay because gay is not okay. God created man, then he created woman for man's pleasure. He didn't create man for man. There is no gay in Islam. It's an immoral act. If it's the law that these lessons have to be taught, we'll accept that, but we want to remove our children from the lessons.' Along with the video, @Macca_0160 wrote: 'Anyone on the left want to condemn these comments? Anyone? *tumbleweed rolling* lololol.'

David clicks through to the comments. @Goldielocks1969: 'Imagine a leftist actually calling out a Muslim for doing something wrong. I think the leftist's head would explode that a Muslim doing something wrong was even possible.' @Tobystyke: 'Can't happen. Because if you condemn a Muslim you're no longer on the left. You're officially on the far right.'

It's true. Precisely this happened to Karl. Still rubbing his temple, David checks out @Macca_0160's profile. Union Jack. Stars and Stripes. 'Facts don't care about your feelings.' In the bios of the users David follows, the only flags are rainbow ones, Palestinian ones. He scans recent tweets. A *Spiked* article with the headline 'The woke-left blind spot' – Zoe and Stephen loathe *Spiked* – loathe it. David has never visited the website before. He takes an Oreo, lies back and reads.

> The woke left is trying to sweep the problem of homophobia among culturally conservative Muslims under the carpet. Yet it is a serious problem. A 2015 Channel 4 poll found that over 50 per cent of British Muslims think homosexuality should be illegal. By pretending that all Muslims hold enlightened views on homophobia, and vilifying anyone who departs from this line, the woke left is giving a green light to homophobia, allowing intolerance to thrive in the name of tolerance.

He wishes he had known about this Channel 4 poll last night. He could have shot Zoe down with it. Even if it is a few years old, it will still be representative. The author of the article wouldn't have used it otherwise. *Spiked* is a famous, reputable online publication, not a Facebook group.

'TAKEAWAY?' DAD ASKS.

'Sure.' David closes the fridge, which is packed, but pointlessly so, with browning cheese and sticky ham slices and a constellation of hummus tubs, empty but for crusty lumps.

'I could pop to the shop,' Dad says. 'But ordering something might be more fun.'

'Yeah.'

He has scaly skin and red patches on his cheeks, thanks to the chilli sauce he bought from Green Street Market. David binned it but Dad retrieved it, insisting it was fine: the effect is temporary.

'Vijay's?' Dad says. 'Panda Cottage?'

'Panda Cottage? We had Vijay's last time. Wouldn't mind some spring rolls.'

'I was thinking Chinese too. Hang on, I'll find the menu.'

A dozen copies lie in a drawer in his room. They first ordered from Panda Cottage using Just Eat. Delivering the food, the courier told them that Just Eat takes 14 per cent commission and that if instead they called up they would receive a 5 per cent discount, and stuck a menu in the bag. Dad now exclusively orders on the phone. The menus have kept coming.

David knows what he wants: spring rolls, sweet and sour tofu, coconut rice. Dad knows what he wants too: spring rolls, chicken chow mein, special fried rice. They don't strictly need a menu. But studying it together is part of the ritual. It makes the takeaway into more of a thing, a family thing, an event. They order a takeaway once a month. Dad's single indulgence (excepting booze).

He returns with two menus, passes one to David. 'You want spring rolls?'

'Yeah.'

'Good last time we had them, weren't they?'

'Yeah.'

'I'll take some too. How about the main?' He runs a finger over the menu. 'Big vegetarian selection. Lot of choice for you. More than I remember them having.'

'The black bean is tempting. But I think I'll have the sweet and sour tofu.'

'Yeah? The chicken chow mein for me.'

'And coconut rice.'

'Let me see. Where's that? Got it. Okay. I'll have the special fried rice. That's the best value: pork, chicken, shrimp . . . So. We have spring rolls, sweet and sour tofu, coconut rice, chicken chow mein, special fried rice. Is that everything?'

'Yeah.'

Dad regards the menu a little longer and calls. 'Hello, it's Richard from Yoxley Drive. Yes, a while. How are things? How's business? . . . Great. I'm telling you, open a proper eat-in restaurant and we would be there night after night. No, I swear, night after night.' How bubbly, lively, he can force himself to sound in situations like this never fails to surprise David. 'Really?' he continues. 'Congratulations. Send him my regards . . . What? Of course. Got sidetracked. Sorry. We'll have . . .'

THE SUN STRONG IN THE WINDOWS of his room in Mum and Stephen's place, steam seesawing from his cup of coffee, David browses Instagram. He stares at the screen – and swears.

Selina. She has a boyfriend. Her most recent post shows her with some wanker, her hand on his chest, his hand on her waist. The caption: a man-and-woman-holding-hands emoji, a hearts-in-eyes emoji. Someone commented: 'aw you guys' with flames. She has a boyfriend.

David clicks on to the boyfriend's profile: a bio that reads 'poet // film photographer // chaser of the light / baroque ideologue // LDN // @ucl' and has heavily filtered photos from literary events, protests. She must have met him at one of the slam poetry nights. A last look at her profile. Unfollow.

He starts his German homework but, struggling to concentrate, soon sacks it in favour of *Stranger Things* in the living room with Coke and hummus chips.

'David?' he hears, three episodes in, and turns round in surprise. Mum is standing in the doorway (a black leather jacket with a silver Amnesty candle in the right lapel), Stephen behind her. After hurriedly pressing 'pause' he mumbles: 'Just leaving.'

'Have you been watching TV all day?'

He tells her that he spent two hours on his German and history homework, finished it a few minutes ago and thought he would watch one episode before taking the Tube.

Mum regards him sceptically.

'Is that *Stranger Things*?' Stephen says. 'Great series.'

'Yeah.'

'Well. Since you're still here,' Mum says, 'why not stay and eat? We're planning to make *fesnjan*. We bought chicken but we could easily use tofu instead. We have some smoked—'

'Don't worry.'

'Are you sure? Because—'

'Don't worry. How was the film?'

'Brilliant. Funny and touching and visually stunning. Just so inventive too.'

'It was really impressive,' Stephen agrees. 'I've never been a big Wes Anderson fan, to be honest, but this one is well worth watching.'

'You would enjoy it,' Mum says.

'Mm.'

She asks whether he has been outside at all. 'Lovely weather.'

'Oh?' He looks out. Three, and a stubborn straw light is rolling in, fuzzing up the succulents on the left of the windowsill. The medallion on the Persian rug glows turquoise.

'Springlike,' she says. 'We'll let you finish watching this episode then. I'll put a five-pound note on the table. You can pick up an iced coffee at Cabal for the walk to the station.'

'Thanks.'

He leaves the sofa at three thirty. Mum was right. It is nice outside. On Whiston Road, a silver convertible sharks past, with two topless guys in sunglasses. He tugs at the neck of his hoodie, hesitates, walks on. A minute later, he stops, slips out of his hoodie and stuffs it in his backpack. This is a free country. He can wear whatever he wants. His T-shirt is emblazoned with 'Karl Williams' across the chest. 'The Alternative Poet Laureate' fills the back. He's worn it out and about countless times, but not since the Islamophobia controversy. He wonders whether someone will confront him and call him a racist – and then smiles twitchily. He is a heretic. Despite Cabal being rammed, he waits with his hands in his pockets, exhibiting the 'Karl Williams' print. When he reaches the front of the queue and places his order, the barista shows surprising restraint – no snarky callout – but he may well be mentally composing a tweet.

Unharmed, David takes the Overground to Whitechapel, Central Line to Newbury Park.

As he leaves the station with his iced oat latte, Eastern Avenue is a warm, buttery white. In front of Ladbrokes, an elderly man in a string vest smokes, considering passers-by. Road workers in orange overalls rest, chat and munch on sausage rolls. The new teenage employee at Gnanam Food & Wine checks the fruit-and-vegetable crates. Passing, David catches her eye. She smiles at him.

Jesus. The Instagram look, with the big eyes and the plump lips. Her breasts. Her legs. She is hotter than Selina. She is way hotter than Selina. Fuck Selina. Could it be that she is a Karl fan – that her smile was in response to the T-shirt? Next time he buys something there, he will strike up a conversation with her. He is still imagining the course it will take when he reaches the underpasses.

HE SLIDES THE VOLUME ON Spotify up to max and enters the first underpass, which is as grubby as ever; nothing of the nice day has got in. A shabby laceless trainer shivers in the cradle of a dim light.

They are sitting on the grass in the square, Mo, Ibrahim and someone else. David has often seen Mo meet him outside the gates of their college. Hassan or Hasim. Hassan.

He can try to sneak past them while Mo and Hassan are facing the other way. Shoulders hunched, hands in pockets, he makes for the second underpass. Nearly there, he hears something over his music. Jeers? He keeps walking. In the second underpass, however, he loses his nerve, sure that he is being followed, and stupidly wheels round, expecting to see them charging towards him.

They're still in the square, but Mo is standing up, hands cupping his mouth, megaphoning.

David tugs the wire of his earphones, forcing them out.

'Hey?' Mo says. 'Can you fucking hear shit or what?'

'Come in. Come in,' Ibrahim says, before turning to the others. 'It's not working. Must be the battery.' He stares at his right hand, as if holding a walkie-talkie. 'Must be the battery. Wait. Come in. Come in? Nah. Nothing.'

David remains motionless in the second underpass, unsure whether to turn and continue home or let them play out their inane set piece.

'He's staring at us,' Ibrahim says. 'Like a rabbit or something.'

'Correction. He's staring at you, bro,' Mo says. 'It's the shirt. Everyone loves that shirt.' A toke from a rollie or a joint – a joint, judging by how they are acting.

‘Nothing wrong with my shirt,’ Ibrahim says, pinching it up. ‘And pass that over already.’

‘Where’s the booze?’

‘In my bag.’ As he gestures towards it, his gold ear stud gleams.

They banter over the shirt. Ibrahim insists that it’s black, with a lightning print. Mo counters that the lightning is pink, orange, green. ‘You can’t be leaving that out of the description. You’re basically wearing a shirt that says “Look at me, boys. Look at me.”’

‘Fuck you, man.’

David continues home. They are out of it.

‘Oi,’ Ibrahim shouts. ‘Oi. Makeup Boy.’ David ups his pace. ‘Oi.’ Footsteps: skittery, trainery. ‘Oi.’ And then Ibrahim is blocking his way. Grinning. ‘You think it’s cool to ignore me?’

‘No.’

‘Yeah. You think it’s *cool* to ignore me.’

‘No.’

Ibrahim can’t even stand straight. He slouches from side to side.

‘You think it’s cool to . . .’ He stops mid-sentence, blinks. ‘Hang on. I know that name. He’s the Islamophobe.’

‘What?’

‘From the news.’ He prods the words ‘Karl Williams’.

‘No.’

‘You saying I’m lying?’ He beckons to Mo and Hassan, who remain in the square, watching. ‘Your wanker bums Islamophobes.’ Hassan whispers to Mo, who slugs from the bottle before whispering back. They too enter the underpass.

‘Look, I’m sorry,’ David says. ‘I’m sorry. Okay? I’m not . . . whatever.’

Ibrahim’s expression changes, as if he is registering something; the vague hostility in his stare swells into a swarming hate. David takes a step back, Ibrahim one forwards. He seizes David by the neck of his T-shirt. ‘Please.’ Nothing. He looks into Ibrahim’s eyes – cloudily raging, small, swallowed up by big, hammocky lids. His teeth skate from side to side.

‘You . . .’ he says. And then a swing. David slumps from the force. Ibrahim draws his arm back, as if about to throw a second punch. David shrinks away, trips and stumbles to the ground.

Ibrahim looming over him, he rolls on to his side and covers his face. He has never been hit before. His cheek stings. He wants to go home. Just wants to go home. Ibrahim, Mo and Hassan observe him. He is determined to keep his face hidden, to not let them see him crying.

'Come on,' Mo says. 'Don't be like that. Get up. He barely touched you. Slap innit.'

'Fuck you,' Ibrahim says.

'Why you slap him?'

'Wanker's a Nazi.'

'What?'

'You not clock what he's wearing? Karl Williams. The one who was talking shit about us. Muslims this. Muslims that.'

'Yeah?' A slobbering sigh. 'And he's wearing his T-shirt like a proper England boy? Well, shiiiiiiit.'

David is wimpy with tears. He hates them, hates them, hates them.

'Lucky I've been wanting one for an hour now,' Ibrahim says. 'I'm fucking busting.'

'Eh?' Hassan says.

'This is going to feel good,' Ibrahim says. 'This is going to feel *gooooooood.*'

Keeping his hands pressed to his face, David sees only the haloed red-black edges of his fingers and, between them, the scummy, tagged side of the underpass.

The spiky sound of flies being unzipped. 'Yeahhhhh.' A jet of vile piss strikes the side of his body. He jolts, draws his knees up towards him and urges his face and hands into the ground.

'What the fuck?' Hassan says.

'Shit,' Mo says. 'You . . . I can't look, man. I can't look. It's on his fucking . . . Oh, man!'

The jet of piss squiggles up, up, up, up, and settles in his hair.

DAVID SHOVES EVERYTHING HE WORE into a rubbish bag, including the Karl T-shirt. No point keeping it. He could wash it a hundred times and it would still reek of Ibrahim's piss. Having tossed the bag into the waste bin, he takes a long, hot shower, kneading his hair with shampoo, conditioner, shampoo, conditioner, shampoo, conditioner. Even so, it feels horrible, mucky. He studies his reflection in the mirror. A small cut on his right cheek, nothing too serious. Dad is unlikely to notice. But Mum or Stephen will. He hangs his head over the sink and swears.

In his room, he picks up his reading lamp and flings it at the wall, cracking the shade. Next, the bedside table. He kicks a wooden leg with his bare foot. Nothing happens to it. Yet his toes cane. He lifts the table and slams it and lifts it and slams it until the leg comes loose.

He tosses his head manically. 'Fuck! Fuck! Fuck!'

When there is nothing left to break, he slumps into his chair. On his desk lies his notebook. It occurs to him that if he means to emulate Karl he should be channelling his emotions into song lyrics. This is an opportunity. Gripping his pen, he leans over an empty page.

He stares at it. He rips it out.

Pointless. He will never be a successful singer-songwriter. There is no longer a place in the music world for someone like Karl or him. Just elite corporate PR bullshit. Why try?

After five minutes spent forcing the nib of the pen into the jagged paint chips on his white desk, he snickers, drops the pen, picks up his phone, opens Twitter and clicks compose.

#Karlwilliams was right to criticise the #farfieldschool protesters and question whether Islam is compatible with Western values. The truth is NO. Islam is NOT compatible with Western values. Stats prove it. Read this: https://www.spiked-online.com/the-woke-left-blind-spot.

Everyone will lose their minds. But who cares? It will be funny.

Having sent the tweet, he runs his hands through his hair, which still feels wrong. Mo, Ibrahim, Hassan. The Muslim cunts. The fucking Muslim cunts.

He takes his towel and returns to the bathroom.

Hassan

'SO.' AHMED BACKS HIS CHAIR out and slowly, effortfully, stands up. 'Shhhhh. Brothers. Brothers,' he says, in competition with Drake's 'Hotline Bling' and pool-table clacks. 'Brothers.' After scratching his silvery beard and harrumphing, he raises his palms. Everyone in the sports hall of the Newbury Park Muslim Youth Centre turns towards him. On his long, hollow-cheeked face, a smile forms. 'It's time for our first semi-final. Hassan and Saajid versus Waleed and Faisal. Step up, competitors.'

Hassan rolls his shoulders. 'Come on,' he says to Saajid. 'Let's have them.'

'Easy.'

He makes his way through five rows of black plastic canteen chairs to the front of the hall, trainers screeching on the wood flooring. Applause, laughter and hollers come from the surprising number of people who have stayed to watch the tournament's closing stages. In the thin rectangular windows a sky the colour of gruel shows. He claims a chair to the right of the fifty-inch projector screen. Saajid sits beside him, rubs his palms on his knees. 'I reckon we can put four past them.'

Ahmed hands them the controllers, his bony frame on the verge of snapping. '*Bil tawfiq.*' Hassan's is sticky, orange crumbs on the triggers. He wipes it with his black Nike hoodie. Maaz, who used it last, can never resist Chilli Heatwave Doritos at half-time. Waleed and Faisal sit to the left of the screen, bringing their intense body odour with them. Neither has started using deodorant.

'We sticking with PSG?' Saajid asks. On the team-select screen, a crackly purple light zips around the edges of a stadium and smoke sweeps across floodlit grass. 'Yeah,' Hassan says, still cleaning his controller. Waleed and Faisal: Manchester United. Being player one, Saajid has control over the match settings. As ever, he changes the ball to the Nike Ordem V. It's sick, white with neon yellow and orange details. The real one was honed over hundreds of hours of testing. Its Aerowtrac grooves deliver true flight. Every time Hassan goes to Sports Direct he admires it on the shelves. Just to take one free kick with it would be incredible. When *FourFourTwo* ran a competition to win one, he entered with a dozen new email addresses.

Saajid proceeds to the team-management screen. 'I'll leave this to you, Hazza.'

Hassan changes the formation to a 3-1-4-2. Mbappé and Cavani up front, Neymar on the left wing, Di María on the right. Tactics. Hmm. Lukaku will pose them problems. He instructs Silva to man-mark him and moves Kimpembe and Marquinhos back. Done.

While Waleed and Faisal tinker with their team, Hassan checks his phone. There is a new message in the Los Galacticos WhatsApp chat with Mo and Ibrahim. Mo: 'Yo Hazza, Valentines Park with Ibrahim & 1/4 of skunk NOW cmon cmon.' He replies: 'It's FIFA tournament night at the yc. I thought you guys were coming? I'm in the semi-final – playing with Saajid. Been fun. You could still make it to watch the final. Loads of crisps etc left.'

'Okay,' Waleed says. 'Ready.'

'Brothers, take a seat,' Ahmed says. 'PSG versus Manchester United.'

Hassan's phone lights up, Ibrahim this time: 'lol Saajid. Isnt he like 14? fuck that shit and get to the park lol. msg when youre here.' Hassan pockets his phone.

The pre-match cut scene begins. A camera pans around the stadium, showing realistic PSG fans holding up red, white and blue cards, and then the players stride out from the tunnel. Ahmed turns up the volume. *And hello to you from a city that is never short on style. I'm talking, of course, of Paris. We're at the Parc des Princes on a glorious day for football. My name is Derek Ray and my commentary partner on this occasion is Stuart Robson. This has all the makings of a highly engrossing match. It's Paris St-Germain up against Manchester United.* The nerves are kicking in. This is the semi-final of a tournament. He has never before made it to a semi-final. 'Come on,' he says to Saajid.

HASSAN STARES AT THE STREET-ART-STYLE West Ham mural on his wall, spray-painted by someone who used to work for Dad. How did he miss that chance? Injury time, and Saajid played a perfectly weighted through ball to him. He controlled it well and took it away from the defender and accelerated into a one-on-one – and then scuffed the shot. Nine times out of ten he would expect to put that away. Nine times out of ten. They lost two–one. Waleed and Faisal won the tournament, and already appear on the Newbury Park Muslim Youth Centre's Facebook page holding mini trophies. Raindrops sprinkle on the window. He should have used a finesse shot or feinted and taken the ball round the keeper.

WhatsApp, Los Galacticos. He flicks the notification away. This many hours in, Mo and Ibrahim will be ridiculously high. Mo's last message made no sense. They are his best mates and will remain his best mates whatever happens. But they've changed. In autumn, having failed to get the grades needed to stay at Oaks Park High School for sixth form, Mo started at Redbridge College, and Ibrahim turned eighteen and got a job as a security guard at Gomora nightclub. They have since concluded that what the three of them used to do together was 'kids' shit' – FIFA, the mosque, everything – and are now waiting for Hassan to catch up.

He embraces the muffling comfort of TikTok – watching a comparison of American and British culture, a 'guess my age' challenge and a West Ham v Watford matchday vlog – then moves on to Twitter. @ArianaGrande: 'thank u australia i love u.' @MehdiFaez2005: 'A lot of respect for the students at #QueenMary for making their feelings clear about the #RachelVine on-campus event.' @DilwarManzoor retweeted a thirty-second video of a protestor outside Farfield school. Since Afria posted about this story, he's been meaning to research it.

'Don't teach our children that gay is okay because gay is not okay. God created man, then he created woman for man's pleasure. He didn't create man for man. There is no gay in Islam. It's an immoral act. If it's the law that these lessons have to be taught, we'll accept that, but we want to remove our children from the lessons.' Along with the retweet, @DilwarManzoor wrote: '17:84: "Say: everyone acts according to his own disposition (nature): But your Lord knows well who is best guided on the way." Gay Muslim brothers & sisters be true to yourselves and ignore these morons. Follow the Quran, the Creator's words.'

Mum calls him. He goes to the top of the stairs. Having just got back, she is still wearing her hijab and her long black coat. She shakes her umbrella, which has a peacock-feathers print, and sets it on the doormat to dry. All her clothes and accessories come from the Oxfam in Bethnal Green. An annual trip. Whatever is available on the day. Throwaway culture annoys her.

She popped to the newsagent's to pick up coconut yoghurt and it started coming down. They can eat in a few minutes: a lemon chicken biriyani she made earlier. As Dad is working late at the restaurant, it will be just the two of them. 'It will be nice. I put pomegranate seeds and cashews.'

'Great.'

'Everything okay?'

'Yeah.'

'Hassan?'

'Just lost in the semi-final of the FIFA tournament.'

A smile. 'Were you playing with Mo or Ibrahim?'

'Erm. Mo.'

'Did Ibrahim's team win?'

'Yeah.'

She laughs. 'I will tell you when the food is ready then.'

'How's the website?' Hassan asks.

A silver saucepan sits in the centre of the table. The whole kitchen smells of cumin. Mum's best friend, Aliya, set up Muslim Voices six months ago, with the ambition to create an archive of Islamic life and culture in Britain. Dad encouraged Mum to help with the project. She had been feeling lonely and frustrated at home and, with an *Evening Standard* mention having made his restaurant more popular than ever, they had the money to hire a cleaner. Aliya put Mum in charge of interviewing. Hassan enjoyed an article about a man who immigrated in the late sixties, like Dad, and another about a woman who owns a record store in Glasgow and plays bass in a metal band.

'Good,' she says. 'This morning I interviewed a man from Bradford. You'd like him. Football is his life, his passion. He coaches an under-fourteens team. I told him that you support West Ham, and he sent his best wishes for the FA Cup.' A carefully calibrated whimper directs her attention to Lina, who is standing by her bowl. 'Don't tell me you are still hungry?' Lina gazes over with her big blue eyes. Mum sighs, and then, of course, takes another pouch of dog food out of the cupboard. 'If only Kala would eat even half as much as Lina.' Jelly and clobbered meat squelch into the bowl. She will upload the audio and the transcript of the interview with the coach tomorrow. She has been incredibly busy lately. 'A lot of homosexual Muslims have contacted us, because of those Farfield school protests in Leeds. We have set up three interviews for next week.'

Hassan casts about for more cashew nuts. 'I watched a video earlier of a protester shouting that there is no gay in Islam, blah, blah, blah. What's up with that?'

She says she wishes she had an answer to this but doesn't – in spite of all her interview research. 'I think, well, the protesters can't find a place for LGBTQ in their faith.'

'Why?'

'They see the Prophet Lot parable as evidence that homosexuality is a sin.'

'But they're wrong, right?'

A sip of water. She watches him through the glass. 'Yes, I would say so. I don't think the parable tells us anything about homosexuality. What happens is rape. Ultimately there are many possible interpretations of the destruction of Sodom, and we should interpret the Quran in a way that benefits society, not holds it back. The protesters are forgetting that.'

He considers this. 'It's just embarrassing. They're giving Islam a bad name, a worse name.' The chandelier's light ripples over the table and across the sea-turtle and oak-tree prints on the wall; a plump shadow from the porcelain vase.

'It is. But. You know. In Britain homophobia was widespread until very recently. You could be fired for being gay. People were given conversion therapies. And AIDS was only taken seriously in the media once it was understood it could kill heterosexuals as well. Now society has changed. And LGBTQ has mainstream acceptance. There are still people in faith communities – Muslims, Christians, Jews – who have not come to terms with this. But they will, in time.'

'Maybe the interviews next week will help.'

She smiles. 'I hope so.'

'YOU WANT ONE?'

'Nah,' Hassan says.

'Bro, it's a smoke. You need to chill out. It's not *haram*.'

'I'm fine.'

Mo rolls his eyes. 'All right, Imam.' He fumbles for his Harley-Davidson Zippo, lights a cigarette. They are sitting outside a five-a-side concrete football cage close to Redbridge College, backs to the metal bars, waiting for a troop of office workers to leave. The air has a spring glaze.

'How were your classes today?' A cheap orange Sports Direct ball between Hassan's knees.

'Same as. My chemistry teacher is so fucking boring.' Mo mimes blowing his brains out. 'Dunno why I bother to turn up.'

'Is Kalila in chemistry?'

'Oh, bro.' He wafts smoke Hassan's way. 'Kalila. Gets hotter every day, I swear.'

Hassan asks whether they have been messaging recently.

'Yeah, course.'

'And?'

'It will happen. Trust. What about you and Afria?'

'Me and Afria?'

'You're into her. You said last week—'

'I barely know her. I said like three words to her outside your college once.'

A floaty clang. They jerk forward, and then lean back as the ball bounces away. The Crawford Place street sign has taken a battering; Hassan wonders whether a car smashed into it. An elderly woman lugs a bucket from her front door to the drain and casually tips out its contents.

'You're into her though. Right?' Mo says.

Hassan concedes that she's hot.

'Yeah,' Mo says. 'You're into her. Okay. How about . . . She's mates with Kalila. They sit together. Shall I get them out? I'll get them out. Just something caszh. Beers in the park or so.'

A coil of sunlight passes over Hassan's retro silver and cherry-red Nike Total 90 trainers. He rubs away a spot of mud. Throughout his life, he has done everything together with Mo and Ibrahim. But can he continue to do so? He knows what would happen on this double date. Mo would pressure everyone to drink, drink, drink, and Hassan would refuse and end up seeming like a loser to Afria. He would rather try to meet her alone.

'Erm.'

'Bro. You can have a beer once.'

Hassan extends his legs on the concrete. 'Get them out, and I'll be there.'

'And you'll have a beer?'

'I'll be there.'

'So you'll have a Fanta. Lemon or Fruit Twist?'

Hassan shrugs.

'All right,' Mo says, and sends his cigarette butt windmilling. A silence settles. Hassan listens to the ball ricocheting around the cage, the calls, the screeches. He tilts his head left, right, left, right, silvering the top of the licence plate of a badly parked Ford Focus.

Gesturing towards a bench across the street surrounded by sorry-looking trees, Mo says, 'Look at him.' A guy from Redbridge College, David, whom Mo seems to hate. 'Seriously. Look at him. He sits there on his jacks day after day and performs the same screwy routine. He's mental.'

'Right.' Hassan is eager to start playing. There is less than an hour until his next class and Oaks Park High School is a twenty-minute walk from here.

'Wait for it . . . Wait for it.'

David rejigs his earphones, taps his phone, unzips his backpack, takes out a fedora, puts it on and starts exuberantly nodding.

Mo slaps his thighs. 'I mean, what the fuck? Every time he sits there. Like clockwork, on comes the hat. Who's he trying to impress? It's weird enough that he wears the shit he wears. But, like, this routine? He's such a faggot.'

'Don't say that, man.'

'What?'

'Stuff like that.'

'Eh?' Mo shakes his head. 'First you're all Imam Miqdad on me and then you're all Frank Ocean. What's happening to you, bro? Just chill. Relax a bit. Jokes.'

Hassan bumps his trainers together. If he were meeting Mo for the first time today, would he want to be mates with him? Better not to ask himself that.

'You there, Hazza?'

'Yeah.'

'This lot's packing up.'

'Okay.'

'Free kicks?'

'Yeah.'

IN FULL-SCREEN MODE, HASSAN OPENS a photo of the mushy leftovers of a falafel wrap in a takeaway box, changes the brilliance, black point and vignette settings, then swishes through others he took.

His art and design homework is to put together a series of photos in response to the theme of the senses. 'A good photographer captures all five senses,' Ms Romano wrote in the instructions. 'They will aim to convey how things sound, how they smell, how they taste and how they feel, as well as how they look. For inspiration, see the attached work by Koudelka, Parr and Halsman.' He will take more tomorrow. His are okay, but not comparable to the examples.

He wants to study media and communications at Goldsmiths, meaning he needs to improve in art and design – and soon. Ms Romano is writing his reference as well. He stares at his laptop. Getting rejected from Goldsmiths would be terrible. The only other interesting courses are at Leeds, Glasgow and Manchester, and university accommodation would cost a shit-ton. With Goldsmiths he could live at home.

Giving up on his homework for the day, he opens Facebook. A post from the Newbury Park Muslim Youth Centre details a forthcoming session with alumni who are now variously practising medicine, teaching English literature and working for a start-up company. It is already in his calendar. West Ham United: 'Remember this? Genius from Paolo Di Canio.' He watches the video. Incredible strike. Legend. He continues scrolling and sees that Afria has changed her profile picture. She is the only person Hassan knows who is active on Facebook. In a light-pink crop top, she smiles at the camera. Her choppily braided black hair suits her.

God, she's hot. He would love to spend more than thirty seconds with her. From the pages she follows on Facebook, it's clear that they are into the same music: Drake, Eminem, Ed Sheeran, The Weeknd, Lana Del Rey, SZA, Stormzy, Migos. She watched *Stranger Things* recently too. They would have stuff to talk about.

Muslim Voices: 'Today brings an interview with Zaara Ahmed, an inspiring 24-year-old lesbian Muslim from Blackburn. (We have changed her name to allow her to speak honestly.) Her story is moving and vital. We urge you to read it. Link below.'

He reads her story. At sixteen, she realised that she was lesbian. But it was only at university, when she grew close to a girl on her course, Phoebe, that she acted on her feelings. They entered into a relationship, and a few years later moved in together. So that Zaraa's parents would think that she and Phoebe were only flatmates, they chose somewhere with two bedrooms. Zaara didn't know whether she would ever find the courage to tell her parents the truth. They might disown her. Their morality was guided by tradition, not faith. If she did ever find the courage, she would quote 10:41 and remind them that the Quran promoted tolerance, understanding, appreciation of difference. But in truth that was unlikely to help. They were stuck in their ways.

He stops fidgeting with the transparent silicone case on his phone, returns to Facebook, clicks 'comment' and writes: '@AfriaBaqri Check this out. Great piece.'

A note exists on his phone with what Mum told him about the Prophet Lot parable and the history of homosexuality in Britain. Just in case the opportunity to speak with Afria arises, he has been reading and re-reading it on his walks to sixth form.

WhatsApp sends him a notification. Ibrahim: 'fucking fucks seriously FUCK them.' Hassan asks what's up. 'Typing' appears, disappears, reappears, disappears, reappears.

Ibrahim: just fucking fuck them who the fuck do they think they are
Ibrahim: FUCK
Mo: ???

Ibrahim: racist cunts
Ibrahim: fucking came to our place pissed through our letterbox shouted their racist shit and then ran away
Ibrahim: pissed
Ibrahim: through our letterbox
Ibrahim: with my parents and my nan in
Ibrahim: FUCK

Hassan has been called a Paki before. Ibrahim has been beaten up before. But this?

He imagines Mum hearing a trickle, walking into the hallway, seeing a puddle forming on the mat. She would never recover from that. They would need to move house. They would need to.

Mo: no way that's nuts
Hassan: fuck
Mo: Nazi scumbags
Ibrahim: You know what?
Ibrahim: Its no longer a minority
Ibrahim: Im telling you every single white cunt in this country wants to send us packing im telling you
Ibrahim: I see it in their eyes
Ibrahim: everywhere Tube bus Tesco I see it I fucking see it
Mo: Yh
Ibrahim: fuck this country
Ibrahim: cunts
Ibrahim: think they can piss through our letterbox
Ibrahim: fuck them fuck them fuck them
Ibrahim: ARGH
Ibrahim: don't mention this to anyone else
Ibrahim: stays between the three of us

IBRAHIM PASSES HASSAN THE JOINT.

'I'm good.'

'None of that, Hazza.'

'Seriously, I'm good.'

'A little toke won't kill you.' As Ibrahim twiddles it between his fingers, smoke crackles up from its orange tip. His bike lies on the grass behind him, metallic-green frame sparkling. 'Oi.'

'All right.' They have been sitting in the square for over three hours, Ibrahim and Mo smoking skunk, swigging Jack Daniels and keying a white powder that is probably coke. Hassan has been taking care to avoid the splodges of sick with which Mo has surrounded them. He takes a brisk pull and then breathes out through his nose, mouth shut, as it said to online. No way is he inhaling.

'That's it,' Ibrahim says. 'That's my man.'

'Knew you were still a Galactico,' Mo says. 'Knew it.'

Hassan passes Mo the joint.

'Galactico,' Ibrahim echoes. 'Always has been. Always will be. You feeling better now, Mo?'

'Yeah.'

'Happens.'

'Yeah.'

Hassan wonders how long he will have to hang out with them. He felt obliged to turn up this time, to show solidarity with Ibrahim. But he is starting to wish he had stuck to WhatsApp messages. Mo stands up, slings out a series of honking laughs, hands fluttering, and says: 'By calculating the intermediate points, plot a graph showing the variation of the tension in a rope. Because, err, ropes are pie squared and pie is . . . And it's important you all know how to calculate intermediate points . . . Because, err, I'm a big posho.' Hassan grins, grabs a grass strand and rolls it round his index finger – unable to comprehend how this can be considered more fun than a FIFA tournament.

When Ibrahim asks who the 'big posho' is, Hassan fills him in: Mo is imitating Mr Roberts, who taught them GCSE maths. 'For each of the cases in part c, express the net acceleration in terms of *m*, *g* and *d*, in terms of *m*, *g* and *d*, express the net acceleration, express it, express it,' Mo says. Ibrahim laughs. 'Fucking stupid white posho.' Mo takes a bow, sits, grabs the Jack Daniels. 'Hazza, I'll message Kalila now and confirm Valentines Park tomorrow. Her, Afria and the two of us.'

'Afria?' Ibrahim says.

'Babe at my college,' Mo says.

'Visuals.'

Hassan tries to change the subject.

'Oi.' Ibrahim forms a camera with thumbs, forefingers. 'Visuals.'

He reluctantly takes his phone out.

'Damn right.' A wrinkling of the nose. A lusty sniffle. A thumbing of ash from his new Superdry shirt, which is black with pink, orange and green lightning bolts.

Hassan has little desire to show them her Facebook page and listen to them rate her. 'GiffGaff's signal is so shit,' he says to buy time. The pages in the Thomas the Tank Engine colouring book, left open on the bench in the centre of the square, flap up.

A rash of footsteps spreads from behind them, the underpass. 'Shit,' Ibrahim says, facing that way. Hassan raises his eyes. 'Shit,' Ibrahim repeats, seizing his bag with a fierce clumsiness.

'All right. Leave it to me to find her socials,' Mo says, too stoned to register the footsteps or Ibrahim's reaction.

Anxiety tingling, Hassan wonders whether it is one of the racists. But Ibrahim soon cracks up. Whoever it is, they are now in the square, passing, walking away.

'Got her Facebook page,' Mo says.

'Fucking hell,' Ibrahim says, collapsing hysterically back. 'This skunk kills me. It kills me. I thought it was . . . Fucking hell . . . And then there's Mo's college mate.'

Hassan looks over his shoulder. David, just David.
'Shit,' Mo says. 'The fedora faggot.'
'Mo,' Hassan says, 'Leave it.'
Ignoring him, Mo shouts, 'Hey!'
'Show Ibrahim her Facebook page,' Hassan says.
'Hey!'
'Let's see it, bro.'
'Oi,' Ibrahim says, sitting back up. 'Oi. Makeup Boy. Oi.'
David turns towards them, twitches out his earphones.
'Hey?' Mo says. 'Can you fucking hear shit or what?'
'Come in. Come in,' Ibrahim says, before turning to the others. 'It's not working. Must be the battery.' He stares at his right hand, as if holding a walkie-talkie. 'Must be the battery. Wait. Come in. Come in? Nah. Nothing.'
'Guys,' Hassan says.
'He's staring at us,' Ibrahim says. 'Like a rabbit or something.'

Hassan looks on. David is weeping, covering his face. A crushed Monster Energy can and what seems to be a condom by his boots. Hassan can't understand why Ibrahim hit him. A Nazi? Really? He wants to say something to stop this escalating even further – but what?
'Lucky I've been wanting one for an hour now,' Ibrahim says. 'I'm fucking busting.'
'Eh?' Hassan says.
'This is going to feel good,' Ibrahim says. 'This is going to feel *gooooooood.*'
Grimacing, Hassan steps back. 'What the fuck?'
Ibrahim swings his cock out. Then—
'Shit,' Mo says. 'You . . . I can't look, man. I can't look. It's on his fucking . . . Oh, man!'
They have lost their minds. They have lost their fucking minds.
Wanting no part in this, Hassan legs it.

Mo: what happened tf u run to?
Ibrahim: bro where r u?
Mo: seriously?
Ibrahim: dnt make us come to urs lol not in this state
Mo: come onnnnnnnnn brooooo

Sitting in bed, with his back to the West Ham mural, knees bent, Hassan stares at his phone. What the fuck has happened to Mo and Ibrahim? What is wrong with them? Unrecognisable. Purple wax blobs up and rises in his lava lamp. He can't continue hanging out with them – that he knows for sure. Who will he hang out with in future then? Saajid? Saajid is fourteen. He stirs on his mattress. They have been his best mates since he was six. He thought that things would eventually return to how they once were, that the three of them would find a way to remain Los Galacticos. Impossible now. Impossible. Will he end up like David, sitting on a bench on his own, wearing a fedora for imaginary friends? There is nothing for it. Ibrahim pissed on someone. He pissed on someone.

Hassan forces his fingers to reply.

Hassan: Guys you went too far
Hassan: I dont want to be involved in stuff like that
Hassan: you do your thing fine I just dont want to be involved anymore ok?

Hands clammy. They have been his best mates since he was six. What will happen when he next runs into them? If Mo hadn't moved to Redbridge College and Ibrahim hadn't started working at Gomora, this might never have happened. Fucking Redbridge College. Fucking Gomora. They have been his best mates since he was six. He will never manage to replace them. How could he?

Ibrahim: erm? i thought we were Los Galacticos
Ibrahim: but i guess i was wrong
Ibrahim: thats cool just wish i had known before
Ibrahim: You can go and hang with the Nazis instead then lol
Mo: Hazza bro? wtf?

Ibrahim pissed on someone. He pissed on someone.

Hassan: Sorry guys i just cant anymore
Hassan: its not just today it's everything lately
Hassan: i know you find mosque boring and the youth centre embarrassing and youre into weed and coke and stuff now but thats not me. just do your thing without me
Hassan: ok?

II

David

IN THE DAZZLE OF A SEVERE, sour light, David rolls a cage trolley into the cheese, yoghurts and desserts aisle. He checks the time: only fifteen minutes until his break. He tears open the first box, clotted cream, a dozen packs. The requirement to wear gloves while stacking the shelves still irritates him. He has got used to everything else about the uniform, even the hideous orange rims on the maroon polo shirt, but the gloves are uncomfortably tight, prickly, sweaty. The second box contains something called boodles, butternut squash noodles, a 'great alternative' to traditional pasta. He kicks the cage trolley towards their spot. The air-conditioning system is meant to extract air from the fresh-fish counter and recirculate air from the bakery counter. He could swear it does the opposite.

'Excuse me,' a customer says. 'Any vanilla-and-banana Müller yoghurts?'

'Sorry, we're out of them.'

'Why bother to make them half price if no one can buy them? I've checked every day this week, literally every day, and haven't seen them in stock once.'

'Sorry.'

The customer asks him to check the boxes on the trolley. He crouches, edges his way around it. 'Sorry. None on here.'

'You know what I think?'

'What?'

'I think this is a scam. Just another scam.'

'Sorry.' He returns to the boodles. A co-worker enters the aisle, pushing her own cage trolley, clanging, rattling. There are three shopfloor sounds he now hears in his sleep: this, the shredding of cardboard and the 'live well for less' loudspeaker announcement. They are becoming a part of him. He exchanges nods with the co-worker, whose name he has forgotten. The boodles are out. What next? He checks the time: eight minutes until his break, eight minutes.

Sainsbury's employees are allowed to smoke in one area, a small rectangle at the back of the shop inaccessible to customers – smoke somewhere else, and you will be in deep shit. He sits on the grub of the step and lights a cigarette. The weather is terrible for late August. It's already dark, wet and chilly. The door behind him jolts open. He fumbles for his earphones. Too late.

'Hey, man.'

'Hey.'

'Joining you cool?'

'Mm.'

'Jamal.' He extends a hand. He's in his late twenties and skinny, with long, oily hair. David now likes the fuzzy bristles on his own head. Showers feel nice. Gusts of wind no longer matter. 'David.'

'Started on Monday,' Jamal says. 'These breaks, man. They're everything.' He takes out rolling tobacco, Golden Virginia. 'You been here long?'

'Six weeks.'

'Fair play. Guy showing me the ropes on Monday said he'd been working here for fifteen years. That's basically a life.' David nods. A skip overflowing with shit, birds on the edges, cleaning their feathers. Delivery vans to the right, covered with images of glazed carrots. And that's it: the sights from the Ilford Sainsbury's smoking rectangle. 'You live round here?' Jamal asks.

'Newbury Park.'

‘Nothing there?’

‘Getting here isn’t too bad. Straight bus. Twenty-five minutes.’ The Tesco in Newbury Park was hiring, but eventually he would have ended up serving Ibrahim, Mo or Hassan.

‘Guess that’s not too long. I only live five minutes away.’ His rollie draws an orange arc through the dusk as he gestures eastwards. ‘By Famz Peri Peri. Living in Newbury Park, you wouldn’t know Famz. But here and looking for a chicken shop. Famz, man.’

‘Right.’

‘Get a chicken shish kebab for a fiver in there . . . You finish school in the summer then?’

‘Yeah.’

‘GCSEs and that?’

‘AS levels.’

‘Didn’t stick it out for A levels? Got to be sticking that out, man.’

‘Just not for me. It would have been a waste of time.’

‘Could have taken you to uni at least. More babes there. That’s for sure. Blondes. Brunettes. Redheads. And from everywhere. Get some Americans, I bet. Whewwweee. No fucking uniforms either.’ He yanks his collar. ‘But I can’t talk. I sacked school off at sixteen.’ A long drag. Before Jamal can say anything else, David cuts in and explains that his break is ending, that he needs to head back inside. ‘Yeah, no worries, man. Sorry for the shit chat. Just good to be talking to someone other than a customer for a minute. You know? Anyway, I’ll see you round.’

‘Yeah.’

Three hours until the shift is over. Three hours.

A VIGOROUS SNORE FROM DAD'S ROOM. No *Only Fools and Horses* tonight then. David changes, waves away the flies in the kitchen, microwaves a vegetable masala, takes it upstairs, opens YouTube on his laptop and watches 'Black Glass' from Karl's Warsaw show. The visuals are jerky and the audio is watery, but the atmosphere is captured all the same. On the last chorus, someone wrapped in a Polish flag crowdsurfs over the person filming to the barrier. Karl is still loved in Poland.

He returns to the homepage, where a Tim Lai video is recommended. David enjoys his videos. Although they tend to be about US culture and politics, they are entertaining. Tim Lai worked for Vice News and won awards for his reporting, actual awards. This one is about Antifa and has 3,783 comments. Wisconsin1848: 'If antifa threatens you you're probably doing something right.' Leadguitarman: 'Antifa is guilty of everything they claim to be fighting against.' Gcal1954: 'I come from Romania. I lived there as a child during the 80s, communist time. Now I live in Portland and see these people calling for communism. They have no idea what communism is, food rations, forced labour, state-controlled business, state owns all property. These people have no clue.' Orange Crush: 'Call the FBI. Seriously, Tim. It's naive to think that they will de-escalate. Seriously.'

David works a wedge of onion bhaji into the thick tomatoey sauce and presses 'play'.

Tim Lai organised an irl event on identity politics and polarisation with four speakers, two progressives and two conservatives, one of whom wrote for *Breitbart*. The venue received death threats from Antifa members, suggesting that if the debate went ahead they would intervene. In panic the venue pulled the event. Tim

Lai is visibly furious. He says that the event was about encouraging debate and reducing tensions and it is outrageous that Antifa did what they did. It shows that the so-called anti-fascists are in fact the real fascists. How can Antifa regard him as a far-right sympathiser? He is a mixed-race second-generation immigrant, for God's sake, a nineties liberal. Is anyone who is willing to engage with other points of view now a far-right sympathiser?

David puts his empty plate on the bedside table, beside three others. His room smells garlicky from globs of left-over Dolmio sauce. There are wilting cucumber slices on the other plates.

He tweets the Tim Lai video: 'Award-winning journalist @timlai1985 showing who the real fascists are today. Don't think Antifa are a threat to free speech? Watch this.'

The up-next video starts. 'Last Laugh?!' An interview with a comedian who made headlines after refusing to sign a behavioural agreement before a show at an American university.

A notification flashes up on his phone. The first 'like' for his tweet. Rory, Eleanor and the other wokies who unfollowed him can do one. He receives more 'likes' now – way more. That Zoe still follows him is surprising. She will unfollow him soon. There is only so much truth she will be able to handle. Having swiped the notification away, he continues watching the video.

The comedian is intelligent, not particularly funny, but intelligent.

'THE BBC IS NOW REPORTING on the Tehran protests too,' Mum says.

'Yeah?' David lounges on the sofa, on his phone.

She takes a pistachio from the snack bowl on the wooden table. 'I'm not getting my hopes up. I have too many times before.' But last night she spoke to a friend in California, who still has relatives in Tehran, and that friend is convinced that teenagers now have far less fear of the regime. A fire-festival celebration called Chaharshanbe Suri with pre-Islamic, Zorastrian roots has become an annual show of rebellion. Across the city – especially in the west – girls and boys gather and drink and dance around bonfires. 'That would have been unimaginable when I was a teenager.'

'Promising.'

Mum says that the Special Court to Fight Social Vice now makes kids pay a fee and sign a letter saying they won't repeat the offence and then releases them. There are too many.

'Promising too.'

'It is.' She pinches the round neck of her knitted top, reaches for her water bottle, white, with a line-print of an octopus. 'That reminds me. I saw something this morning, while I was browsing.'

'What?'

'Hang on. I'll email it to you.'

'Okay.'

'. . . Sent.'

Jesus. A link to something called Open College. 'Mum.'

She asks him to check the website out. He can enrol any time – no set terms – and study at home. They supply everything necessary: textbooks, lessons, assignments, practice papers. And he will be offered a dedicated one-to-one tutor he can email with questions whenever.

'Mum.'

An enraging kindness in her eyes. 'Just an option. Still, it is an option. You could achieve what you need to study English at university. I know Redbridge College didn't work out. But Open College—'

'Mum. We've been through this.'

'But with Open College you could study at home. There's no need to worry about the money. We have the money. We'll pay for it.'

He still winces every time she uses 'we' to refer to her and Stephen. 'I don't want you to pay for me. I'm seventeen. And anyway – no. This is not what I want.'

'What exactly do you want? To close down all your opportunities? Because if you stay at Sainsbury's too long, you will. Trust me.'

'Good.' He sweeps his arms out across the sofa. 'I don't care right now. I really don't care. Why can't you understand that?' He looks away, out of the window. Now that autumn is approaching, the eggshell-blue bistro set in the garden looks lonely, glum.

'I guess it hurts. That's why. I wanted my child to go to university. It was one of the things that motivated me to leave Tehran.'

He closes his eyes.

'Baba always said that it was the best time of his life. The people he met. The experiences he had. I missed out on all that.'

'Why?' he spits. 'Why, Mum?'

'When I was your age, dedication to the regime and religion were the most important entry criteria. You had to take tests in Shia theology. And that was fine. I would have been willing to study for any test. But with Baba's reputation, there was no way I was going to be let in.'

'Right.'

'But with Open College ... There is nothing stopping you from studying what you want to study, from spending three years reading books.'

'I don't want to. I didn't say there was anything stopping me. I didn't say that. Listen to me. I don't want to go to university. I don't *want* to.'

'You would rather work at Sainsbury's than read novels and meet interesting new people?'

'Yes.'

There would be no reading novels anyway, he thinks. There would only be criticising novels for their heteronormativity, their whiteness, their Europeanness, their whateverness.

'Fine then. I suppose I wasted my time researching this.'

'I suppose so.'

She taps the table with her nails. 'You're—'

'No. Argh! Fuck. Fuck you, Mum.'

She stalks out. He returns to his phone.

'Where are you?' she asks.

'Not now.'

David is sitting on the toilet. It's nine thirty. He has been listening to Karl and reading the subreddit in his room. Stephen is home.

'Are you in there?'

'. . .'

'Look, it's not okay for you to shout or swear at me. But I'm willing to put your shoddy behaviour aside for now.'

'Just wait two minutes.'

She must have spoken to him through a bathroom door a hundred times in his life. When she is excited about something, she has to share it immediately – immediately, immediately, immediately.

'David.'

'What? What?'

'I was thinking about something Baba said to me before I left—'

'Oh my God.'

'He asked me to make a pact. If I read an interesting work of fiction or philosophy, and was ready to discuss it, I would call him. Otherwise, I wouldn't bother. For five years after moving here, I stuck to that. I made sure to read something interesting every few weeks—'

'Go away. I'm not listening to this.'

'You can't throw away the chance to spend—'

'I'm not fucking listening to this!'

He beats the wall pointlessly with his right fist and reaches for more toilet paper.

THE TOP POST IN THE SUBREDDIT is a photo of Karl embracing a middle-aged fan on stage in Warsaw with the caption 'Karl is not perfect I know but a lack of humanity is not one of his faults' – fifty-five upvotes. The next most popular posts are a photo of a plectrum with the caption 'Caught one. Karl and his touring musicians played their asses off tonight. Great show' and a screenshot of 'Black Glass' streaming on Spotify with the caption 'Wedding coming up in august. My gf suggested this for the first dance. She's a keeper all right.' David arranges the posts in chronological order. There is a text-only post from an hour ago with the ominous title 'I was in Antwerp last night and this will be bad' and twenty replies. He presses two fingers to his temple. What now?

My 16th time seeing Karl last night in Antwerp and it was up there with the best. I'll never get bored of 'Silhouettes' as an opener. When the riff kicks in, MAN! His voice was sounding as good as it's ever sounded too and there was loads of crowd interaction. BUT he said some pretty controversial shit about halfway in. Doesn't bother me tbh but know the UK media will pick up on it. I saw tons of people videoing (I was videoing the whole gig so have footage but won't be posting it just yet). He said 'Thank you for having me, Antwerp. It's a pleasure to be here, to be somewhere sane. England has become a mad place. The Monster Raving Loony Party could be running it and it would be less mad than it is now. We have Muslim parents pulling their kids out of schools because of the teaching of LGBTQ lessons. And everyone thinks that's fine. Here in Belgium that would be seen for what it is, reactionary homophobic madness. But you are far ahead. You have after all already banned halal slaughter and the burqa. You care about women's rights, animal rights. You're prepared to fight for Western civilisation. For that Belgium an Englishman salutes you.'

Heymoon replied: 'SHIT.' Depressed_aesthetic: 'Oh God. Just wait until the Grauniad hears about this.' K3nerak: 'And there I was thinking Karl had decided to keep his mouth shut after Leeds.'

David blinks. Karl is escalating, not retreating.

After a short clammy spell, he concludes that this is the right call. The woke police would never have accepted an apology anyway. He wouldn't have been un-cancelled. So why not escalate?

When Zoe learns about this new controversy, she will be relentless in tweeting about it. Not willing to listen to any more anti-Karl crap, he unfollows her.

'WHAT TIME ARE YOU WORKING TOMORROW?' Dad asks, wedging a hand into a BBQ Pringles tube.

'From seven to three.'

'I'll be out in the afternoon but should be back by six.'

'Got something?'

'Chadwell Heath. Girl booked me for four hours. I don't know what she's expecting me to do. Probably move a mountain or so. There was nothing in the comments box.'

'Good luck.'

'It'll be fine.' An easy smile.

David says that there is a two-for-one offer on ready meals at the moment: Thai vegetable curry, sweet potato katsu curry, lentil cottage pie, chana masala and cauliflower pilau rice. They thrash out what to choose: David settles on the sweet potato katsu curry, Dad the lentil cottage pie.

After reinvestigating the Pringles tube Dad taps his thighs and makes a low humming sound, a sound that seems to signal comfort. In the background the TV shows an image of Del, Rodney and Grandad in the Nag's Head and plays the *Only Fools and Horses* theme tune over and over.

A stupid thought enters his head: One day, Dad will be gone and he will have to live exclusively with Mum and Stephen. 'Great episode,' he says to flush it away.

'Great episode,' Dad echoes.

The belly. The spider veins on the nose. The fluttering lower lip. Bad signs. He jerks his shoulders. 'Yeah, Del's idea for Rodney's film – a killer rhinoceros escaping from London Zoo . . .'

'Hilarious.' A mosquito lands on the screen. 'Well . . . Guess it's bedtime. I should be back by six tomorrow. We should watch the "Jolly Boys' Outing" episode. That's brilliant too.'

'Sure.'

'Can you see to the TV and the switches?'

'Yeah.'

'Night then.'

'Night.'

Leaving, Dad says: 'I think the lentil cottage pie will be the best value.'

JUST THE TEA BREAK SECTION: *That's Life, Fiction, Psychologies, Simply You, Closer, Heat, Healthy Living, Take a Break, Pick Me Up, Chat, Elle, Love It*. David wonders who buys all these magazines. The cover of *Pick Me Up* promises these stories: 'My Photo Shame! I was Bigger than my Pregnant Sis!' 'Roller Coaster of Love! I Doooooo!' 'Beaten for Saying No to Sex!' 'I've Got a Toe in my Face!' 'Britain's Most Evil Carer?' He shakes his head. At least this is a straightforward stock task. He spent his morning in the meat-and-fish aisle: chicken fillets, lamb chops, turkey meatballs, and so, so many halal-certified stickers. He longed to prise open a pack of wings, take one out, wave it in a shopper's face and shout, You want it? You want it? and then force it into their big, fat, stupid mouth.

Did you know you can save twenty-five pence on a hot drink if you bring a reusable container? Please see one of our employees for more information. Sainsbury's. Live well for less.

He is all for reusable containers. But he has now heard that six times today.

'All right, Doc?' Jamal, and a cage trolley. 'Doc' because David wears Dr Martens to work, over the maddening dress pants. Everyone else wears trainers. On the first day, the store manager told him that trainers might be more suitable, a 'friendly' suggestion. But David is not going to give away the smidgeon of individuality that he is allowed to express. No way is he going to give that away.

'On the magazines?' Jamal says.

'Yeah.'

'Lucky shit. I'm rolling these fuckers over to the back-to-school section. Nothing worse. Questions. Questions. Questions. Do you have this in medium? Do you have this in large?'

'Yeah.'

'Anyway, see you later on, Doc.'

David nods, then turns his attention back to the magazines. He wishes Jamal would stop talking to him. They are not friends. They will not be friends. They have nothing in common.

'WHAT DO YOU WANT?' Zoe asks.

'Don't worry,' David says. 'I'll get mine.'

They find a table outside. Zoe presses the rod on the ashtray, sending butts spinning into its belly, and starts rolling. A warm fuzz from the lantern string lights overhead. The messy tangle of vines on the fencing. If there were fewer Queen Mary students, The Rose would be a nice pub. A heavily tattooed waitress strolls past with a pizza, calling number nine, number nine, number nine.

Zoe asks him how things are going. He shrugs. Fine. The shifts drag. But he is earning money. That's something. How are things going for her? Fine too. Her third year is starting in a few weeks. She desperately needs to get her head together. She went on a boozy road trip around the Balkans in August and has read fuck-all since. The upcoming modules should at least be interesting: Writing Modern London, Postcolonial and Global Literatures, Decadence. And the dissertation will be fun to write. She is planning to do it on someone called Helen Achebe.

'That reminds me. Did you have the chance to read those books?'

When they last met up, she lent him two. 'Yeah.' He takes them out of his bag.

'Thoughts?'

Reading them was a struggle. One is a 'courageous book' about 'race, identity and belonging' in Britain. The other is about intersectionality. He managed only a few chapters. But he was intent on showing Zoe that unlike her he is willing to engage with other points of view.

'Not for me.'

'Oh.'

'Glad I read them anyway. It's important to know what everyone is saying, the right and the cultural Marxists.'

'Come on. Don't use that phrase.'

'No, I'm serious. Thanks.'

Their glasses sit empty on the table, foam clinging to the sides.

'Another one?' Zoe asks.

'Okay.'

'Let me get both. If you go up on your own the bartender will ID you. Same? San Miguel?'

'Okay.'

When she returns with the drinks, she asks him whether he will download Bumble when he turns eighteen. He says he hasn't thought about it. She presses. He should be mentally putting together his profile. It will be a way for him to meet interesting girls. 'One word of advice though – choose a profile picture with your fringe. I'll never get why you shaved your hair.'

'Does it matter?'

'Remember when you were starting college and you would retweet the West Ham account every day?'

'I retweeted that account twice.'

'What I'm saying is – that wasn't you back then and this isn't you now.'

'This is me.'

'You looked properly cool with the fringe.'

'Just leave it. All right?'

'No need to be so touchy. Want to see what Bumble is like then? Here.'

'I can imagine what it's like. I've read about Tinder.'

'Forget Tinder. Only fuckboys use that.' She opens Bumble. A man appears. She swipes him away. A man appears. She swipes him away. A man appears, stroking a Siberian husky. She reads his bio. 'He's dog-fishing. Guaranteed.' She swipes him away. 'Anyhow. This is what it's like. Swipe left or right. And then wait and see what matches materialise. You're lucky. The girl will have to message you first. You won't even need to come up with an exciting opening line.' She swiftly opens and closes her inbox. 'In five months I bet you will be spending half your life on this.'

'I'm not sure.'

He knows what would happen were he to use it. Despite swiping yes to hundreds of girls, he would fail to get a single match. He is unattractive, and works at a supermarket.

'Trust me,' Zoe says.

'Do you use it a lot then?'

She has a love–hate relationship with it. 'I have spells where I use it every day – I'll admit to some Bumble tourism in Kosovo together with Eleanor – but I also have spells where I forget about it. There are so many new people to meet at Queen Mary anyway.'

'Right.' The waitress is back, now with nachos, number six, number six, number six.

Zoe removes her phone from the table. 'Sorry, I thought Bumble might interest you.'

'Oh well.'

'You're tough work now. You know that?'

'Yeah.'

'Come on . . . You can still . . . Do you want to become another guy who spends his evenings alone watching Joe Rogan interviews and playing *Call of Duty*? You're better than that.'

He sees off the rest of his beer in one gulp. 'Thanks for the concern.'

'David—'

'Bye.'

'Hey. Don't be like that—'

'I said I'd be home by nine. Newbury Park's miles away. Thanks for the beer and everything.'

LAZING IN BED, DAVID WATCHES a new Tim Lai video.

A left-wing columnist tweeted a photo of a man sitting next to her on a plane along with the comment 'close your legs ffs. Im so fed up of this. It drives my anxiety to spike.' Tim shakes his head in dismay. Is this the state of Western feminism? Going into meltdown over non-issues like manspreading, while turning a blind eye to actual issues like female genital mutilation? This columnist previously wished all her Muslim followers a Happy Ramadan. Why is there never a peep about the brutal oppression of women in Muslim communities the world over, from the Middle East to Europe? What is behind the pact Western feminism has made with Islam?

Enraged by the hypocrisy, he browses the comments. Shayan: 'Lololol manspreading. US women you have it so bad. You should share your experiences with women in Saudi Arabia. Let them know how bad you have it.' Thewomanwithnogod: 'Tim's right. Feminists in the West make me angry. I live in Pakistan and I can tell you what causes my anxiety to spike, the knowledge that I will soon be forced into an arranged marriage, not the way men choose to sit.' Dr. Strangelove: 'I've had it up to here with white women who are totally awol on Islam and just spend all day tweeting how they are victims because they saw someone manspreading or they have too small hands to hold the newest iphone or they only get paid $200k a year whereas their male co-worker gets paid $201k etc. omgthehorror! Do you hear this? I got the world's smallest violin and I'm playing it for you.'

Having tweeted the video, David checks out what is trending on YouTube. 'Extreme Moments before Disaster' and 'I Spent 32 Hours Breaking World Records' and 'I Survived on $0.01 for

30 Days' – and a trailer for the new *Call of Duty*. He laughs. Fuck you, Zoe. He clicks on the thumbnail.

Soldiers creep through a dark forest. *The rules have been bent. The line between right and wrong has become blurred. We have been sent in to find it.* One takes a drag on a cigarette, flicks it away and declares that he is going in. A medley of battle scenes follows, soundtracked by AC/DC: shots are exchanged in Piccadilly Circus, its curving LCD screens glowing in the gloom; tanks stream into a ravaged Middle Eastern city. *We get our hands dirty. So that our leaders can keep theirs clean. That's the mission.*

He marvels at how realistic everything is. That the series has reverted to *Covert Ops* instalments is news to him. An Xbox 360 plus the original *Call of Duty: Covert Ops* was his thirteenth-birthday present, much to Mum's fury: not only was *Call of Duty* unsuitable for him – it was an eighteen-rated game – but the bundle was also obviously stolen; Dad had got it from a client. Still, they had split up by then, so there wasn't much she could do. David kept it in Newbury Park and played it whenever he was there. He vividly remembers the missions in Russia. Unfortunately he never got the chance to play it online, as an Xbox Live subscription was required for that. After a few months, he told Dad to sell the bundle on eBay. Mum would never stop moaning otherwise. Besides, games were expensive and he couldn't keep playing the same offline missions over and over.

Apparently *Call of Duty: Covert Ops 2* has a campaign mode that courts controversy and a multiplayer mode that takes things to a whole new level. The reviews are positive. The *Guardian* went for the headline 'Great Game, Pity about the Politics' and gave it four out of five.

Well, if the *Guardian* has a problem with the politics . . .

He investigates how expensive a console would be. Not that expensive, it turns out. He has the money for a refurbished PlayStation 4 – and has been looking for something else to do. *Only Fools and Horses* sessions are now all that give structure to his free time. He relies on them as much as Dad does.

SPENDING HIS BREAK UNBOTHERED, for once, David reads a hot thread on the Karl subreddit: 'If Karl was Far Right this wouldn't be so painful' – nineteen upvotes, forty-six comments.

> Karl is a screwed-up, contrarian, depressed, passionate animal rights and LGBTQ+ rights activist. He's not far right so he can't go & join them & claim a new audience. He clearly knows he's gone too far and regrets saying what he said but he'll dig himself further in because he's great at feelings and not so great at the complexities of politics. Or, worse, he'll run away and socially isolate himself when what he needs is friends. It's disgusting that the media/social media is doing this to him when anyone who listens to his work knows how depressed he is and the amount of trauma he's had in his life. He sings songs no one else could ever have written, songs that have saved people's lives and mean everything to them, literally everything. Why is the media/social media so hell bent on taking him out now? He's in his 50s. Why can't they show some gratitude and respect?

The highest-rated comments: 'Karl is vegan, pro trans/LGBTQ+ rights, feminist, anti-monarchy and anti-gvt so definitely not far right' and 'He IS repeating far-right propaganda. But I think he did get to it from an animal welfare/feminism/LGBTQ+ angle. I just hope he gets out before his reputation becomes unrecoverable in the UK. The media hates him for being difficult and is loving this.'

David has read none of the recent press coverage, but he can imagine it.

At his show in Amsterdam, Karl said: 'Your support means the world to me. Thank you for ignoring the *Guardian*. The person they are describing is not me. It is someone else. *C'est la vie*. They are having fun. They will not stop. But nor will I.'

Squinting, he breathes out smoke. A nice morning. The sun has found its way into the rectangle. A gold glint from a Twix wrapper. Heavy shadows dangle from the skip.

He thumbs through the other comments.

Dr Benway: Reading most of the UK press you would think Karl was a serial killer who needs to be caught and stopped at all costs rather than an ageing artist with an opinion.
Happygib: Fuck me. The wilful ignorance of the majority of Karl fans in this sub, attempting to whitewash his mostly revolting political views, is seriously, seriously depressing.
Dr Benway: No one is trying to 'whitewash' his political views. We don't mind that he has different political views to us and take issue with the sensationalism of calling him far-right.
Happygib: Look at the state of you. Facepalm.

Why can't users like Happygib pack their bags and leave the subreddit to the true fans? It will become a bickering swamp otherwise. Having a few minutes to spare, David opens Safari. Argos on eBay is selling refurbished PlayStation 4s for 120 quid with a twelve-month warranty. A thousand and forty-two have been sold. There are fifteen left, with fifty-five watchers.

Tempting. The next-cheapest buy-it-now listing is 140 quid and is being sold by a randomer in Leicester with three feedback ratings. On the bus to work this morning, David watched more *Call of Duty: Covert Ops 2* videos. It would be fun to play. Tempting. A refresh of the page shows there are now fourteen left. Fuck it. He snuffs out his cigarette and clicks 'buy'.

'I HEARD YOU WENT FOR A DRINK with Zoe last week,' Stephen says.

'Yeah,' David mumbles, searching for a snack in the freezer, which is comically well stocked. Getting the shopping in must be like playing Tetris.

'Whitechapel?'

'The Rose.'

Stephen says that Zoe took him there too. He likes it.

Mum is running late, due to delays on the Central Line. In the forty-five minutes she spent waiting on the eastbound platform at Holborn only three Tubes came and each was rammed. She is now on a bus back but could still be a while. Of course, Stephen arrived home unusually early.

As clothes leap from side to side, the washing machine screeches, clanks, sobs. David sticks a vegan sausage roll in the oven.

'Keep some room for the five-bean chilli later,' Stephen says.

'Yeah.'

On the trellis outside, solar string lights shake with a soft twinkle. From the bistro set, only the criss-crossing table legs are visible. While Stephen precisely waters the plants on the window-sill, David recalls the slug he saw in the kitchen in Newbury Park, big, black, twitching tentacles. After taking it out and placing it on some weeds, he wondered what else lived in the kitchen. The slime trail suggested it had come from under the cooker. He chose not to look there.

'Got any more concerts booked with Zoe?' Stephen asks.

'No.'

'Shame. Do you use Dice?'

'No.'

'I've heard that's the best way to see everything that's on.'

'Oh.'

As David is leaving the kitchen, Stephen mentions Open College. David tenses up. In Stephen's opinion, it is worth considering: A levels would be valuable to have, and money wouldn't be an issue.

'Pass.'

'David—'

'Pass.'

He is not letting Stephen parent him. He is not letting that happen.

'I have a responsibility now to look out for you, and I really think your prospects would—'

'Just let me be. Jesus. You're not my . . . Just fucking let me be.'

'Sure you don't want any of the chilli?' Mum presses.

'No,' David replies without looking up from his phone.

'Sorry I was so late.'

'Don't worry.'

'You can't live on sausage rolls.'

'Mum. I'm fine.'

'. . . Can I come in for a minute at least?'

'Do what you like.'

He stares at the smiling blue whale on the wall. It may have had a calming, soothing effect on the previous owners' baby, but it is not having that effect on him. Stephen is a wanker, a grade-A wanker. Mum sits at the end of the bed, prompting him to pull in his knees.

'Reading anything interesting?'

'Reddit.' Although he has mentioned Reddit countless times, he still isn't convinced she understands what it is. She has never been tech savvy. Just mastering the differences between Facebook, Instagram and Twitter took time. She still uses Gmail to message friends.

He wonders whether Stephen has told her what happened. Hopefully not.

She says nothing. Stretches out her hands, which lie in her lap. 'I finally, finally, finally opened the box with Baba's things. I would like to show you some.'

'Not now.'

'I won't mention Open College, and it would mean a lot to me.'

'. . . Fine.'

'I'll be back in a second then.' The windows are taking a beating. Streetlights give the raindrops a glittery glow as they run down the glass. A gurgle from the radiator in the corner of the room; Stephen must have turned on the heating. David kicks away the duvet, which has a new cover, with white, blue and turquoise squares. She returns with the box, sits on the edge of the bed and passes him two small, foxed photographs. 'The first one was taken in London in the sixties.'

'This was him?'

'Mm-hm.'

'In London?'

'He won a scholarship to study at Saint Martin's. You know that.'

The photo shows him standing in front of a large canvas, wearing a ragged white shirt and black trousers, left hand in a pocket, right casually holding a cigarette.

In the next one, he is sitting at a wooden table, wearing gold-rimmed glasses and the sort of ivory-white suit David associates with safaris. 'That was later in life,' Mum says. 'The early eighties.'

'Interesting style.'

'He loved that suit. I have no idea why.'

Feeling compelled to show some interest, David asks what sort of artist he was. She takes out a notebook, with sketches. 'Here. Take a look. He was part of the Saqqakhana movement. It was a big thing in Iran in the sixties. He and other artists drew on Iranian popular culture, Islamic religious objects, literary works from the pre-Islamic period, Persian folk art and even household items like bowls and beads. Basically they were interested in celebrating the diversity of Iranian society, showing how rich and unique it was.'

David pauses on a page with calligraphic swirls.

'Mm,' Mum says. 'He used letters and numbers decoratively like that a lot. He exhibited a much larger version of that sketch at one of the Tehran biennials in the mid-sixties.'

'Right.' David should have asked a closed question.

'But he ended up turning away from the Saqqakhana movement,' she continues. 'He came to the conclusion that it was helping the Shah, helping to paper over cracks in Iranian society, covering up the social and economic inequality with the idea of a unified country. He returned to Picasso and Matisse and European artists for inspiration. The image of the man and the woman that got him in trouble with the Islamic regime – the one that landed him in prison for a week – was more cubist than Saqqakhana.' She takes out a smaller black notebook, prompting David to release a tight rasp. 'This will be the last one for now, I promise. It's from the late seventies. That blood-red sketch of the rooftops is very cubist. You know, even seeing it here today unnerves me a little. There was a time shortly before the Shah was overthrown when the Ayatollah instructed his supporters to take to their rooftops in the evenings and chant. You would hear the chanting from everywhere, and I mean everywhere. It was impressive ... or at least intense.'

Intrigued, David takes the notebook.

'I'm surprised he never burned it, to be honest,' she says.

'Hey, what's this?' A watercolour *Mona Lisa* – in a veil.

'Oh ... There's a series of those. Reproductions of famous paintings. But with veils. Just him venting his frustrations. Nothing serious.'

Frida Kahlo in a veil, a Picasso-like woman in a veil, Marilyn Monroe in a veil.

'Awesome.'

KNEELING ON THE LIVING-ROOM CARPET, David unboxes the PlayStation 4. It's sleeker than his Xbox 360 was. Jet black, an inch or two thick, light. He picks up the controller, spins the thumbsticks, raps the buttons and rests his middle fingers on the triggers, which are pleasantly sandpapery. The box also contains an in-ear headset, for chatting online, and power and HDMI cables. He switches it on. A PS logo materialises on the screen. The controller's rectangular touchpad illuminates an icy blue.

He raises the volume: forty, fifty, fuck it, fifty-five. There is no amount of noise that would wake Dad, and the neighbours can deal with some loudness for once – God knows he deals with enough moaning and shouting and baby-bawling from their side. He clicks on 'new user' and scrolls through categories for an avatar. Creatures? The polar bear is all right. He likes polar bears. There is something poetic about them, totally white creatures making their way alone through a totally white world of snow and fierce cold and weak sun and frosty stars. And when they feed on carcasses, and bloody their white snouts, they look brutally cool. Watching *Planet Earth* with Mum, he enjoyed the Arctic segments. He selects the polar bear. Next, a username. There are 'a few suggestions' on the right of the screen: *eventful-scrub*, *enough_shadow*, *speedy_auntie*, *scratchylibertyuk*, *adequate-swearer*. What to choose? David, David, David1702? He saw Karl at Brixton Academy on the seventeenth of February. It's taken. How is that possible? On a whim, he tries it with UK, and that works. David1702UK it is then.

He has a PSN profile. He is ready to play *Call of Duty*.

As Jamal was around to approve the age-restricted sale, he was able to buy it in-store after his shift. He tears the shrink wrap from the jewel case and inserts the disc. Swallowing it, the PlayStation

4 makes a satisfying sound, somewhere between an eep and a click, and starts whirring. The *Call of Duty* cover art appears, a well-built, rugged soldier sporting a buzz cut and a neck tattoo and holding an assault rifle over a ballistic vest. David will be him for a while. He surveys the room. Now that the ceiling bulb has got going – a sharp yellow rather than a dull, lazy orange – the atmosphere is wrong for gaming. Whenever the screen goes dark, he sees his awkward face and he doesn't want to see that. He slaps the light switch, takes a sip of Heineken and presses 'start'.

'HELLO.' DAVID PUTS ON AN EXAGGERATED, fake smile.

The customer nods but says nothing. He scans her shopping, a 'friendly, professional face' on a checkout. The store manager cautioned him for not making customers feel welcome. 'Remember, the most important part of our jobs is to do right by our customers, to offer them the best shopping experience possible, so that they develop brand loyalty and come back again and again. I know you have it in you. Just put in a bit more effort, will you? I want to see you put in a hundred and ten per cent when you're on the checkouts this afternoon.' Whenever he slides a product on to the scanner, a shrill bleep sounds. He is barely halfway through her shopping.

'Did you scan the correct barcode on those olives?'

'Yeah.'

'Are you sure?

'Yeah.'

'Because I will check.'

'Okay.'

'I only bought them because they were reduced.'

'Oh.'

He watches her stalk over to the seats by the window and study the receipt, before he turns to the next customer. 'Hello.' An exaggerated, fake smile, even more exaggerated, even more fake.

He can't wait to return to *Call of Duty*. Last night he played into the early hours, completing five missions in the campaign mode. The first one was a highlight. He wended his way through the fictional country of Vezikstan in awe. The sooty blue evening light. The thick, snaggling smoke. The black cinders. The sinister fires. The piles of rubble. And the sounds. The staccato clip of bullets. The military cries. The dramatic, atmospheric music. Set in London, following an Al-Qafada terror attack, the third mission was another highlight. There were a couple of elementary mistakes in the map: the phone boxes shone red and were really phone boxes, and the Piccadilly Circus Underground station was weirdly dilapidated and run-down, more like a US subway. But there were nice touches too, like blue finger-post street maps and ads on the sides of buses.

The pace was more addictively frenzied than he remembered. He scored his first kill before even figuring out the controls. After his first deaths, he read the quotes that appeared – by a curious mix of people: Cyrus the Great, Bob Marley, Winston Churchill – but he soon took to hammering 'X' the instant the colour had drained from the screen. The two-second break felt too long.

Quinoa, chickpeas, washing-up liquid, bananas . . .

He feels bitterly restless. At least on the shop floor he can move and check things on his phone. There is fuck-all escape here. 'Receipt?'

'No, I'm fine.'

'Okay. Thanks for shopping at Sainsbury's.' He turns to the next customer. 'Hello.'

'DO YOU REMEMBER *Call of Duty*?' David says, the *Only Fools and Horses* title screen rolling. 'You bought me an Xbox 360 bundle with it for my birthday once.'

'The Xbox?' Dad says. 'I remember. Your mother wasn't a fan.'

'No. Anyway, it came with *Call of Duty*. We played some missions together.'

'It took place in Russia?'

'Exactly.'

Visibly pleased with his memory, Dad takes some nuts.

'So. I bought a PlayStation 4 and the new *Call of Duty*. It's a sequel to that one.'

'Did you tell your mother you bought that?'

'She wouldn't mind me playing *Call of Duty* now.'

'Maybe skip mentioning it to her anyway. Just in case.'

'Sure.'

'Good then?'

'Great. Really enjoying the campaign mode. It's similar to the one we played. Excellent story. You play as CIA and SAS soldiers, fighting the Russians, alongside rebels from a fictional country, Vezikstan, which Russia has invaded. There are missions in London too.'

'London?'

'Yeah, this one is set all over. The missions are more varied too. Lots of straight-out shooting, obviously, but more complicated things as well. Defusing bombs and what not.'

Dad picks at a molar. 'Got a nut stuck.' His face contorts with the effort to unlodge it. David looks away, wondering how to go about asking what he wants to ask. The Swiss Army knife Dad bought him lies on the cracked wooden cabinet. He can't remember which features it has. Definitely a corkscrew. What else? There were at least ten features. Scissors? Keyring? Light? Next to the Swiss Army knife sprawls a constellation of shiny celluloid Fender plectrums, which he ordered when he was thinking about learning the guitar; a Red Stripe can from the first time Zoe invited him to hers; a whisky flask; and a stack of music magazines with Salomé or Karl coverage: *NME*, *Q*, *Kerrang!*

There are no wall prints, no bookshelves, no nice ornaments in the living room. Dad has nobody to impress. If David hadn't scattered some of his things around, it would be totally bare.

Having successfully extracted the nut, Dad tongues the spot where it was. A sedate fly buzzes beside him. He elbows it away. 'These nuts, eh.'

'Mm. So. Anyway, I was playing the new *Call of Duty* last night and in one mission I had to defuse a bomb in the US embassy in Vezikstan, and it made me think . . . It must have been exciting working as an electrician in the British Army.'

He knows Dad has no interest in speaking about his past, but he is now curious. As interesting as Mum's father might be, Dad is on a whole other level. He is main-character-level interesting.

There is also something that has stayed with David from the stupid thought he had – the thought that one day Dad will be gone. It is hard to understand exactly what. Just something.

'Sure,' Dad says. 'I was in the army, an electrician. I never had to do any bomb-disposal work. But I was in the army.'

'How long were you in the army for again?'

'Nearly a decade.'

'And did you always want to join?' SAS Captain Steve Garrett had wanted to since he was six.

'No, until I'd done my exams and started looking for a job, I'd never considered it, not for a second. But the army was . . . I don't regret joining. It's something I don't regret. The culture, spirit, humour. The travel too. Germany, Canada, Cyprus, even Kenya, Africa. I'd never left England before. I'm not sure I'd even left London.'

'Amazing.'

‘Plus, it felt worthwhile serving then.’

‘I can imagine.’

‘I’m not sure it would feel that way now, with the way the country is.’ Dad nods, lips sliding right and left, clipping each other. It seems as though he is trying to form a forgotten phrase. But he soon returns to reality. ‘Anyway. Xbox. *Call of Duty*. Have you completed it? The new one?’

David says that he has a few missions left.

‘Great . . . Well, I suppose we better head to bed then.’

‘Actually, I’m not that tired. Shall we watch one more episode?’

‘Yeah?’

‘Sure. I’m only starting at eleven tomorrow.’

‘I might have a lie-in tomorrow too.’

They settle on ‘A Losing Streak’ – a ping and the theme music chimes.

'YOU WORKING THE MORNING or evening on Friday?' Jamal asks.

'Morning.'

'Yeah? Me too.'

David nods.

'Pass me that lighter a sec,' Jamal says. Its big, slurping flame licks his rollie. 'Cheers. Don't know where I put mine. I could have sworn I left the house with it. Going to have to suck it up and buy a new one. Kills me sinking one twenty or whatever it is we charge on a lighter. Guess shit happens.' It's bleak outside, the sky covered with sparkling bruise-purple clouds. While rain hisses into the smoking rectangle, David stares into the murk. 'So,' Jamal says. 'You free Friday night?'

'Me?'

'Got any plans?'

'I think so. Why?'

'Ah, man. That's not the banter. What you up to?'

'I'm meeting some mates for a meal.'

Jamal spits on the concrete. 'Allow that, man. I can offer a better Friday night. I'm throwing a house party at mine. Good lads coming. Bringing a shit ton of weed with them. And there'll be babes. I can promise you that, man, babes. Go on. You can meet your mates for a meal any time.'

Even Jamal has friends. Enough to throw a house party. 'I haven't seen them for a while, so I'd feel bad cancelling,' David says. 'But I'll try to pop by afterwards.'

'Where are you eating anyway?'

'Pizza Express.'

Jamal shakes his head. 'You're choosing pizza over pussy? Not cool, man. Oh well. I reckon the party will still be swinging late into the night. You have my number? You can WhatsApp me when you're done. See how things are looking. How many mates are you meeting?'

'Just two, three.'

'You can bring them too then.'

'Thanks.'

He will now have to spend Friday stressing over an excuse.

'Back into the workhouse then?' Jamal says.

'Guess so.'

'Did you say you were on the magazines again next?'

'Yeah.'

As David stands up, his Dr Martens grate on the wet tarmac.

'Lucky shit.'

DARTING INTO THE LINE OF FIRE, David takes stupid hits. The screen turns black and white, and blood spatters throb in the corners. His controller vibrates. He retreats, crouches behind a military truck, crackling with sparks, windows shattered, and waits for his health to increase. A grenade icon appears. He drags the left thumbstick down to get out of the strike zone. The grenade explodes, gravelling and smoking the air. Once colour has seeped back into the screen, and the spatters have gone, he stands up, mounts his AK-47 and shoots around the truck.

'Fuck!' Dead. Again.

He is close to completing the campaign mode. Yet for the past two hours he has been struggling with the final mission. The only other comparably hard one was Captivity. In that, he hurled rock after rock after rock at the brick walls and carted a chair from window to window to window before figuring out how to break free from his cell block. When he did, though, and released Zayna's sisters and smashed open the gun locker and killed the Russian guards, his skin grew tight with goosebumps. He hammers 'X' to return to the last checkpoint, intent on completing this tonight.

If no progress has been made by 2 a.m. he will consider downgrading the difficulty level to Hardened. But that is not a concession he's willing to make yet. He completed the original *Call of Duty: Covert Ops* on Veteran. He can complete this on Veteran too.

'Fuck!' Dead. Again.

He throttles the controller. A Martin Luther King Jr quote appears: *Injustice anywhere is a threat to justice everywhere.* Having started the night on the sofa, he is now sitting cross-legged on the floor, less than a metre from the screen. It's freezing. He and

Dad never turn the heating on in autumn though. December is fair game. Not before. The radiator barely does a thing anyway. It would take hours to heat up the room. Even in the dark he can make out the red dribbles on its ribs. Ketchup? Sriracha? Dolmio? Too many meals eaten huddled up to it. How can it be this cold in September?

A groan. He's looking for excuses. The problem is him, not the cold; nothing else, him. He needs to show patience, make smarter decisions. He needs to reload his gun at regular intervals, slide more while sprinting and save his grenades for opportune moments.

He presses 'X', sprints towards the factory pipeline, sidestepping the sniper's laser sight, and hides behind a roadblock. *At the stairs!* someone shouts. He stands and fires, fires, fires, killing three Russians. But there are more, many more. They aren't surrendering the pipeline without a fight.

Just past three, he makes it to the factory pipeline and sets the charges. A cinematic scene plays, wrapping up the narrative. The gas facility has been demolished, Ivanov has been killed and the Russians have disowned him. The allies have taken a big bite out of the problem. Left unchecked, however, it will rise again. Lebedev will want Ivanov's throne after all. SAS Captain Steve Garrett wants to set up a task force to ensure the problem never arises again. Diaz is hesitant. She can fund assets, but not outlaws. He insists: the problem must never arise again. She reluctantly agrees. What does he want to call the new task force? He will call it 7-0-7. The credits roll. Game complete.

In bed, he opens the *Covert Ops 2* subreddit and, too wired to sleep, spends an hour there, by the end of which he has resolved to take out a PlayStation Plus subscription. He needs to experience *Call of Duty* multiplayer, needs to. The subreddit is filled with users sharing videos of their Killstreaks and giving shout-outs to randomers they enjoyed playing with. A hot thread: 'Down to the wire. Had to show up for the boys!' and a clip of the user killing four opponents in a matter of seconds to help his team win by three points. 'Shiiiii those knife throws were cleaner than mountain valley spring water bro,' someone replied. 'Fuck me I wish I had teammates like you!' someone else replied. He will take out a fourteen-day free PlayStation Plus trial tomorrow.

'THOSE ARE ALL SKETCHES he made at our neighbours' place,' Mum says. 'When it had become clear that exhibiting his work was no longer a realistic possibility, he had some bad spells, really bad spells. I was so grateful for our neighbours . . . He'd go over and drink whisky with the husband – they always had it somehow – and he'd sketch their animals, pull himself out of his mood.'

David is leafing through a notebook with weird sketches of weird creatures. Mum explains that their neighbours cared for rescue animals, a curious mix, including a cross-eyed cat, a hedgehog with a missing leg and a paraplegic dog. 'It's funny, now even healthy dogs are *najes*.' They are in his room, David sitting up in bed, Mum perched on the edge. Her fine, sparse, chestnut-brown hair rests on her sharply outlined collarbones, fuzzy with light from the standing floor lamp. She relates how kind their neighbours were to one particular cat. They were told it would live six months, max, but took it in regardless and built it a huge structure in the shed, complete with a climbing frame and a scratch post. Because it was a particularly harsh winter, they even put a wood stove in there, so that it could sleep comfortably. Somehow when she left Tehran it was still alive. 'When I phoned home, my mother would always say, "And it's still alive, would you believe it?" She must have told me that a hundred times.' Droplets zigzag across the window through an orange street smear. The soughing of the trees. A screech. Honks. 'I wonder whether it was the cat's diet. They used to feed it and all the other animals left-overs. The shed would smell of cinnamon.' She frowns. 'Although, thinking about it now, I'm not sure how healthy that would have been.'

'Mm.'

'They were one of the few Jewish families in our neighbourhood who stayed after the revolution. They were really something. Baba loved them – them and the whisky.'

David passes the notebook back to her. 'Do you have the one with the sketches of the famous paintings with veils? It would be cool to share them on Twitter.'

Mum shoots him an inquisitive look. 'Oh. Sure. It's in my bedroom. I can get it now . . . I'm not sure it would be wise to share those sketches online though.'

'Why?'

'Well, with the current political climate in the UK, the anti-Muslim sentiment . . .'

'The anti-Muslim sentiment?'

'It's so widespread now . . . and . . .'

'What?'

'And I know this is nothing, but—'

'What?'

'Stephen said he stumbled on your Twitter profile and saw that you had been sharing *Spiked* articles and that some of them were . . . It's not that he was worried. But he thought . . . Obviously. I know it's nothing. And you're free to share whatever you like. But you don't want to add to the anti-Muslim sentiment . . . Those sketches have a complex context. If shared without it, they might send the wrong message.'

David experiences a sensation of beetles crawling on his skin. Stephen 'stumbled' on his Twitter profile? After reading in the *Guardian* or the *New York Times* about the controversy surrounding Karl, he must have started monitoring David's social media activity, ready to call Prevent. Karl is Islamophobic; David loves Karl. Ergo, David must be Islamophobic too.

Unbelievable.

'Fine. Forget it.'

'I can still get the notebook and we can discuss—'

'Forget it.'

'David—'

'Forget it. Just show me more sketches of cute animals or whatever.'

'FUUUUCK!' DAVID SAYS, screwing up his face and swinging his controller. He has let the opposing team take the overtime flag and win the round, putting them five–one in the lead. *Match point* flashes up. *We lost that one* comes the automated voice. *Step it up.* He seethes with self-reproach. How could he have let them take the flag? He really is shit sometimes.

Close Combat has become his favourite multiplayer mode. It's exhilarating. In tiny, cage-like maps, using the same random weapons, over multiple rounds, two players fight two others. There are no respawns and each round lasts only forty seconds. If the forty seconds elapse and neither team has been eliminated, an overtime flag appears for ten seconds, providing a new way to win the round. But as the flag is in a perilously exposed spot, attempting to take it can be a death sentence – should be a death sentence. The first team to win six rounds is victorious. He loves the intimacy, the pressure. The countdown to the next round begins: ten, nine, eight, seven, six, five . . .

David and his Alliance teammate, Corey(515), can still turn things round.

Go. David sprints to the east side of the map, mounts his AK-47 on the edge of a ceramic shower and presses his controller's right stick to look down the scope. He inches closer to the screen. Where are his Federation opponents? Flickering lamps sway from the ceiling, spraying sickly light.

House of Meetings is the smallest map. It has dozens of destroyed showers to take cover behind, but that cover can be negated by flanking. The showers only offer protection from one side. Where are his Federation opponents? He wonders whether they are on the west side of the map, intending to flank him. The rat-a-tat-tat of bullets being exchanged. Shit. Corey(515) has been killed. It is up to him. Everything is on him. Abandoning his cover, he makes for the north side of the map, where the Federation spawned. Not there. They must be on the west side then. He has to try to flank them. Quickly too. He runs – and sees someone. He fires frenziedly. Dead. But only a second later he's under fire. He takes cover behind a shower. Where was he being shot from? He mounts his AK-47 and peeks round the shower. Fuck. He sees him – and shoots, shoots, shoots.

Dead. He has won the round for the Alliance and made up for his shocking showing in the last round. They have narrowed the lead to five–two. Game on. He watches the final-kill replay with pride, relishing the vibrations. *This round is ours. Stay sharp for the next one.*

A few mad minutes later and somehow it is five–five, thanks to him. This is his best online performance. Nine kills racked up. What a comeback. Last round: five, four, three, two, one . . .

Go. He has to try something new, something the Federation won't see coming. He moves to the east side of the map but rather than head for cover behind a shower keeps sneaking forward, right stick pressed, aiming, waiting for one of them to enter his line of sight. He stops and listens out for footsteps. Nothing. Just the sizzle of the steam vents. He sneaks further forward – to where the Federation spawned. Gunfire. Gunfire somewhere. Corey(515) has killed a Federation player. Shit. Corey(515) has been killed too. David looks round frantically. Blood spritzes into the screen. Hit. He crouches behind a shower. His opponent is still shooting. The bullets crackle past and ping the wall behind him. The shooting stops. David's character moans – health low. But his opponent might be reloading. This might be his chance. He has to risk it. He comes out from behind the shower, crouching, and furiously fires, fires, fires, fires, fires. Got him. *Federation eliminated / Alliance victorious* shines in blue on the screen. They have won. They have fucking won.

Eager to bask in the victory, he leaves the lobby he is placed in with new players. What a Close Combat. He balls up his fist.

Come on. A notification flashes up. Corey(515) has sent him a PlayStation Network friend request. A warm tingle shoots up his back. Accept. Another notification. Corey(515) is inviting him to a voice chat. He scrabbles behind the TV for the PlayStation earphones, plugs them in – a fiddly task in the dark – takes a nervous breath and joins the party.

'Dude?' Corey(515) says.

American.

'Hey.'

'Dude. You still buzzing from that Close Combat too? Fuck me.' A gruff drawl to his voice, though he doesn't sound old – maybe in his early twenties.

'Yeah. That was a hell of a game.'

'Your performance. Olympic shit. Olympic. We were losing five–one, right?'

'Yeah.'

'And to then win six–five. Fuck me.' He whistles. 'Take a bow. Because, man, it was all you. I was a spectator for ninety per cent of that match. At least I got to witness a *COD* masterclass.'

'Thanks.'

'Yeah. Take a bow. Deserved, man.'

'Thanks.'

'British? You sound like Beckham.'

'Me?'

When meeting someone new, David is used to a curious 'Where are you from?'

'Yeah. You. Who else?'

'Sorry. Yeah, I'm British. I live in London.'

'Ohhh. London? Londonistan now. Right?'

'Erm. Right.'

'Read too many stories about that place, too many. I feel for you, man. I feel for you.'

'It's—'

'Corey's the name. David. Yeah?'

'Yeah.'

'Sweet. Dude, I still can't believe that. Six–five. Get the fuck in.'

David laughs, relaxing into the conversation. He can't remember the last time he relaxed into a conversation. 'Close Combat's my favourite multiplayer mode.'

'Love it. Everything that makes *COD* what it is.'

'Yeah.'

'You tend to play with mates?'

'Just on my own.'

'Same. Sucks. I wish I had regular teammates. I hate ending up with camping noobs.'

'Yeah.'

'... You wanna join a lobby together and try to re-create the magic?'

'Sure.'

'All right, Beckham. Let's mess some shit up then. I'll pull my weight this time.'

Hassan

'WHAT DO YOU THINK the first game will be?' Dad asks, standing by the wall mirror, combing his wavy hair, which shows no signs of thinning. Hassan inherited the emphatic monobrow, but that's a price he's willing to pay for a full head of hair in old age. Saajid has early-onset baldness in his family.

'Chelsea v Liverpool.'

'Even though it was only one all? We beat Man United three–one.'

'Yeah, but the BBC loves Liverpool, and they scored a late equaliser.'

His side parting neatened up, Dad slips the comb into a shirt pocket and comes to sit on the sofa. After work, he swapped his Tariq's Grill polo neck for a white shirt, a claret tie and a black sweater – any social occasion, even watching *Match of the Day* with Hassan, calls for formal wear – microwaved the leftovers of the meal Mum had cooked and rushed to the living room. Although they have a smart TV with iPlayer, they never miss the live broadcast: Saturday night, ten thirty.

'Mm,' Dad says. 'There's some real flavour in this.'

'It's lovely.'

'Sabiha's the one who should be running a restaurant.'

Hassan ate earlier with Mum, who is now upstairs, snoring. For some reason, she can never manage to stay up later than ten, regardless of how well rested she is or what the occasion is. Even on New Year's Eve she celebrates with Hassan and Dad at nine thirty and then steals away to bed.

'I'm sure West Ham v Man United will be second,' Hassan says.

'It better be,' Dad says, spooning up sauce, mutton, coriander leaves.

A warm welcome to BBC One this Saturday evening. It's time for Match of the Day. The opening titles. The bouncy orchestral theme song. Hassan cracks his Fanta. A packet of cheese-and-onion Walkers lies on the coffee table, ready for the West Ham highlights. For once, they will be fun to watch.

'You've finished the sociology homework. Right?' Dad says.

He is never carefree. Even on a Saturday, after a long, exhausting day at the restaurant, it occurs to him to check this. Hassan has lost track of the number of times he has heard Dad say, 'If you don't work, you won't get anywhere in life,' or something to that effect.

'Yeah,' Hassan says. This is not strictly true. But he has started it.

Dad reminds him how important A levels are and that he can help – that he wants to help.

Some big hitters in action tonight, Gary Lineker says. *First, to Stamford Bridge.*

'Just let me know when you need any help.'

'Sure.'

Dad nods and they settle into the highlights.

'Fair play,' Hassan says, as Hazard scores.

'He's an incredible player.'

'The swerve on that . . . You know, the Nike Ordem ball will have helped him there. It has a fuse-welded casing and Aerowtrac grooves to help players put it exactly where they want it to go.'

Hassan figures that if he mentions the ball every time they watch *Match of the Day* Dad will eventually relent and buy it for him. Even in Sports Direct it is still ninety-five quid.

During Chelsea v Liverpool, Kala paws into the living room.

Dad clicks his tongue and beckons her over with a palm. His cufflinks shine. A hesitancy in her eyes, but she comes. 'Good Kala,' he says, taking her grizzled snout in his leathery hands. 'Good Kala. That's it. You can relax. This is your home now. This is your home now.' He pats the sofa. 'Sit here.'

'Kala,' Hassan says, reaching for her too. 'Kala.'

In the background, Alonso heads the ball on to the crossbar from a corner. 'What a chance.'

'Big chance,' Dad says. 'Sit here, Kala.' She appears to consider her options, then leaps up on to the black faux-leather fabric, between them. 'Good Kala.'

Hassan scratches her back. They have had her for eight months. At the outset, any and all sounds spooked her and she barely ate a thing, but she seems more comfortable now.

'I wish Muhsin could see this,' Dad says. 'Kala watching TV with us.'

'I bet.'

As a child in Lahore, Dad bonded with a skinny, scruffy stray Labrador. For months, he would squirrel away scraps of meat from the meals his mother cooked and later give them to the dog. One night, with his parents in Karachi, he let it sleep in his bed. The next morning his uncle, Muhsin, unexpectedly turned up at the house and saw it on the stairs. He chased it, caught it and maniacally beat it. Dad protested through tears but couldn't stop Mushin. The dog eventually managed to break free and run away. Over the following weeks, Dad searched the streets. Yet he never saw it again. The experience must have stayed with him because Hassan has heard it recounted multiple times.

'Muhsin was convinced that angels wouldn't enter a house with a dog in it,' Dad says, tickling Kala under the snout. 'And that after touching a dog you had to take a bath before you could offer your prayers. He thought he was a pious man. But he didn't know anything about the Quran.' Dad tells Hassan that when the Prophet was leading his army to Mecca and stumbled on a female dog with puppies he gave orders that they should not be disturbed and posted a sentry to protect them.

'Yeah?' Hassan says, flicking his eyes between Dad, Kala and *Match of the Day*.

'If Muhsin were here today, he would be protesting outside Farfield school. That's the sort of man he was. Zero understanding of Islamic history.'

And now we take a trip to the Olympic Stadium for West Ham v Manchester United, Lineker says. *The Irons made a dreadful start to the season, losing their first four games, but were much improved against Everton and Chelsea. Can they continue their resurgence against Mourinho's men? Let's find out. On lead vocals: Steve Wilson.*

'Here we go,' Hassan says.

'Yes. Here we go.'

As Dad strokes Kala, she sheds white hairs. They settle softly on his suit trousers.

'HANDS UP FOR *CASINO ROYALE*,' Ahmed says.

Hassan raises his, Saajid too.

'That's seven, eight, nine, no, eight.' Waleed raised his, only to change his mind seconds later. 'Anyone else?' Ahmed sweeps a finger over the sports hall, at chest height, thanks to the tightness of his blazer around his armpits. 'Okay, eight for *Casino Royale* then. *Jaws*?'

Hassan swings round. He's seen *Jaws* twice.

'That's five, six, seven.' Despite stirring, Waleed keeps his hands in his pockets. Ahmed smiles. Then, really straining his blazer, claps his hands together. 'We have a winner. *Casino Royale* it is.'

'Get in,' Hassan mutters.

'A classic of British cinema,' Ahmed continues. 'James Bond. The first of Daniel Craig's Bond films. I'm sure you'll all enjoy it.' He checks his watch, a cheap black Casio. 'It's six thirty now. Let's start at seven. In the meantime, there are paper plates on the table. Load them with the food Abu Hassan was so generous to provide us tonight. Lamb chops. Methi chicken. Karahi tarka dhal. And much more. Tariq's Grill is the best Pakistani restaurant in our city, bar none. You're in for a feast.'

Saajid slaps Hassan on the back. 'Tariq's a legend.'

He laughs. 'Yeah, he's all right.'

Saajid presses him for his recommendations. Tandoori chicken is a must. Peshwari naan too. They join the queue, which Maaz is leading, as ever. 'Hey,' Saajid says. 'I was meaning to ask, Hazza. I'm having a party at mine on Friday. For my birthday. Just five, six close mates. Fancy it?'

'Sure.'

'Yeah?'

'Sure.'

'Sweet. We have Sky Sports, so I'll put Brighton v West Ham on in the background. I've made a Spotify playlist with some banging tracks too.'

'Great.'

'My mates from school are banter. You'll like them.'

They load their plates, then take a seat in the front row. 'This naan,' Saajid says. 'Really, Tariq, he's something else, bro, something else.' Ahmed tinkers with the projector until a black rectangle takes shape on the wall. A house party. Hassan has only ever been to one.

LISTENING TO DRAKE, Hassan explores UCAS.com. He has been meaning to start work on his application for weeks. Saajid's party has convinced him of its urgency. He likes Saajid, but his mates – God, they are immature. He lost count of the your-mum jokes. He must get into Goldsmiths and make some new friends his age. The website explains that a personal statement is an important part of any application: a chance to describe one's ambitions, skills and experience. How to explain why he wants to study media and communications? He opens Notes, then takes a Twitter break.

After a few minutes of scrolling, he lands on something interesting. @NewburyParkMasjid: 'Can you #help? We're looking to recruit telephone befrienders. If you have 30 minutes a week spare to chat to someone in our #community who feels lonely and needs a little extra support, please reply to this tweet or email us at volunteering@npmasjid.com and we'll be in touch.'

He remembers his careers adviser saying that volunteering experience would help his UCAS application stand out. This might be worth doing. It sounds easy too. He can spare thirty minutes a week. The retro single-use Kodak camera he used on GCSE results day lies on the window ledge, covered in cobwebs. A white van with a stepladder on top pulls up and squeezes into a tight parking space outside the house opposite. Someone with a JD King of Trainers drawstring bag over their shoulders spits on the Lil Meep graffiti that appeared on the pavement overnight. Hassan composes a short email and sends it. Done. His procrastination has brought him progress.

Anything else interesting on Twitter? @EASportsFIFA: 'Last Chance. Claim this EA Play-exclusive Epic Storm Stadium set in #FIFA now through October 31!' @iamcardib: 'I have a new behind the scences clip coming out today. It's soooo funny!! Make sure you watch it on Instagram & Messenger!' Not really. He returns to UCAS.com. A personal statement needs to be personal. It should be written in an enthusiastic, concise, natural style. It should not include jokes, just in case the admissions tutor doesn't have the same sense of humour. He wonders who would risk cracking a joke in their personal statement, and smirks: Mo would, without a second thought, and it would work for him. Is Mo still planning to apply for City University? He has no idea.

He follows the steady flow of the purple wax in his lava lamp, reads on. Candidates should get their teachers, advisers and family members to read over their personal statements, and should double-check that the spelling, punctuation and grammar are correct. The 296 bus rolls by, with an ad for *Call of Duty: Covert Ops 2*. He's seen countless ads for it on YouTube, as every Sky Sports video seems to come with one. But first-person shooters aren't his thing; he's never played a *Call of Duty* title. Ibrahim loved the series and went on about it all the time.

Mo . . . Ibrahim . . . Does he miss them? Irrelevant. He would never be able to speak to them again without imagining the incident in the underpass anyway. He rolls the blinds shut.

Later that evening, the mosque replies, thanking him for his interest in the telephone befriending scheme and attaching two forms, one with more information, one to fill in and return.

The first form emphasises the positive impact the scheme is having, explains why there is so much loneliness in Britain, reveals that befrienders will be matched with befriendees on the basis of shared interests, and includes dos and don'ts for calls. Nothing too surprising. On the second form, he completes the sections asking for his personal details, availability and interests. The wind rustles the bins outside. He swivels the 3D moon lamp on his desk, feels the craters on the other side, opens a stick of Starburst and sends the forms back. He is going to get a place at Goldsmiths. He is.

ON SUN-CHIPPED GLASS, Westfield glints red. A swarm of people waiting on the far platform with John Lewis, M&S and Apple shopping bags. 'No Smoking' lights up the electronic display in their carriage. Outside the window, a National Rail employee packs up a wheelchair step-up ramp. He says something to his colleague, who raises a baton. The train zips away.

'Do you have any memories of Southend?' Mum asks.

She is interviewing a groundskeeper at Roots Hall for Muslim Voices. Hassan has a soft spot for Southend United and is joining her for a tour of the stadium. Then he will go to the seafront alone and take a series of photos for his art and design homework. The theme is faded glory.

'Some.'

'We went for your sixth birthday. You loved Adventure Island.'

'I remember the turtle in the logo.'

Mum recollects how relaxed Tariq was about riding the Fireball roller coaster with him – and how sick he felt afterwards. In the restaurant, he could only stomach a few chips and even went to the bathroom twice to throw up. 'I took a lot of videos, but we had a Fujifilm camera back then, with a memory card. I wonder whether the videos can be transferred to our laptops.'

Hassan says that he'll investigate. He'd love to see footage of Dad there in a suit.

The train pulls into Romford. A group of girls his age get on and take the booth opposite – hot, especially the brunette, who is wearing a cropped Nike sweatshirt and light-blue jeans with rips at the knees and slurping a McDonald's milkshake. She flicks her eyes over to Hassan and Mum and then whispers something to her friend, who looks over too. They crease up. The sun illuminates scratches, smut on the windowpane. A spark of buttery light speeds along the overhead lines.

'I am proud of you for volunteering for the befriending scheme,' Mum says.

'Oh, thanks.'

Do they think he's hot? Unlikely. No one thinks that. He swabs his chin and cheeks, in case there are any salsa smears from his Pret wrap.

'Have you been matched with someone?'

'Guy called Zulfi Khan. They sent me his number this morning.'

'Any more information?'

'He's from Azad Kashmir, immigrated in the late sixties, likes cricket.'

Do they find his clothes funny? He's wearing a padded black West Ham jacket, black jeans and white Adidas sneakers. Nothing eccentric. Vehicles negotiate a multi-lane roundabout. Pets at Home, Halfords, Big Yellow Storage, Community Foods. A water treatment plant, with huge tanks and plenty of pipes. They must be laughing at something else. He puts them out of his mind.

He has been meaning to speak to Mum about the befriending scheme. The mosque sent him a link to a Dropbox folder with training materials and 'good practice guidelines' for volunteers. He grew anxious reading them. This might be harder than he first anticipated. What if it is impossible, literally impossible, to maintain a phone conversation for thirty minutes? The only people he ever calls are Mum and Dad and that is never for more than a matter of seconds. He is starting to wish he hadn't signed up for the stupid scheme. He stretches his legs out.

'Do you ever find it hard?' he says. 'Your phone interviews.'

'In what way?'

'Just in terms of speaking to someone new like that.'

A stripe of sunlight cuts across the tabletop. She withdraws her hands and brings them together in her lap, with a smile. 'I forget how scared your generation is of using the call function on your phones. Trust me, it's not that scary.'

'Hmmmm.'

Mum tells him not to overthink things. It is a friendly chat, nothing less, nothing more. Tips? Be respectful. Empathise with his befriendee. Remember that hearing their stories and feelings is a privilege. And let them share as much or as little as they want. Don't worry if there are silences.

'Okay.'

The train judders past Gidea Park and Harold Wood: a timber mill, pylons, roadworks.

'By the way,' Mum says, 'I ran into Aqsa.'

'Aqsa?'

'She hasn't seen you for a long time.'

'Oh.'

'She told me how many happy memories she has of you and Mo playing in her hallway with the small football with the blue stars. It made me think . . . I haven't seen Mo for a while either.'

'Mm.'

'Are you two still friends?'

'Yeah.'

'Really?'

'Sure.'

She seeks his eyes. 'You should invite him round sometime. It would be nice. I can buy those Masala Munch crisps he used to like.'

Hassan promises he will. Then opens Instagram. Mum reaches for her handbag and takes out her lipstick. More commotion from the girls. A new possibility prickles at him. Is it Mum they find funny? That she's wearing lipstick and a hijab? Despite knowing they are wrong, he has never managed to shrug off Ibrahim's comments about the way white people in Britain see Muslims. He chews his mouth. Is it Mum they find funny? No, this is paranoid nonsense. He is imagining things.

As she rolls on her lipstick, he turns towards the window.

‘HI, IS THAT ZULFI KHAN?’

‘Speaking.’

‘This is Hassan. I’m calling as part of the mosque’s telephone befriending scheme.’

‘*As-salamu alaikum.*’

‘*Wa alaikum*, erm, *assalaam.*’

‘Thank you. I was told you would be calling.’

Hassan is sitting at his desk, with two pages of notes splayed out in front of him, questions to ask, questions not to ask, potential conversation topics, other prompts. In the morning, he panicked, studied the training materials properly and read the latest cricket news. This volunteering work is causing him too much stress and costing him too much time. It was supposed to be a piece of piss.

‘Yeah, I’ll be calling every week for a thirty-minute chat.’

‘Wonderful.’

‘Erm. How are you today?’

Zulfi laughs. ‘Oh, I am not too bad today. I was looking forward to this.’

‘Great.’

Hassan checks how long has passed so far: just under a minute.

‘So, Hassan, let me give you a bit of background as to why I signed up for the scheme. I am sure some of this will have been shared with you already. But I thought it would be nice to tell you myself. I have osteoarthritis in my right knee. Back when I was a teenager, like you, I tore my meniscal cartilage playing cricket. I had a series of operations that went, shall we say, badly, and I was told that in old age I would be in trouble. Well, now I am sixty-nine, and I am in trouble. I can barely walk from room to room any more. Going upstairs is like climbing Everest. It takes me ten minutes to muster the courage. I am hoping to have a knee replacement, but that could be eighteen months away. The NHS waiting list is long. In the meantime I will not be leaving my house too much.' He pauses, a wobble in his voice. 'And, well, I miss our mosque. I used to see so many kind people there. It is a special place.'

'Sorry to hear that.'

'It is okay. That is life. I feel a bit lonely sometimes. But nothing more serious. And once my knee has been sorted you will not be able to keep me away from our mosque.'

'I bet.' Rustling, as Zulfi moves his phone.

Hassan asks whether the pain can be eased with medication. Not really. Some foods supposedly reduce inflammation though: spinach, kale, broccoli, walnuts. Zulfi has made a list. He prints it out every Monday morning and crosses something out once he's had it. He is still waiting to see any results but hopes that it will eventually help.

'I'm sure it will.'

'*Inshallah.*'

They haven't even been speaking for two minutes.

'What do you like to do in your free time?'

A chuckle. 'All my time is free time now. Hmm. What do I like to do? I read a lot. In my early years here, I used to read a book a week. But then, between eighteen and sixty-five, I must have read fewer than ten. I was working, working, working. Now I dip into the Quran every night, and I always have a novel on the go as well. What else? Oh, I watch TV, too much TV. *Only Fools and Horses*, *Fawlty Towers*, *Blackadder*, other sitcoms. And the cricket, of course. It continues to give me great pleasure. My career might have ended before it began. But I will never tire of watching it.'

Hassan slides closer the bottom page of notes. 'Have you been following England's tour of Sri Lanka?'

'Of course.'

'Great win in the last One Day International.'

'Ah. You care for cricket too?'

'Yeah.'

Zulfi makes a warm, satisfied noise. 'Magic.'

'The, erm, catch from Rashid was something else.'

'A sight to see.'

'The partnership that Foakes and Curran have formed too.'

'They are finding their rhythm.'

'And the bowling was spot on for once.'

'Everything seems to be coming together.'

Even on the phone, Hassan feels comfortable speaking about sports. This is better.

'The first test match is next week, right?'

'Yes, I am expecting a fiery encounter.'

Ideally, Zulfi would be a football fan rather than a cricket fan. But Hassan can get into cricket. He is willing to do that in exchange for a place at Goldsmiths.

'Thursday,' Zulfi says. 'I have it marked in my calendar. Will you be watching? The mosque said you were studying for your A levels. I imagine you must be very busy.'

'I have classes, but I'll manage to watch some of it.'

'Excellent.'

'I know we've only been speaking for a few minutes,' Hassan says. 'Just to get it out of the way, though, shall I call again on Thursday, after the first day of play? Like, five or so?'

'Please . . . I'm embarrassed to say, once the Sky Sports coverage has finished, I tend to turn on TalkSPORT and listen to their analysis too. I like hearing voices. It makes me feel less lonely.' He clears his throat. 'Sorry. What I meant to say is . . . A post-match chat would be a pleasure.'

III

David

Dysruptz Today at 22:09
Kno her musics shit etc etc but worth watching this: https://youtu.be/Laoes7ac65I hot af

Nmoos Today at 22:10
You're sharing Rina Demianova on Jimmy Fallon? ok lol

Nmoos Today at 22:12
SHIT lolol watched the first 30 secs fair play those legs

Chilozzi Today at 22:14
Damn when she said FIRST TIME ON THE COUCH all I could think was PORNHUB

TRXDripp666 Today at 22:15
Haha imagine it a Fake Agent job lolol

Chilozzi Today at 22:15
1000x yes

Mix Today at 22:17
oO

Corey(515) Today at 22:18
wow she's fucking smoking

WarriorCorgi Today at 22:21
I read these comments before watching and I was like DAMN

there are some thirsty mofos in this server *rolls eyes* and then I watched it and now I'm like ok legs legs legs legs legs legs legs legs legs legs legs legs legs legs legs legs legs legs legs legs legs

Nmoos Today at 22:23
I had to go back and watch the rest I would fuck her all day all night all millennium

David1702UK Today at 22:25
She is really hot

Having contributed to the banter, David goes to the kitchen. The bin is surrounded by gross morsels: a slice of onion peel, a pasta twist, a shrivelling lump of gherkin. He steps on the pedal, grimaces, holds his nose and drops in an empty crisp packet. Then he takes a Stella out of the fridge. Ten thirty. Hopefully someone will suggest a Team Deathmatch soon. He is working from seven tomorrow, meaning a six wake-up. At least the sun will have risen by the time he leaves the house. The morning shifts in January were hell. As the server is US-dominated – and it's still afternoon there – the boys will be in no hurry to let go of Rina Demianova though. The only other European is Nmoos, and he's nocturnal. When David wakes up, Nmoos is routinely still online. He pops open his Stella, slugs and wonders how many Rina Demianova links he'll return to.

It's funny: Discord has 250 million users worldwide, more than Snapchat and nearly as many as Twitter. Yet before Dysruptz invited him and Corey to join his exclusive Dark Fury Gaming server, he hadn't even heard of Discord. A notification the other day let him know that it is now his most-used app, and almost always the first he opens after picking up his phone. (It's on his laptop as well.) Setting a limit on his usage was suggested to him. No thanks.

He bears the Dark Fury clan tag in front of his username in *Call of Duty* with pride. Obviously some users in the server are better than others. But everyone is proficient, with a K/D ratio of 1.5 or higher. Dysruptz doesn't invite just anyone to join. He has made that clear. David is relieved that teaming up with randomers is a thing of the past. He enjoys the banter, semi-political chat and shitposting in Dark Fury too. Last week he and six other users were playing Search and Destroy, and Dysruptz netted the final kill. During the replay, WarriorCorgi made a callback to a meme David had shared in the text chat in the morning and everyone in the voice chat cracked up.

When he first googled Discord, he read that its mission was to 'bring people together around games' and it seems to be nailing that. He is grateful to Dysruptz.

Back in his room, he scrolls through the messages he has missed.

Nmoos Today at 22:27
@David1702UK lolol 'really hot' the proper Englishman

WarriorCorgi Today at 22:28
legs legs legs legs legs legs legs legs legs legs legs legs legs legs

Chilozzi Today at 22:28
Yo. Sry to break up the Rina Demianova stanning here but got some proper stan shit. U boys seen the new Stan Tyler vid? He went inside a no-go zone in Malmo, Sweden. Crazy.

Chilozzi Today at 22:29
https://youtu.be/cxeLapDE6bc

TRXDripp666 Today at 22:30
Yeah, I saw that. Stan's all right, actually speaks the truth lol. Europe's lost. The vid reminded me of the Scandinavian chicks who went to Morocco to show that the rumours were exaggerated etc and then they got beheaded.

Dysruptz Today at 22:30
Stan's OK. Kind of like Tim Lai but not a PC pussy.

Corey(515) Today at 22:30
Amazing lol. I have to watch this^^

Dysruptz Today at 22:31
I kinda wanna watch it now but also kinda wanna get some COD going hmmmmmm . . .

He recognises the name Stan Tyler. It's come up in his recommended videos on YouTube. There was something about the aesthetic of the thumbnails that didn't sit well with him – the titles in block capitals with a single key word in blood-red – but perhaps he is worth checking out after all.

David1702UK Today at 22:32
@Nmoos haha

David1702UK Today at 22:32
@Dysruptz Never seen Stan Tyler's vids before but seen a fair few Tim Lai. Quite enjoyed them. Is Lai PC? I'll check this out. Keen for some COD first though?

Dysruptz Today at 22:33
Lol Lai is 300% PC

Dysruptz Today at 22:33
Hmmmmmmmmmm

Dysruptz Today at 22:33
OK OK how abt watch this to make Chilozzi happy & then TDM in 15?

Corey(515) Today at 22:34
Yh

David1702UK Today at 22:34
Cool I'm up for that

DAD NEVER CLOSES THE CURTAINS in his room. David stares out. The streetlights cast lolling orange shapes. A delivery driver waits outside number twenty, into which a Muslim couple moved last week. They enthusiastically introduced themselves when he walked past them in the street; he has forgotten their names. Pointless knowledge.

'Hm?' Dad slurs. 'Who is it?'

'Me.'

'David?'

'Yeah.'

The musty smell causes him to cough. He suspects mould is growing somewhere: Mum once said it can be hidden in walls or under a carpet. He steps over a heap of newspapers, moves the Rammstein cap from the chair to the already cluttered desk and takes a seat. This time he must remember not to lean back: the chair's legs are coming loose. Dad props himself up and experimentally hinges his mouth about. A burp. He wipes his lips with the hairy back of his hand.

'Okay?' David asks.

Dad admits to falling asleep for a minute. He started reading and his exhaustion got the better of him; David sees no book. Dad scratches a cheek with a turmeric-coloured nail. 'How's work?'

'Same as. Got some interesting Kettle Chips for us.'

'Salt and vinegar?'

'No. New flavour. Sheese and Spring Onion. Like the ones we used to have ages ago. But with vegan cheese instead of real cheese.'

'I used to like those cheese-and-onion ones. Walkers.'

'Those were,' David says slowly. 'These are Kettle Chips. They should be nice.'

Dad urges his legs over the side of his bed, rubs his knees, reaches for his Sports Direct mug, sips, winces. 'What time is it?'

'Just past eight.' As well as the mug, the bedside table hosts a heap of loose change, mostly coppers, a fluorescent-orange lighter, Snickers bars, the padlock Dad took to the gym – its numbers showing David's birthdate – a gnarled Savlon tube, a paracetamol pack and an ibuprofen pack.

'Where's your clock?'

'It was there, but . . .'

Rather than using his phone, like everyone else in the twenty-first century, Dad inexplicably uses a small white plastic travel alarm clock which runs on AA batteries. Whenever he goes out, he pops it in his tool bag. There's nothing special about it, as far as David can see. It's the sort of clock an airport W. H. Smith's would sell. But Dad has a curious sentimental attachment to it. 'Let me have a look.' He kneels on the earthy-brown carpet and slithers under the bed: empty Sainsbury's vodka bottles, a ready-meal tray, dustballs, piss-stained Y fronts, a red XL tag. He spots it, by the headboard. Outstretching a hand, he pings one of the bottles. 'Got it.'

'Mm,' Dad says. 'Quarter past eight.'

'Episode of *Only Fools and Horses* in twenty minutes?'

'Shall we say eight thirty to make things simple?'

'Sure. We'll try the crisps.'

'Walkers. Which episode? Maybe "To Hull and Back"?'

David opens his mouth. Yet says nothing. They watched "To Hull and Back" only last night, and this isn't the first time Dad has suggested an episode that would be a repeat. It has happened three, four times in the past month. David wonders why; Dad never used to make mistakes like this.

Hate swaggers into his chest. The Muslim on TaskRabbit is to blame: Aisha R. She left a shitty, unfair review for Dad. Okay, David is willing to believe that Dad may have turned up hung-over, but not that he was rude and performed the work poorly. No way. *Don't use! I had a horrible experience!* He knows her type: the type who puts on reading glasses to check whether their reduced items are going through at the right prices. He wishes he could un-read her review, wishes he had never checked Dad's Task-Rabbit profile. But he had to find out what was up, why he had gone from working on average twice a week to once every few weeks. Of course his drinking accelerated afterwards. Why not drink all day when there's no work to do?

'Great episode,' David says after a long pause.

'I like that one.'

'Me too.' He stands up. There is nothing else to say. He can't correct Dad, can't inform him that they watched 'To Hull and Back' last night. 'I'll see you in a bit then.'

Dad reaches for his mug. 'Mm. Eight thirty.'

DAVID SHAKES HIS HEAD. Unbelievable. Unbelievable.

He screenshots a meme Zoe posted on Facebook, opens Discord, and copies and pastes it into the Dark Fury text chat.

David1702UK Today at 17:30

^ Can you believe that?

David1702UK Today at 17:30

There are genuinely people out there who think like that.

Chilozzi Today at 17:33

Hahahahaha

TRXDripp666 Today at 17:35

omg

Runningngunning Today at 17:35

But the person who reposted that meme is . . . white . . . no?

David1702UK Today at 17:35

Yep

Runningngunning Today at 17:35

lololol what a world

Dysruptz Today at 17:36

You're facebook friends with someone like that?

David1702UK Today at 17:36

She's my stepsister

Dysruptz Today at 17:36

Ah yh remember you said before . . . Just wow

Corey(515) Today at 17:37

Hilarious

Zoe has unfollowed and blocked David on Twitter and Instagram. Yet they remain friends on Facebook. He never posts, and she only reposts – mainly memes from left-wing pages. Nonetheless, he's pleased they remain friends on there, as she is supplying him with incredible content to share on Dark Fury. No one else knows a real-life SJW.

David1702UK Today at 17:40
Want to see something else mind-boggling?

A popular Scottish actress, Janice Johnson, lost her role in a BBC drama after a supposedly racist joke she'd sent to friends in a private WhatsApp thread was leaked. Zoe has reposted a meme on the controversy with the text 'notice how many of the people defending Janice Johnson have usernames like @whiteethnostate69? I hope she knows these are her new friends.'

Runningngunning Today at 17:42
omg

Corey(515) Today at 17:43
So Janice Johnson is now a white supremacist?!

Dysruptz Today at 17:44
Lolol Guess we're all white supremacists. Oh well.

WarriorCorgi Today at 17:47
https://youtu.be/NaFN1c-XADc

WarriorCorgi Today at 17:47
legs legs legs legs legs legs legs legs legs legs legs legs legs legs

Chilozzi Today at 17:48
Haha You LIVE for Rina now

WarriorCorgi Today at 17:48
Rina Demianova ftw

BonkRipper101 Today at 17:50
That Janice Johnson thing is crazy^ I miss the 90s

David sits back. He is really pleased they remain friends on Facebook.

IN THE WEEKS LEADING UP TO EASTER, David re-stocks the shelves in the homeware aisle with 'too hip to hop' napkins, paper plates with interchangeable ears, Sophie the Sheep balls, gold rabbits and honeycomb carrots. By Good Friday, all of these items are sold out. Kevin, his boss, calls him over.

'Yeah?'

'Gonna need you on something else.'

'Okay.'

'You might not like this but 'fraid that's life.'

'Okay.'

Kevin scratches his stubble. 'So. There was a fuck-up with the rota. Janet is actually only working until one today, and she won't budge on that. Doing something with the family. Good Friday and all. Anyway, Cynthia, who's supposed to be taking over from her, starts at three. I need someone to fill in for two hours.' A callous twinkle in his eyes. 'And that someone will be you.'

'But isn't Janet—'

'Yep.'

'I'm restocking until three. It says—'

'I know what it says on the rota. I'm making a change.'

'But—'

'Oi.' He jabs David in the chest. 'Don't no or but me. You're filling in for Janet from one, which is in ten minutes, until three. She will be waiting for you in the storeroom.'

'Seriously?'

He says nothing. Disdain rustles in his smirk.

'Why me? Why not . . . someone else?'

'Enjoy.'

*

David stands by the bakery counter sporting light-brown bunny ears – made from a headband, pipe cleaners and string – and offering customers complimentary hot-cross-bun samples. He hates everything and everyone.

'Go on,' a father encourages his son.

David holds out the tray.

'Thank you,' the boy says, taking one with a nervous smile.

'Give the Easter bunny a wave,' the father says.

The boy waves. David refuses to wave back. 'Thank you for shopping at Sainsbury's,' he says through his teeth. 'Happy Easter.' The boy waddles back to his father and takes a bite. A tannoy announcement: *Have you been to our bakery counter today? We are giving out free hot-cross-bun samples courtesy of the Sainsbury's Easter bunny. Go to our bakery counter now to get yours. Sainsbury's. Live well for less.* He watches two girls in matching white dresses lead their mother – and then he spots her: Selina, and her boyfriend. Shit. She catches his eyes, smiles and comes over. Shit. He hasn't seen her since college. The girls gaze up at him, their mother's hands on their shoulders. He lowers the tray, lets them take their samples. Expecting something more, they idle, until their mother ushers them away, sarcastically muttering, 'Great service,' under her breath. The baroque ideologue looks as imbecilic today as on Instagram: orange beanie, white oversize sweatshirt, white sneakers.

'Hey,' Selina says.

'Hey,' David replies, fretting over the bunny ears. The embarrassment flushes his cheeks.

'You working here then?'

'Yeah.'

She introduces him to her boyfriend, Stewart. 'Nice to meet you, man.' Gaudy silver signet rings on his index and little fingers. A thin pencil moustache too. And flesh-tunnel earlobes. She tells him that David was the only other student in her English class who read more than SparkNotes summaries. 'You a big reader too then?' Stewart asks.

'Not really.'

'No time?'

'No.'

'That's a shame,' Selina says. 'Hey, what happened to the hair? You used to have a cool fringe. Like, an indie one, noughties, Strokes-esque, right?'

'Got bored of it.'

'I like the bunny ears anyway,' Stewart says.

Selina playfully tells him not to go getting any ideas – his head is long enough as it is – before turning her attention back to David. 'Were you always planning to leave after AS levels?'

The tray wobbles in his hands. 'I couldn't be bothered staying for A levels.'

'I hear you,' Stewart says.

David briskly moves the conversation on, asking whether she applied to university.

She has an offer from Goldsmiths for English. 'It's not UCL, where Stewart is, but it should be fun. New Cross is cool, at least. I can't wait to leave this shithole. Sorry, I—'

'It's fine. It is a shithole.'

She fidgets with a zip on her leather biker jacket, whose lapels are studded with metal pins: Wolf Alice, HAIM, Goat Girl, Glass Animals, The 1975.

'All right to swipe one?' Stewart says, motioning to the tray.

'Go crazy.'

Having set his basket on the floor – Punk IPAs, Prosecco, orange juice, Galaxy chocolate, strawberries – he takes a hot-cross-bun sample. Selina follows suit, glossy black nails gleaming. She really is hot, even hotter than in college. It has been ages since he unfollowed her on Instagram. Her eyes. Her cheeks. Her lips. And the wine-red streaks in her long black hair. In his opinion, she is hotter than Rina Demianova, way hotter. Why is she with this idiot?

'Thanks,' Selina says. 'Well, Happy Easter.'

'You too.' David says.

'Happy Easter, man,' Stewart says. 'Nice meeting you. Good luck with everything.' Ogling the cakes, Selina says something.

He replies. Then his voice splashes into laughs and they amble away.

David wishes he and Stewart could play a Close Combat for Selina. His polo shirt feels gummy around the armpits. His fingers are red at the tips and the knuckles. He bungs the tray with the hot-cross buns on top of the bakery counter and flings off the bunny ears. House of Meetings, Factory, Hanger, Cave. Any map. David would show Selina that he is more of a man than Stewart.

ON THE BUS HOME, he phones Mum. He is in no mood to speak to her – to speak to anyone – but he has little choice. Four missed calls. He squashes a 7up can rolling towards him. The bus hits a red light. Sports Direct has on an 'Easter Bonanza' sale. KFC is heaving. He read on Facebook that it is trialling a plant-based popcorn chicken bucket in Mexico. Bizarrely, there was a slew of excited comments. He has never bought something in KFC. Kentucky Fried Chicken? Kentucky Fried Cruelty more like. Its employees cram tens of thousands of chickens into shit-filled, windowless sheds, make them eat until their legs break, no longer able to support their weight, and then seize them by their broken legs and murder them. Karl plays footage from KFC suppliers' slaughterhouses at every show, before the encore. It is a twenty-first-century holocaust. The bus pulls away. A cyclist slashes past. Mum picks up. 'Hey,' he says, feigning cheerfulness.

'Finally.'

If he neglects to speak to her for forty-eight hours, she will act as if they haven't spoken for months. 'Sorry, I was too exhausted last night, the night before, whatever.'

'You could have briefly returned my call.'

'Yeah. Okay.'

'Okay?'

The bus stops at Gants Hill station. It is filling up. A cute blonde girl sits next to him. He is tempted to hang up, just hang up. He hates speaking to Mum with so many people around, able to see him losing his temper. Later would suck too though. He wants to relax at home. He grinds round the 7up can. 'Look, I'm calling now. So. Erm. You had a day off, right? How's that been?'

'I may as well have been working, to be honest. I spent most of it feeling miserable.'

'Why?'

'You know.'

He cracks his neck. 'What about the book? Did you start it?' Last time he was in Haggerston, she told him she wanted to write something about her father and the Saqqakhana movement.

'No, I'm leaving that for now.'

'Why?'

'I'm not in the right frame of mind.'

'Why?'

'You know.'

He stabs his tongue into his right cheek and takes a long breath. 'Okay, Mum. Go on.'

'I'm so worried about you that—'

'Oh my God.'

'It's true. I've raised a son who has every opportunity in the world but is choosing to—'

'Stop worrying about me.'

'How can I not worry about you? You're stuck at Sainsbury's. You're not meeting anyone. You're not reading anything. You're not doing anything any more.'

'I'm fine!'

'Are you?'

'Yes.'

'Hmm.'

'Mum, I'm fine, I'm fucking fine!'

'You're stacking shelves. You could be reading books and—'

'Fuck reading books! I'm fine. For God's sake. I'm fine.'

'Maybe now. Trust me, though, there might be something romantic about working at Sainsbury's as a teenager, but there's nothing romantic about working there in your forties. I sometimes find my job at Action Aid mind-numbing. Can you imagine how you will feel about yours one day? You still have the opportunity to go to university, get a rewarding job. You could write

TV scripts, video-game scripts – something. But that will become harder and harder and eventually—'

'Who cares!' He is worried he might be visibly shaking. He lowers his voice and huddles up against the window, away from the cute girl. 'Listen to me, I'm fine, I'm fine. You're worried about me? Then stop moaning at me. That's one thing that would improve my life. You think I like working all day at Sainsbury's and then phoning you only for you to have a go at me?'

'Don't phone me in that case.'

'Awesome.'

'Goodbye then?'

He grits his teeth. 'Wait. Am I coming over at the weekend?'

'Are you?'

Jesus. 'Yes. Sunday. I'll come on Easter Sunday.'

'Thank you. That would be nice.'

'Okay.'

'I will make a special meal. Zoe will be there too.'

'Okay.'

'. . . Is everything all right between the two of you?'

An elaborate groan. 'No more. I'll see you on Sunday, Mum.'

'OI,' WARRIORCORGI SAYS. 'Stop spraying me. I look like I went paintballing and had my ass handed to me.'

'Pink,' Chilozzi says. 'Yellow. Blue.'

'Oi.'

'This is hilarious. Guys, I've transformed Corgi into a rainbow soyboy.'

'Ahem,' Dysruptz says. 'You two are supposed to be sniping.'

'Tell that to Chilz,' WarriorCorgi says. 'I'm trying to concentrate.'

'Okay,' Chilozzi says. 'I've had my fun. Actually. Hang on. One more spray of pink. What's it called? Electro spray. Oh man. Hilarious. Okay. I'm back. Don't worry.'

'Dave, let's take B,' Dysruptz says.

'Roger that. Right behind you.'

He is playing a Street War with Dysruptz, WarriorCorgi and Chilozzi. Street War is an intense, chaotic mode, a thirty-two versus thirty-two battle on a huge, sprawling map, with significant verticality, various ways of engaging enemies, and even vehicles. The goal is to capture objectives (A–E) spread across the map. Holding them provides points. The first team to reach 250 wins.

WarriorCorgi and Chilozzi are sniping from the roof of the skyscraper by E, while David and Dysruptz are on the main street, making their way to the parliament building, B.

Their team, Alliance, currently holds C, D and E and has 190 points. The opposing team, Federation, holds A and B and has 170 points.

'Guys,' WarriorCorgi says. 'Chopper.'

'Shit,' Dysruptz says. 'Where?'

'Near us. Wait. Don't worry. Someone took it out.'

Looking up, David sees a helicopter spinning in a frenzy of flame. It smashes into the TRK Comm building and vanishes in black smoke. He sprints on, past piles of rubble, a crashed truck, sawn trees and upturned traffic cones, staying close to Dysruptz. Gunfire rattles in the background. With so many players, shots are constantly being exchanged. Objective B is 33 metres away, only 33 metres. But it will be guarded. Federation won't give it up easily. He and Dysruptz hide on either side of a dumpster and mount their guns. The street is littered with leaves. Outside the parliament building stand stone columns. He trains his scope on the entrance.

'Just took out three up here,' Chilozzi says.

'Their little Federation corpses look like Jackson Pollock paintings,' WarriorCorgi adds.

'Ready to make a play for B?' Dysruptz says.

'Ready,' David says.

Dysruptz hurls a frag towards the parliament building; David follows with a Molotov. 'Okay, three, two, one.' They abandon their cover – and are met with a spray of bullets. Dysruptz dies, swearing. David retreats, bronze sparks zipping about his feet. 'Don't worry,' he says. 'I'm still alive.' The screen black and white and smeared with blood, and his controller vibrating feverishly, he makes it into a nearby building and crouches there, regaining health. Dysruptz spawns on him. 'Back.' Golden rockety hell strikes the parliament building, killing three Federation players.

'Get in,' David says. 'Someone on our team came through with a rocket launcher.'

'Okay,' Dysruptz says. 'Second time lucky.'

'Let's have it for real this time.'

An incredible headshot and a scrappy melee kill later, David and Dysruptz have cleared the area and captured B. Alliance now holds B, C, D and E and is on 210 points.

Chilozzi promises to eliminate any Federation players heading their way. WarriorCorgi directs his attention to a jeep on the main street. 'Got the driver.'

'Got bonnet boy.'

'Shit. The way he flopped. You took him out like that jihadi in the news.'

'Eh?'

'You know. The fat fuck. There was that photo of him shot on the bonnet of his truck in Iraq.'

'Na na na na na na na na na na na na Musman!' Dysruptz says.

'Ah, of course,' Chilozzi says. 'The fat fuck.'

'Putting the fat in fatwa. Best headline I've ever read,' Dysruptz says.

'What was that tweet, Dave, the fat-shaming one?' WarriorCorgi says.

'He might have been a heinous human being who committed unforgivable crimes,' David says, repeating the tweet word for word, crouching by one of the stone columns, waiting for a Federation player to step into his line of sight, 'but there's no need to fat-shame—'

Dysruptz bursts out laughing.

'Ah, man. Stop. You're killing me here,' WarriorCorgi says, laughing too.

'No need to fat-shame him,' David continues. 'Just condemn him for his—'

'Hahaha.'

'Haha.'

'Hahahaha.'

'Was that tweet legit?' Chilozzi asks.

'Shut up,' Dysruptz says. 'Don't ruin it for me.'

Grenade. David attempts to edge out of the way. Too late. Dead. 'Damn.' He lost concentration. He shakes his controller by its handles and whacks it on the floor. 'Sorry.'

'Down as well,' Dysruptz says. 'That was too funny.'

B has been lost – and Federation has taken back D and E, putting it on 200 points. Closing up. Chilozzi tells David and Dysruptz to spawn on him; there's a helicopter on the roof of the skyscraper, which he can pilot over to one of the objectives. 'Sounds like a plan,' David says. Reunited with Chilozzi and WarriorCorgi, he marvels at the view. It's possible to see swathes of the map: the snow-capped mountains, the stadium, the fire station, the military base, the river.

'Right,' Chilozzi says. 'Get in.'

'Wait for me,' Dysruptz says. 'Okay. I'm in.'

'Sweet,' Chilozzi says. 'Let's move. D?'

'Yep,' Dysruptz says.

The blades whirr. They take flight.

'Federation's up to two hundred and twenty,' Dysruptz says. 'We have to take D.'

'We will,' David says as the helicopter passes a warehouse pumping out smoke. 'We will.'

'Parachutes ready?' Chilozzi says.

A notification flashes up: enemy cruise missile incoming.

'Go. Go. Go,' Dysruptz says.

Now unmanned, the helicopter explodes and smudges the sky black.

'Let's fuck shit up then,' Chilozzi squeals, firing his AK-47 towards D.

There's no choice. They have to take the objective, and take it now.

David slams the R2 trigger. 'Come on, boys!'

DAVID WORKS FROM TWELVE until eight on Saturday, and every second is torture. The store is teeming with lazy shoppers. Questions. Questions. Questions. *Have you got . . . Do you have . . . Are there any more?* Just look at the shelves, he wants to tell them. You have eyes. Not on the shelves? Then funnily enough the answer is no. He is still bitter about the bunny ears, the meeting with Selina, Stewart.

When he returns home, he watches *Only Fools and Horses* with Dad and then heads straight to bed, because no one in Dark Fury is free for *Call of Duty*. He plays an early Salomé B-side which he hasn't heard for months, closes his eyes and concentrates.

The simple melody. The harrowing lyrics. No one else has the bravery to write a song from the perspective of a serial killer. In the music industry, what passes for bravery is saying racism is bad, the Tories are bad, climate change is bad. That's not bravery: it is guaranteed to get the artist more sales. Although he prefers Karl's solo material, 'A Stranger' is an incredible track.

He closes his laptop and lies down. It has been under three hours since he finished work, and he is already dreading Monday morning. He rolls on to his side. The outlines of his posters are darkly visible. It would be easier to sleep if the room stank less. In future he will take his dirty dishes downstairs straight after eating. He won't leave them for days and days. That the bottom-right corner of his poster from the 'Ultimate Guide to Salomé' special issue of *Uncut* has ripped upsets him. His favourite poster, it shows Karl sitting on a bench in the woods, wearing a fedora and waves of necklaces, fiddling with a lighter, lost in thought, the tattooed phrase 'Don't Help' visible across his knuckles. The rest of the band are standing in the background, chatting. There is something about Karl in the image: enigmatic, poetic and simply cool as fuck. David frequently summons it up in his cigarette breaks. He sighs. He needs to stop his mind returning to work.

'Bret. You. You take it. No. You take it. You take it.' David raises his head. 'You take it. You were the best in training. You take it.' Dad. He is sitting outside, monologuing. Over the past few months, David has heard this too many times. The bedroom window is right above the green plastic chair they keep in the back garden. He knows Dad is down there, smoking and sipping from his Sports Direct mug, and motioning, to no one. 'You take it,' Dad continues, in a mushy voice. 'Go on, Bret.' He seems to be playing out memories from his past. Why? It's so late. Nearly two thirty. Who is Bret? A childhood friend? An army colleague? 'We've won. We've won. Four–three.' David curls his toes. He feels uncomfortable overhearing this. 'What a penalty.' He presses the side of his head firmly into the pillow. 'Woooooo. Weeeeeeeeeee.' Oh God. The sounds are the limit. They kill him. 'Weeee. We've won. We've won.' They are so . . . wrong. They are wrong. Not Dad. What is happening? David can't take it. He opens his laptop and puts Salomé back on.

Runningngunning Today at 10:15
OH FOR FUCKS SAKE

Runningngunning Today at 10:15
HOW MANY TIMES?

The Frosted Strawberry Sensation Pop Tart David is having for breakfast is making him feel sick. It was a mistake to buy so many packs, even though they were half price. His black sleeping T-shirt is covered with purple sprinkles, icing shreds. He gives it a brush. On the windowpane a fly twitches, rubbing its legs together. He gets up, takes the post-office slip and the glass he keeps on the windowsill, covers the fly with the glass, seals it with the slip, opens the window and releases the fly. A bright blue sky, no clouds. The top of the back wall is glazed with sunlight. The stems of the dead creeper plant rattle. Waiting for Runningngunning to elaborate, he finishes the Pop Tart.

Runningngunning Today at 10:16
https://twitter.com/NightWaters83/status/
1222991785963724800?s=20

Runningngunning Today at 10:16
Easter Sunday morning too FFS

He wonders why Runningngunning is even awake. It's 4 a.m. in Texas. He opens the link. Oh shit. Something is going down in Paris: a shooting, Chappe Gallery. Apparently blood everywhere – bodies everywhere. The tweet is from an eyewitness. He keys #chappe into the search bar. Oh shit. Hundreds of tweets in the past minute. Oh shit, shit, shit. He gnaws at his right thumbnail.

David1702UK Today at 10:18
Fuck! #chappe is everywhere. Looks like it's real.

Runningngunning Today at 10:18
Yea. Nothing in the mainstream media yet but its real for sure. Seems like it only happened 20/30 mins ago. CNN probs fact checking (finding a way to pretend its not Islam)

David1702UK Today at 10:19
Yeah. It's Paris, so it will be Islam for sure

David1702UK Today at 10:19
Depressing

David1702UK Today at 10:20
Being reported on BBC News now. An 'incident' at Chappe Gallery in Montmartre. The 'suspect' has been shot dead by the police. 'A number of people' believed dead.

Runningngunning Today at 10:20
Lol BBC News. You might as well watch Al Jazeera.

Runningngunning Today at 10:20
Seriously you guys in Europe need to sort yourselves out. We used to look up to you with all your art and music and books. Then you opened the gates to millions of migrants and now you can't even go to an art museum without being gunned down. Fuck that! What happened to all your culture and civilization? You guys have really pissed things away

BonkRipper101 Today at 10:21
Woah. Just woke up randomly and saw this shit.

BonkRipper101 Today at 10:21
I mean, this photo: https://twitter.com/DamianZGray/status/1223241991020116096?s=20

Runningngunning Today at 10:21
Christ I feel sick. That won't be up on Twitter for long.

BonkRipper101 Today at 10:21
Bastards

David shudders. He wishes he hadn't seen the photo. It's too much. Just too fucking much.

David1702UK Today at 10:22
That's horrific

Runningngunning Today at 10:23
Seriously Im so sick of seeing this every week everywhere. And everyone's like Why is it happening? Its so strange! I just dont get it! ITS FUCKING OBVIOUS

Runningngunning Today at 10:23
ISLAM

Runningngunning Today at 10:23
& You know what the worst thing is. In an hour Twitter will be flooded with SJWs saying Islam isn't to blame and expressing their sympathy for Muslims everywhere. You just know that #IslamisPeace will become the top trending hashtag.

BonkRipper101 Today at 10:24
100% the police/mainstream media/politicos will force the parents of the victims to release statements saying they forgive the terrorists and have only love and respect for Islam etc

BonkRipper101 Today at 10:24
fuck that if this ever happened to someone I knew I would go on the news and say some real truth shit no love and respect and forgiveness bs

Runningngunning Today at 10:25
Lololol. I would love to see someone do that.

Runningngunning Today at 10:28
Who knows. Maybe one of these Parisians will step up to the plate?!

David1702UK Today at 10:30
Ha! Fingers crossed

BonkRipper101 Today at 10:30
Man I'm so revved up I might have to get on COD and let off some steam. In?

David1702UK Today at 10:30
Can't now unfortunately but later for sure

Nearly ten thirty. He needs to be in Haggerston by twelve for Mum's stupid Easter lunch. A waste of an afternoon. Zoe will be there too. He hopes Mum at least got him the Moo Free Easter egg she got him last year. That was all right. He grabs a Karl T-shirt and goes to the bathroom to shower. There is so much light shining in. The grimy smudges across the window look like shooting stars.

On the Overground he refreshes Twitter obsessively, itching for updates. The bars in the carriage blaze a sweaty orange. The terrorist shouted '*Allahu Akbar*' before opening fire. A string of witnesses attested to that. Yet the BBC is still concealing the truth. It sounds as if there was total carnage. He was armed with a Kalashnikov. The police managed to 'neutralise' him within three minutes, but in those three minutes . . . There is speculation that the death toll could be in the dozens. The train rattles past a park with kids playing football. A bright green ball loops over a heap of backpacks. The Dark Fury server seethes.

Runningngunning Today at 11:30
Lolololol. Its begun

Runningngunning Today at 11:31
https://twitter.com/becca_hogwarts/status/1254212256447693825?s=20

Runningngunning Today at 11:32
https://twitter.com/lululalu/status/1254213304365411328?s=20

Runningngunning Today at 11:32
https://twitter.com/asifrno092/status/1254214203281534976?s=20

Runningngunning Today at 11:32
https://twitter.com/DrRuthWright/status/1254215303902773249?s=20

Runningngunning Today at 11:32
https://twitter.com/Tinuvie61893/status/1254216937031245826?s=20

Reading these tweets, David feels a flush of heat in his face. ‘Dont even know whats happening at #chappe yet but have already found people blaming Islam for it, can you just try and hold in your islamophobia for one minute people?’ ‘There’s been a shooting at #chappe and again people are saying Oh let’s blame Muslims! No! Don’t blame Muslims. Only blame the person who did it. The background is irrelevant. Whoever did it is an asshole and there’s really little more to it than that.’ ‘What happened at #chappe today is scary af but please don’t use this as an opportunity to spread your ignorant agenda. The guy was NOT a Muslim. He was a terrorist. Have some respect.’ ‘1 person has committed a mass shooting so now let’s start an agenda against 1.8 billion people who follow their religion. OK. Yeah. That makes sense.’

Zoe and Stephen will express the same sentiments. Even Mum might. He rubs his hands on his thighs. He will tell them where they can shove their Islamophilia, because he is not in the mood for Guardianista bullshit today. He squeezes out a slab of spearmint gum. He is sick of being bullied into silence and will stand up to them. They can call him Islamophobic. So what? Bring it on.

'CAN YOU TAKE THE AUBERGINE OUT?' Mum asks.

'Sure.' Stephen puts on oven mitts.

'Hm,' Mum says, tasting the soup. 'Yes, I think everything's ready.'

Stephen tugs open the oven. The kitchen fills with an aroma of spices.

'David,' Mum says. 'You can sit.'

He is leaning on the pale wooden surface by the toaster. No breadcrumbs. It's weird how clean they keep the house. Mum and Stephen – they *are* weird. The early-afternoon sunlight oozes into the kitchen. Translucent blue glasses glint in the display cabinet, through the spotless sliding glass doors. Lettuce growing in pots on the porch sways in the breeze. He has never understood why people grow things like that. You can buy lettuce in a supermarket.

The table is laid with Easter things: a vase with spring flowers, a mini wooden rabbit and colourful eggs, painted by David as a child, or so Mum claims. He has no memory of painting them. In the midst of all these Easter items even the trendy Ikea pendant lamp hanging over the table today reminds him of a shoddily reconstructed egg. Sitting, he checks Discord, Twitter and – warily after Runningngunning's comment – BBC News. No interesting updates.

Mum gives Zoe a shout to let her know the food is ready. Then asks David and Stephen how long it's been since they were all here together. 'It feels like forever. It must have been months.' She is wearing contact lenses, lipstick and an elegant navy top with a floral print. When he arrived, she even had on a long, floaty silver-white shawl.

'Christmas,' Stephen says, placing the oven tray on the table.

'Boxing Day.' He is wearing his normal officey outfit, an unbuttoned shirt and black suit trousers. Mum rearranges the flowers. Their petals are pale blue, like the veins in her wrist.

Zoe appears in the doorway. 'Sorry, I was noting down a new idea for my dissertation. I had a thought as to how I could link . . . Anyway, I'm now done for the day.'

Stephen jokingly checks his watch. 'At one? I know it's Easter Sunday but . . .'

'You know, I never work past one any more. I've come to the conclusion that putting in more than two or three hours of dissertation work a day is counterproductive.'

'Well, the tortoise and the hare, I suppose.'

'Funny.'

There are two dark-silver studs below the right side of her lower lip, a spider bites piercing. After running her eyes expressionlessly over his Karl top, she takes a seat next to him.

'Hey,' she says, as if they were still on talking terms.

'Hey.'

'There's roasted aubergine,' Mum tells Zoe, 'stuffed grape leaves and *ash reshteh*, a soup my mother used to make, with noodles, chickpeas, beans and a lot of herbs.'

'I need some home-cooked Iranian food in my life,' says Zoe. 'I've fallen into the habit of using Just Eat every other night. It's embarrassing.'

She, Mum and Stephen share their favourite Just Eat restaurants – Sake Sushi, The Breakfast Club, Yard Sale Pizza, Dhaba Kitchen – and Mum puts the soup pot on the table. Zoe photographs it for Eleanor, who has started making soups and will 'lose her shit' when she sees it.

'Just a warning,' Mum says, ladling it into the four bowls. 'It might be too minty. I ended up putting in several tablespoons. But hopefully it'll be okay.' David goggles at it. He has never seen something so green. This is the sort of food people probably imagine he eats every night, as a vegan.

Stephen plunges a corkscrew into a bottle of white wine. 'David?'

'Any beers?'

A faint tightening of his features. 'I think white wine would go better with the meal.'

David shrugs. He would prefer a less feminine drink. Dysruptz called Runningngunning out for admitting he likes white wine. But at least there is booze, some succour for this shitshow.

Having put the grape leaves on the table, Mum sits next to Stephen, opposite David.

Stephen makes a lame attempt at a toast. 'Happy Easter. And *Eide Shoma Mobarak*. Amira told me that it was Nowruz, the Iranian New Year, yesterday. So this is really a double celebration.'

'*Eide Shoma Mobarak*,' Mum echoes.

'Yeah, cheers,' David says. The sun spreads the kitchen with thick, buttery light. He would kill to be outside, on his own, relaxing and smoking a cigarette.

'Okay, I can't promise the soup will be edible,' Mum says. 'But let's see.'

'Amira, it's so nice,' Zoe says, trying it.

'Lovely,' Stephen says.

'Hmm. Not a patch on my mother's *ash reshteh*,' Mum says. 'She always got the flavour just right. But it's not bad, actually. David, do you like it?'

'Mm.'

'Yeah?' A smile. Then Mum clears her throat and turns to Zoe. 'Are you still enjoying the research for your dissertation?'

Zoe coughs, thumps her chest. 'Sorry. This roasted aubergine is great, too, Amira. I'm stuffing my face. I need to slow up.' She takes her wine glass. The research is exciting. She has read Helen Achebe's novels before but not thought critically about them. 'It's criminal how little known she is.'

While she bangs on about Helen whats-her-face, David spoons up the soup. It's too healthy for his liking. The roasted aubergine is all right, but would be better with a battering of Bang Bang.

He is inclined to stop Zoe in her tracks and tell her that she's as thick as pig shit. Helen too. But now is not the time to speak up. The conversation will turn to Paris. He stabs his toes into the

Persian rug under the table meantime. The small black-lacquer birds on the windowsill are beaming. A malnourished pigeon lands on one of the lettuce pots, bobs its head and coos among the leaves.

'How was the run-up to Easter at Sainsbury's?' Stephen asks.

'What?' David says, snapping back to the conversation.

'How was the run-up to Easter at Sainsbury's?'

'Fine.'

'Busy?'

'Yeah.'

'It's cool how many vegan Easter eggs supermarkets are selling this year,' Zoe says. 'Eleanor went fully vegan a week ago. She said there are loads, even white chocolate ones.'

'Yeah.'

Zoe raises her eyebrows conspiratorially to Stephen, as if to say: He's being difficult, isn't he? She may as well have said it out loud. David can read her signals all too easily. Stephen's phone rings. He reaches into his pocket. 'Sorry, I might need to take this. Things are a bit hectic at—'

'Don't worry,' Mum says. 'Go for it.'

'So what exactly is in the soup?' Zoe asks Mum. 'Eleanor will press me for the recipe.'

David takes out his own phone. Still no real updates. Just more SJW tweets. Everyone is waiting for Nmoos. Living in Paris, he will be able to provide unique, informed insights.

'Everything okay?' Mum asks Stephen when he returns, opening a hand to the sunlight.

'Dominic. He wanted me to have a final look over our statement on the incident in Paris today before posting it. What are we talking about?'

While Mum fills him in, David opens Amnesty's Facebook page. The statement is there.

> Amnesty International condemns in the strongest possible terms the heinous and cowardly act committed in Paris today, which has taken so many innocent lives. The thoughts of everyone at

Amnesty International are with all those affected. In responding to this attack, it is important that politicians and the media refrain from using language that will further fan the flames of hatred in society and instead stress that we have far more in common than that which divides us. Amnesty International urges more love, not more hate.

More love? More love? David bursts out laughing.

Stephen turns to him. 'What's up?'

'Don't worry,' he says, shaking his head.

'No. What's up?

He knocks back his wine and weighs up whether the moment has come, the moment to take the leap. Corey has spoken the truth to his parents, Runningngunning to his wife. Dysruptz has spoken the truth to his boss at Qwikwash. He can speak the truth too. 'I read Amnesty's statement.' A crackle in his voice. 'There was no mention of . . . There was no mention of Islam.' The sentence swings out into the kitchen and sizzles. He has said it, really said it. His heart is pounding. Stephen regards him uneasily. 'Yeah,' he stumbles onwards, breathless. 'There was no mention of Islam.'

A hot-faced silence. Then Zoe groans. 'What are you talking about?'

'What am I talking about?' David says, turning to her. 'Honesty.'

'David,' Mum says.

'The terror attack may have been Islamism-inspired,' Stephen says, 'but—'

'Fuck me.' David theatrically throws his head back.

'David,' Mum says, placing both hands on the table.

'Didn't you hear that, Mum?' he says. 'Islam*ism*? Islam*ism-inspired*?'

'Watch your language,' Mum says. 'And think about what you're saying.'

'But Amnesty's Islamophilic!' His thoughts are running too fast. He knows what he wants to convey but can't convey it. 'Don't you see? Mum! Everyone's Islamophilic.'

'David. You're. We'll talk about this later,' Mum says. 'This is Easter—'

'Pffff.' He pushes his plate away. 'Great. Censorship.' He mimes zipping his mouth shut. 'I'll stay silent then, nice and politely silent. Let's pretend that the terror attack was not committed by a Muslim in the name of Allah. Let's pretend Muhammad was not a warlord and a . . . You know what.' The air turns clammy. His molars are crunching together. His fingers trembling.

'What's happened to you?' Zoe asks.

'Me?'

'David,' Mum says. 'You need to. You've become a real handful. You've become . . .'

'What? What?'

She takes a long breath. 'It's Easter. This is not the time.'

'Don't worry,' Stephen says. 'Don't worry. We can talk about this amicably, as adults. There's no reason we can't have a calm, sensible chat about the terror attack.'

'Are you sure?' Mum says. 'We were looking forward to this.'

'It's okay.' He makes eye contact. 'David, explicitly mentioning Islam in our statement would have granted the terrorist religious legitimacy, and that would be wrong – terrorists have no religion.'

'No religion? He shouted, "*Allahu Akbar!*" *Allahu Akbar! Allahu Akbar!*'

'Enough,' Mum says. 'Get a hold—'

'Speak up!' David says, pivoting to Mum. 'Speak up for once. You saw what happened to Iran. You saw it. You want that to happen here? You want there to be an Islamic revolution in the UK? Because there will be. My grandfather went to prison for freedom of expression. No?'

He picks his fork up, shakes it and sticks it into the wooden table and rakes, rakes, rakes. Mum reaches over the table to grab it from him. He bats her hands away and lets it clang on to his plate.

'What? What?'

She looks aghast at him. 'You're losing the plot.'

Stephen spreads his palms and suggests that everyone take a

deep breath. He inspects the table and confirms to Mum that it's fine. The scratches can be covered up. A warning to David that if he wants to take part in adult conversations he needs to learn how to act like an adult. 'Okay?'

David looks away.

'Apologise.'

'Oh. Fu—'

'No. Apologise.'

'David,' Mum says, her voice feathery but firm. 'You're losing the plot. Baba cared about freedom of expression. But he was not anti-Islamic. He hated the Ayatollah and his regime. And he hated the Shah and his regime too. He hated repressive governments, not Islam. Those sketches I showed you, they have a context. I wanted you to know more about your heritage and your history and to share Iran with you, to share Baba with you. I should have done that more when you were younger, but . . . David, your grandmother was a devout Muslim. She prayed five times a day. If she were alive now and knew her grandson were becoming anti-Islamic . . .'

He rolls his eyes.

'Listen to me,' she continues. 'Listen to me. You're losing the plot. The problems with Iran. They're political, not religious. What happened in Paris today was not religious either. Islam is not the enemy. For your grandmother, Islam was something profoundly personal, something that helped her. It helped her after – well, too many times. It was a source of hope and comfort for her. There are people who think every word in the Quran should be read literally, who think the world hasn't changed since the seventh century. But all religions have those people. God knows Christianity has them. There are many, many beautiful, compassionate, progressive passages in the Quran.'

'Amira's right,' Stephen says. 'We can't let terrorists control the narrative of Islam in the UK. Terrorists may claim to be Islamic. But they're not, not really. They're violent opportunists who co-opt religion, nothing more. It's wrong to respond to terror attacks by stigmatising moderate Muslims and Islam.' He pauses. 'Think about it like this – how is a moderate Muslim who, I don't know, owns a record store in Glasgow responsible for a terror attack that happened in Paris?'

David has never heard of a Muslim owning a record store.

'Yeah?' he says. 'So. So.' His thoughts are still running faster than he can speak. He wants to be more eloquent. 'How come none of these so-called Muslims ever condemn terror attacks? Two thirds of British Muslims wouldn't report a terror plot to the police. Two thirds.'

'Bullshit,' Zoe says. 'That's a made-up statistic.'

'It's not.'

A snort of laughter. 'How do you know? Do you have a source for it?'

He stares at her.

'Thought so,' Zoe says. 'Oh, and wanting moderate Muslims to condemn terror attacks? Firstly, we can't expect one point six billion people to apologise on behalf of a few violent psychopaths. Secondly, do you know how many do? Just look on Twitter. Right now there are millions of moderate Muslims condemning the attack in France – millions. I see it all the time. And they shouldn't even be—'

'I never see *any* moderate—'

'You're stuck in a far-right echo chamber. That's why.'

'Me? I'm stuck in an echo chamber? You're—'

'No. Listen to me. Moderate Muslims. They should not feel compelled to speak out and condemn the attacks. Because it is nothing to do with them. They have nothing to apologise for. They are the ones suffering. You want real facts? Last year, a record number of anti-Muslim attacks were reported in the UK – a record number. They never make the news because they're classed as "hate crimes" rather than "terror attacks" and don't tend to result in headline-making fatalities. But we are talking hundreds. That's why it's so important to respond to terror attacks in the right way, and for politicians and the media and everyone to be careful about the language they use. Rather than saying Islam this, Islam that.'

He sarcastically mimes Zoe speaking. She sighs. Mum stares disbelievingly at him.

'Grow up,' Stephen says.

'Argh!' David says. 'This is impossible. You're Islamophilic, Islamophilic, Islamophilic!'

'You really are being childish today.'

'I'm not. You are!' He tosses his fork away. It stabs a floor tile.

'David,' Mum says.

'Pick it up,' Stephen says cooly, calmly.

David kicks back his chair, stands up and shouts, 'Fuck you!' He chucks his plate at the wall, and it smashes into pieces. A second pigeon is now cooing outside loudly. Mum is screaming at him, screaming. He spins round and storms out, out of the Godforsaken house, out of Godforsaken Haggerston, out of Godforsaken la-la land – raising a middle finger to them on his way.

DAVID SLOUCHES AGAINST A WALL, tugging on a cigarette. The weather has turned. It's so bad now that he can't even sit on the step in the smoking rectangle. A fifteen-minute break spent entirely on his feet. He screws up his face as hailstones pelt the building – hailstones. At least Jamal is no longer here to bother him and louse up his breaks with inane chit-chat. After he left, Jamal sent David a couple texts. 'Yo. Hws stuff at the wrkhouse? sme old shit?' 'Houuuuusse Paaaaaaaarty @ mine on Sat. Keen, mate?' 'Hws Oberfuhrer Kevin? hahahaha. Still runnin the place like a cunt?' He never bothered to reply.

The skip is sponged in an eerie white-blue light, a broken cage trolley headstanding out. A constant pinging, as hailstones strike concrete. He browses the Covert Ops subreddit, shielding his phone from the weather as best he can. A video clip with the title 'teamwork makes the dreamwork, we all know how this would have played out in a game of randoms'. So true. A heated ninety-five comment thread with the title 'friendly reminder: If youre playing hardcore and you run in front of your teammate while theyre shooting, its your fault if you die.' He skims the comments, then checks Twitter, where he finds an interesting *Spectator US* article on the Paris attack, arguing that progressives are using 'pretzeled language' and have to stop making excuses. He shares it. Since the hellish Easter Sunday, he has been tweeting a lot. The way Zoe and Stephen and Mum all piled on him with their propaganda – fuck them. Mum has tried to call him five times and left multiple voicemails, which amuses him. Who listens to voicemails? He has no intention of calling her back this week: maybe next week, maybe. He is not submitting to a patronising lecture.

He stubs out his cigarette. It would have been nice to sit on the step. His feet are killing him. He lifts his heels off the ground and grimaces. He lowers them. The Dr Martens might be to blame. But trainers – no way, not happening. He spends his last three minutes on the Karl subreddit. There are rumours that Karl will release a new song later in the week. A reliable source claims to have seen the press release. It is embargoed until Friday but reveals that the song will be called 'Because Of My Views' and see 'one of the country's most provocative voices hitting brave new lyrical heights'. David cannot wait. He literally cannot wait.

THE FRONT DOOR GRINDS OPEN, stuttering, halting, stuttering. David pushes it with all his body weight. It expanded in summer and no longer fits properly in the frame.

'I'm home,' he says loudly.

It smells as if something is burning. He leaves his bag at the bottom of the stairs. A hob is on, flames lapping a pot. He lifts the lid, releasing gobs of steam. Dad has forgotten about his rice. A crusty mess. Other than some grains glued to the sides, all are black, burnt to a frazzle.

He opens the window and goes to tell Dad the bad news.

'Dad. Hey, Dad.'

'I'm here.'

'So,' David says, bursting into his bedroom. He stops in his tracks. 'Shit! Dad. Are you okay?'

'Mm-hmm.'

He lies in the middle of the room, staring up at the ceiling, his hands knitted together over his chest, his big, bulky shoes on, a mist of ash on his trousers, an empty vodka bottle beside him.

'What happened?'

'I'm fine here. But there's some rice—'

'I've sorted that,' David says, kneeling on the carpet. 'What happened?'

'I put the rice on and then realised I had left my phone upstairs so I went to get it and . . . I don't know how it happened but I fell and . . . for some silly reason I'm having trouble getting up.'

When David makes to help, Dad tells him to wait a minute and sucks his lips. There are specks of mustard on his cheeks. '*Only Fools and Horses*? Maybe a Christmas special?'

'Sure.' David wonders why Dad can't get up. He put on a

significant amount of weight over the winter. Even his hands are bigger now. That might be why – or there might be another reason, a worse reason. 'Come on,' he says, his voice taking on a pleading tone. 'Hey, Dad, come on.'

'Mm?'

'Come on. Let's try.'

'I'll be there in a minute.'

He edges behind Dad, puts his hands under his armpits and tries to pull him up. Too heavy.

'Come on.'

'Just a minute.'

'Dad!' His voice is shaking. 'On three together. Okay?'

'Mm.'

Slowly, David manages to haul him up and help him over to the bed. The ink-blue bedsheet has a spiky cigarette burn. 'Lie there ... How are you feeling?'

'I'll be there in a minute.'

He has barely registered the move from carpet to bed. The lamp on his bedside table casts a charcoal shadow over the bridge of his nose, obscuring the spider veins. David tells him to rest for a while. He will cook pasta. They can have that and then later watch *Only Fools and Horses*.

Dad reaches for his hand in a way he never has before.

'Don't worry,' David says. 'Just rest.'

In his bedroom, David considers keying 'fall on the floor can't get up dangerous' into Google. But is worried that the results will not make for good reading. His phone rings. Mum. He clicks 'decline'. From the bathroom comes a plopping sound. The toilet tank has a crack. Water is leaking out into a bucket squeezed underneath to prevent the bathroom from flooding. He empties the bucket every evening. He pockets his phone, storms into the bathroom, empties it, and tosses it at the tank.

'Just fucking stop leaking!' he shouts. The bucket lands on its side. 'Just fucking stop!' He clenches his fist and smacks the tank.

'Arghhh. Fuck.' His knuckles sting. Nonetheless, he lashes out a second and a third and a fourth and a fifth time. 'Just fucking stop. Just fucking, fucking stop.'

Nmoos Today at 21:00
Hey guys

Nmoos Today at 21:00
Sorry I havent been around recently

BonkRipper101 Today at 21:00
NMOOS IS BACK

Runningngunning Today at 21:00
shit where u been bro

At last. David leans into his laptop. What is the vibe in Paris? What are real Parisians saying?

Corey(515) Today at 21:01
cmon then hit us man

Dysruptz Today at 21:01
#:-S

Nmoos Today at 21:03
Yeah sorry guys

Nmoos Today at 21:04
I dunno what to say really, everythings pretty shit atm

Nmoos Today at 21:04
so

Nmoos Today at 21:04
my cousin was killed in the Chappe thing and im feeling kinda overwhelmed

Nmoos Today at 21:04
I just wanted to log on to say that im ok but i think ill lie low for a while

Nmoos Today at 21:04
take care and im sure ill be back at some point

David puffs his cheeks out, processing this.

David1702UK Today at 21:05
Shit

David1702UK Today at 21:05
I'm so sorry to hear that man

Corey(515) Today at 21:05
@Nmoos omfg no way?

Corey(515) Today at 21:05
Fuck thats heavy dude

Dysruptz Today at 21:05
@Nmoos wow thats fucking shit

Dysruptz Today at 21:05
take all the time you need we'll be waiting for you

Runningngunning Today at 21:05
no way im not fucking having that

Runningngunning Today at 21:05
those fucking scumbags

Runningngunning Today at 21:05
nmoos man . . . fucks sake

While more Dark Fury users send their condolences, David sits back, feasting on his little finger. This is serious, really serious. Nmoos's cousin has been killed. He was at the Chappe Gallery on Easter Sunday – and he was killed. David thinks back to the photo he saw on Twitter. The blood. The bodies. He might have seen Nmoos's cousin, lifeless. He crooks his finger far into his mouth and sinks his teeth in until it crumples up. Nmoos is one of them. They cannot let this slide.

Mix Today at 21:10
@Nmoos that sucks sorry dude if theres smthing we can do holler?

WarriorCorgi Today at 21:10
@Nmoos yeah anytime u wanna stop thinking for a bit we can get a street war going I promise i wont start piloting the helicopter without u this time

Corey(515) Today at 21:11
@Nmoos or if you can get over to the states come visit theres a shooting range near me which literally has a jihadi as a target

WarriorCorgi Today at 21:11
lolol

Dysruptz Today at 21:15
Dont think nmoos is reading these messages anymore guys i think hes tapped out for now let him sort his head out he'll be back when hes ready

Mix Today at 21:16
that shooting range sounds hilarious – the ones by me are so pc

Runningngunning Today at 21:18
https://www.illuminating-islam.org/Quran/Themes/violent_passages.html

Runningngunning Today at 21:18
just some quotes from the religion of peace ^

Runningngunning Today at 21:18
read them, seriously read them

Corey(515) Today at 21:19
wow some of those are fucked

David1702UK Today at 21:20
Really messed up

He opens his third Heineken of the night and contemplates how anyone can claim Islam is a religion of peace with a straight face. He is sitting in the dark, except for the screen's faint glow and the blue light bubbling up from below the keyboard. The laptop no longer charges properly. He fiddles with the power cable. The plastic has frayed near the end, exposing the metal wires.

It's late, but a *Call of Duty* session will be suggested soon, and, regardless of how many hours' sleep it means losing, he will have to take part – for Nmoos.

He is, anyway, eager to try a back-button attachment he's bought for his controller, which provides two extra mappable buttons and so helps to shorten response times: apparently all pro gamers use one. He intends to assign 'jump' to the right paddle and 'crouch' to the left one. That will help with his drop-shooting and make it easier to dodge bullets while turning corners.

Runningngunning Today at 21:21
its more than messed up its fucking sickening shit

Runningngunning Today at 21:21
i think ive actually finally had enough i cant take it anymore its too much for me

Runningngunning Today at 21:23
@Dysruptz i know theres a no linking to other Discord servers rule here and i totally get that but could we make an exception once?

Runningngunning Today at 21:23
Im on another server that i think you guys would dig and everyone there would be cool with you guys joining

Runningngunning Today at 21:23
its not a COD server at all so no competition dw. Just political chat and stuff but there are like 200 members so loads of good content and theyre actually pretty serious about things and i think we need to start getting more serious

Runningngunning Today at 21:23
I mean Nmoos's cousin ffs

Dysruptz Today at 21:25
go on then

Dysruptz Today at 21:25
but we are not making this is a regular thing

Runningngunning Today at 21:23
https://discord.gg/48URfde

Runningngunning Today at 21:23
i know its more serious but these are serious times

Runningngunning Today at 21:23
everything cant just be for the lulz

Runningngunning Today at 21:23
we have to realise that or we'll all end up like Nmoos's cousin

The link leads to a server called W.O.T.A.N. ϟϟ whose cover photo is a horizontal tricolour black-white-and-red flag emblazoned with the server name. When he clicks on the #chat channel a 'red-light' message pops up informing him that he doesn't have permission to read or post messages and pointing him towards #rules. There are new messages in Dark Fury.

Mix Today at 21:25
is this for real?

Corey(515) Today at 21:26
what is this place?

WarriorCorgi Today at 21:26
wow u werent faking when u said it was serious shit

David returns to W.O.T.A.N. ϟϟ and opens the rules.

1. W.O.T.A.N. ϟϟ is a Muslim-free zone ***Aryans only*** Sorry not sorry.

A squeezing sensation in his chest. Aryans only? He scans the other rules.

2. W.O.T.A.N. ϟϟ is a server for media guerrilla warfare, meme sharing and real chat about news, race, religion, traditionalism, spirituality, philosophy, art and literature. Shitposting is welcome but should be kept to the appropriate channel (W.O.T.A.N. ϟϟ is not Kekophobic).

3. MISSION STATEMENT: FIGHT BACK AGAINST THE ISLAMISATION OF THE WEST AND STOP THE GREAT REPLACEMENT/WHITE GENOCIDE BEFORE IT IS TOO LATE.

4. You will start out as a Rekrut. You must be prepared to participate in social media raids, sniper missions and other campaigns. Members who demonstrate commitment and loyalty to the cause of TRUTH will rise in rank (ranks range from Rekrut to Supreme Commander).

5. You must NOT be identifiable from username or avatar. ANONYMITY. No facefags.

7. Discussion must be ENGLISH.

7. Sharing fake news links **New York Times, CNN, BBC, Guardian etc** is forbidden. Screenshots/PDFs only. Every visit to MSM websites = $£€ for Soros.

9. Sharing loli/cub porn WILL result in a permanent ban.

10. Use of Nazi, Antisemitic, anti-Islamic, homophobic, racist terms WILL result in a 24 hour ban (the server can be auto shut down). **But there is nothing wrong with creativity**

***DISCLAIMER W.O.T.A.N. ϟϟ in no way endorses Nazism.

DISCLAIMER The use of military phrases/ranks is only for LARPing purposes END DISCLAIMER ***

Before you can access the members-only W.O.T.A.N. ϟϟ channels, your account will need to be authorised. Take a photo of your right wrist with **ϟϟ** **username** and **date** on it. Then answer this questionnaire:

(1) Do you know your DNA? Are you 100% Aryan?
(2) How old are you?
(3) Where do you live?
(4) Do you use GAB or Twitter? What is your handle?
(5) What are your political and religious views?
(6) What is your favorite film, book or musician and why?
(7) Why do you want to join W.O.T.A.N. ϟϟ?

Send the photo and questionnaire to Supreme Commander @RitterKreuz

The authorisation process may take up to 48 hours. Sorry, but checks need to be performed. We know there are msm elites out there looking to infiltrate W.O.T.A.N. ϟϟ and silence the TRUTH. Defending the TRUTH is all kinds of risky. Once your photo and questionnaire have been assessed a W.O.T.A.N. ϟϟ General will be in touch to arrange a voice chat.

In the meantime, here is some recommended reading and viewing material:

https://www.thepeacelovingreligion.com/pages/quran/violence.aspx (non-partisan fact-based website which examines the ideological threat that Islam poses to human dignity and freedom)
https://altpedia.org/wiki/White_demographics (fact-based article on white demographics)

https://www.bitchute.com/video/SAZPXDSFAXt5 (interview with Julius Evola)
https://infonebula.org/info/Martin_Heidegger (introduction to Heidegger)
https://infonebula.org/info/Friedrich_Nietzsche (introduction to Nietzsche)

Welcome, KEK, H.H. KEK.

What is Runningngunning into? Aryanism? Other than by Mr Gupta in history, he has never encountered the word 'Aryan' being used seriously. Is Aryanism still a thing? In a non-ironic way? Or is this ironic? Question one. He is not eligible. Thanks, Mum. A twinge of hate. If she were English, rather than Iranian, his life would be so much simpler.

The media guerrilla warfare is enticing. He could lie and claim to be a hundred per cent Aryan. Checks are, however, being performed, meaning his heritage might be uncovered. He pinches his neck. How does he always fall short? What is wrong with him?

He returns to the Dark Fury server. Maybe no one else will want to join anyway.

Runningngunning Today at 21:34
Give it a try trust me.

Runningngunning Today at 21:34
The way they organise media guerrilla warfare, its real no messing

Runningngunning Today at 21:34
Good chat too. News, art, philosophy. Ive learnt a lot. People from Europe and the US on there. Lots have PhDs. Scholars lol they actually got me to buy a book 1984.

Runningngunning Today at 21:34
We owe it to Nmoos anyway imo

Runningngunning Today at 21:34
We cant just lay down and let muslims qwn us

Runningngunning Today at 21:34
While SJWs post shit like this: https://twitter.com/Lace_Flye/status/1217185465482201242?s=20

Corey(515) Today at 21:36
fucking sjw

Corey(515) Today at 21:36
hmm It looks a bit intense man aryanism?

Runningngunning Today at 21:36
I thought that at first too but now im like you know what? this is a time for taking sides

Runningngunning Today at 21:36
ultimately it's up to you whether you wanna tho

Corey(515) Today at 21:36
ill give it a try then

Corey(515) Today at 21:36
For Nmoos

Corey(515) Today at 21:36
ive always said dont knock something until youve tried it

Corey(515) Today at 21:36
Muslim-free zone is funny lol

WarriorCorgi Today at 21:37
Dysruptz? Thoughts?

Runningngunning Today at 21:37
You wont regret it, man

Runningngunning Today at 21:37
but like i said no pressure

Dysruptz Today at 21:38
Im in

AT THE KITCHEN TABLE, Dad butters toast and reads a week-old copy of the *Sun*.

'Hey,' David says.

Dad looks up. 'How was work today?'

'All right. Not starting until twelve tomorrow at least.'

'You can have a lie-in then.'

'Yeah.'

Since finding Dad on the floor, David has been keeping a close eye on him, searching for signs, symptoms, something. But he seems normal. His tongue poking through his lips, he covers his toast with a second layer of Utterly Butterly, considers it, then squeezes on a zigzag of Bang Bang sauce.

'Your mother called earlier.'

David freezes. He is still ignoring her. 'Oh.'

Dad relates what she told him. On Easter Sunday David behaved terribly. He made Islamophobic comments. He smashed a plate.

David explains that she, Stephen and Zoe ganged up on him.

'. . . Was it a fancy plate?'

'Yeah.'

'They like fancy plates.'

David laughs. 'It was so fancy. You should have seen it, midnight blue, ceramic.'

Dad brushes breadcrumbs from his lower lip. 'She thinks I'm feeding you Islamophobic views at home, saying irresponsible things. She thinks I'm a bad influence. Not fit to parent you.'

'Seriously?'

'She's very sensitive. She likes to work herself up.'

David says that Stephen must be encouraging her. 'He's such a . . . pussy.'

'Does he still work at Amnesty?'

'Yeah.'

Dad picks his teeth. 'You should maybe call her anyway. Otherwise she will really get the hump with me. You know how much she likes to get the hump with me.'

'I will – sometime.'

'Does she know you bought a PlayStation?'

'No.'

'*Call of Duty*?'

'No.'

'Maybe skip mentioning that.'

David spends the next forty-eight hours weighing up what to do about WOTAN.

He concludes that it is unlikely his heritage would be uncovered as there is nothing on his social media to give the game away. Yet claiming that he is a hundred per cent Aryan is a prospect that makes him feel uncomfortable. Plus, he is unsure whether he even wants to be a WOTAN member. Is the server too out-there or is out-there now what is needed? Nmoos's cousin . . .

At various points, he finds himself unable to think clearly, blames the stench of onion and sprays Lynx Africa all about him. He has not been taking his dishes down straight after eating.

Corey messages him to say that he has submitted to a 'pretty serious' voice chat with a moderator and been allowed in. 'I went for the username LobsterSins68 – dont ask haha.'

He neglects to reply. His most pressing concern is that he will be shut out from the *Call of Duty* voice-chat banter. In a recent session, TRXDripp666 referred to a meme in WOTAN and everyone cracked up and riffed on it and he felt shitty and all at sea. Having not seen the meme, he couldn't contribute and had to wait for the conversation to move on. He wishes Dysruptz had never let Runningngunning share a link to WOTAN.

'SO,' MUM SAYS. 'You're finally calling.'

David leans on a lamp post, five minutes from home. The shops to his right are smeared with a warm hazel light. He kicks an empty sandwich wedge into the street.

'Yes.'

'Okay.'

'What?'

'Okay.'

A hot blonde girl is vaping and texting outside Rebecca Beauty. According to its black-and-red fascia, the salon offers waxing, threading, facials, manicures and pedicures. Three guys his age with hoods up cycle down the street, whooping. He retreats to the centre of the pavement.

'You told Dad I'm Islamophobic. You said it was his fault. You said he wasn't parenting me well. You ordered me to call and now . . .'

'He isn't parenting you well.'

'Fuck you, Mum.'

'Mm.'

He can visualise her stupidly shaking her head. She will report on this call to Stephen later and he will stupidly shake his head as well. He hates them.

'Go on then. Why are we speaking? What do you want me to say? I'm sorry for breaking your fancy plate. I'm *sorry* for breaking it. There. Are we done?'

'No. We're not.'

'Fine. I'm sorry for the table too, so, so sorry. Did I leave a little mark?'

'Don't take that tone with me. Do not. I'm warning you.'

David spits on the pavement.

'Just listen to what you're saying,' Mum continues. 'What's wrong with you? When did you become so nasty and bitter? When did you change?'

The window stools in Spice Hut are occupied by an old man in a white robe and two kids in football kits, socks and all. David turns back to Rebecca Beauty. 'You tell me, Mum. You tell me.'

'David, I'm not worried about the plate or the table. I'm worried about you, about what you're becoming. The plate. The table. Fine. That's teenage hormones. But some of the things you said. What you seem to think. That's more serious. I was embarrassed hearing you—'

'You think I'm Islamophobic?'

'. . .'

'You think I'm scary? Dangerous? Monstrous? Is that it?'

'I think you're young and you have—'

'I'm eighteen!'

The bin beside him is overflowing. It lolls out a white trainer like a tongue.

'I just don't understand where this hate comes from,' Mum says.

'Life.'

Silence. He hears her breathing. She sighs. Then in a twitchy voice says: 'David . . .'

'What?'

'You know . . . You can tell me what really happened in college. You say that nothing happened and that none of the other boys bullied you. But I can't forget—'

'We're not talking about this.'

'I can't forget that time I found you at Haggerston station crying.'

'I was not crying.'

'Yes. You were. Tell me. Did the boys bully you at college?'

'No.'

'You can tell me.'

'No.'

'They never bullied you? They never hurt you?'

'Fuck you!'

'David.'

'Fuck you! Argh. Fuck you, Mum. Fuck you. Fuck you. Why can't I hold opinions without them coming from some weird unconscious root? I'm not the only person in the world who sees a link between terror attacks and Islam. I'm not the only person who sees that Muslims are changing Europe, transforming Europe into . . . Eurabia. You're the one who's insane.'

A man limps past, clutching a Stella in one hand and a blue plastic bag in the other. He signals to a bus to wait. It pulls away. 'Well? Why?' David presses her.

'Do you remember primary school?'

'What?'

The man sends the can spinning towards the bus.

'Do you?'

'No.'

'You were badly bullied there.'

He feels his stomach knotting up.

'You were so badly bullied there. It was . . . I'm sorry. It still breaks my heart. I've never felt as powerless in my life as then. It was a thousand times worse than when I received racist abuse myself, a thousand times worse. I'm sorry. I'm . . . What I'm saying is . . . David, the boys there were white. English. If something happened in college, and whoever was responsible was Muslim, and that's where this hate comes from, it's not because they were Muslim. Some boys—'

'Arghh!' He moves his phone away from his right ear and tightens his grip. He is fighting the temptation to throw it at a bus, as the man threw his can. Mum is infuriating.

'In primary school I was the one who had to—'

'Shut up!' She is crazy. He barely remembers primary school. 'Just fuck you!'

'Don't be—'

'No! I'll call you in a couple of weeks. You can speak to Stephen and Zoe in the meantime. Get them to keep you company. Get them to. Don't call me. Don't call Dad either.'

'Please. Stop being childish. I—'

'No!' David says. 'I'm warning you. Don't call us. Don't ever call us.'

He hangs up and, panting, lashes out at the lamp post.

Corey(515) Today at 20:05
Yo?

David has to reply. He rakes his chin, which is stubbly, even though he shaved in the morning. The bristles on his upper cheeks are becoming more and more noticeable, too, but he is worried that shaving them will lead to their returning even thicker, even blacker. He has to reply tonight. A scattering of feathers on the paving stones outside. He googles 'Aryan meaning now'.

The first result is from Wikipedia. Its preview reads 'that is in contrast to Indo-Aryan usage, in which several secondary meanings evolved, the meaning of ar- as a self-identifier is preserved in Iranian usage hence . . .' The related entries are 'Aryan race' and 'Aryan (disambiguation)' and 'Graeco-Aryan' and 'Indo-Iranians'. He stares at the screen in bewilderment. Iranian usage? Indo-Iranians? He opens the 'Indo-Iranians' entry.

> Indo-Iranian peoples, also known as Indo-Iranic peoples by scholars and sometimes as Arya or Aryans from their self-designation, were a group of Indo-European peoples who brought the Indo-Iranian languages, a major branch of the Indo-European language family, to major parts of Eurasia in the second part of the 3rd millennium BCE. They eventually branched out into Iranian peoples and Indo-Aryan peoples.

This is too complex. What is the connection between Aryanism and Iran? He opens the main 'Aryan' entry.

> Aryan ('ɛəriən/) has its roots as a term used as a self-designation

by Indo-Iranian people. The term was used by the Indo-Aryan people of the Vedic period in ancient India as a religious label for themselves and for the geographic region known as Āryāvarta, where Indo-Aryan culture is based (in this region). The Iranian people used the term as an ethnic label for themselves in the Avesta scriptures, and the word forms the etymological source of the country named Iran.

The name Iran comes from the word Aryan? What? How can he have not known this before? Why did no one tell him? The entry is too long, too crabbed. Reading it would take ages.

He clicks back and frenziedly searches for 'Aryan Iran Iranian'.

Ten thirty. David has spent the past two hours reading posts on Reddit and Quora and articles on dozens of science and history websites and watching YouTube – and he is tingling with excitement.

Aryan. He is Aryan, totally Aryan, as Aryan as anyone. Iran is the birthplace of Aryans.

The Persian king Darius I was buried in Naqsh-e-Rostam in 486 BCE and his rock-cut tomb read 'I am Darius the Great King, King of Kings, King of countries containing all kinds of men, King in this great earth far and wide, son of Hystaspes, an Achaemenian, a Persian, son of a Persian, an Aryan, having Aryan lineage.' Died in 486 BCE – and that was inscribed on his tomb: an Aryan, having Aryan lineage.

David has learned so much tonight, so much that Mum has hidden from him. For the first time since he stopped writing song lyrics he has used his notebook.

In 1768 the European scholar Anquetil-Duperron discovered that ancient Iranians referred to themselves as Aryan. Then, in unrelated research, the English philologist Sir William Jones discovered that Greek, Latin, Sanskrit and Persian derived from common roots, that the similarities between these languages couldn't be coincidental. Then the German philosopher Schlegel theorised that this linguistic 'Indo-European' relationship was due to a long-ago Aryan migration from Iran to Europe. This theory spread widely throughout Europe and was confirmed by other philosophers: Max Müller, Ernest Renan, Adolphe Pictet, Arthur de Gobineau. David has looked into them. Each has published loads – there is an eighteen-volume *Collected Works* for Max Müller – and has a well-referenced Wikipedia page. They are serious philosophers.

And that is how Europe came to be Aryan. Because there was an Aryan migration to Europe.

He came across a discussion on one website about the innate differences between Iranian/European Aryans and non-Aryans, an argument being made that whereas Aryans had creativity, sensitivity and innovation, non-Aryans were lazy, barbaric and unthinking. Reading that, he winced and clicked away. But then he cast his mind back to Mo, to Hassan, to Ibrahim, and reconsidered.

He scans his notebook.

Seif Azad: 'Iranian, German, English, French, these are the names of different kinds of Aryans, who have not renounced creativity in thought and deed, and are known for these qualities in the realm of science, although appellation, location and time have made them distinct.'
Mohammad Reza Shah: Iran member of European family. Just accident of geography that Iran is in Middle East, not among fellow European nations. Together in spirit.
Friedrich Max Müller (English lecturer at Oxford): 'thought still runs in our thoughts, as their blood may run in our veins . . . our true ancestors in spirit and in truth.'
Read something by Gobineau?
DNA ARYAN = R1A. IRAN = R1A M420. EUROPE = R1A Z93 + R2A.
Persia was a world power – an Aryan power – until the conquest of 651 CE. Its infiltration by non-Aryan peoples led to its decline. Read up on this?

With English-Iranian heritage, he has pure Aryan blood.

Unbelievable. Questionnaire time. (1) Yes, he does know his DNA. He can confirm that he is a hundred per cent Aryan. (2) He is eighteen years old. (3) He lives in London, England. (4) He uses Twitter. His handle is @DavidBlackGlass. (5) He believes in free speech and animal rights. He is an atheist. (6) Karl Williams. He is a musician willing to alienate his own target audience. He has the courage to speak his mind whatever the consequences. (7) David wants to join WOTAN because he is fed up of being censored and told that saying anything about Islam is Islamophobic.

He rummages his desk drawer for a felt-tip pen. There are printouts from college and highlighters and paperclips and an issue of Q and his old click-wheel iPod, which Dad got for him ages ago. He remembers opening it. Even though it was refurbished, it came in a cool glossy white Apple box, which he kept on his bedside table for years. He still has the Apple stickers somewhere. Having at last found a pen, he sketches two Bowie-esque lightning bolts on his right wrist. Given the strict anonymity requirement, David1702UK might not be an acceptable username, so, instead, he writes BGMP5 – BG for 'Black Glass' and MP5 for his favourite *Call of Duty* weapon – and 17 April. A smile and he adds R1A: BGMP5R1A. He takes a photo, clicks 'edit' and applies a monochrome filter. From the bathroom comes the sound of water trickling out of the toilet tank and slapping the bucket. BGMP5R1A. He sends the materials to Supreme Commander @RitterKreuz.

Hassan

'HEY, ZULFI, I was meaning to ask. What were your first impressions of Britain?'

'Grey. Grey. Grey. The sky. The streets. Everything. I was stunned that all the houses were one colour. It wasn't like that back home.'

'Yeah, I read an interview on Muslim Voices with a woman who immigrated from Azad Kashmir in nineteen sixty-nine, too, and she said the same. The cold was a shock.'

'She made my mistake? She came in winter?'

'January, I think.'

'Maybe we took the same flight to London. There were so many other kids on my flight. I have never since seen a plane on which ninety per cent of the passengers were under sixteen. The boys sitting on either side of me were wearing name tags. I remember wondering where mine was and whether I would be lost without one. Actually. You know. My very first impression? My very, very first impression? Feeling blinded by the bright, white light in Heathrow Airport. It was overwhelming. It hurt my eyes. I kept blinking. There was no electricity in the village I grew up in.'

'Really?'

'It only arrived there in the mid-seventies. So all the light in Heathrow Airport, that was quite something for me. But then I travelled to Leeds, where my uncle was living . . .'

'Grey.'

'My first morning in Leeds, I went looking for a tree. I could not understand why there were no trees on our street, how my uncle could have lived there for so long without planting one.'

A lovely spring morning. Diamonds of light have settled on the white bedding, which is patterned with silhouetted players running up to kick silhouetted footballs. Dust swirls over the mattress. The phone pressed to his ear, Hassan stands and looks out of the window. He has never before registered how many trees there are on his street. Obviously, he can't say which trees.

'He came in the early sixties?' Hassan asked. 'Your uncle.'

'Yes, nineteen sixty-one.'

'Do you know what made him leave Azad Kashmir?'

'The Mangla Dam. It flooded Mirpur and Daydal, as well as hundreds of small villages, including his. He was offered financial compensation and a passport by the British contractor responsible and told that he could move to Birmingham, Bradford or Leeds, because there was plenty of work there. As far as I know, he thought about it for a week and then just went, together with some friends.'

'Ah wow.'

'My father tried to convince him to come and live with us. But he never liked the rest of my family. They couldn't spend more than a few minutes together without . . . And then, when my parents passed away, I went to Leeds to stay with him. It's funny how things pan out in life.'

'Yeah.'

Zulfi breathes thickly into the phone. Hassan is unclear how it happened but he has grown to quite enjoy these conversations. He asks what seventies Britain was like in terms of racism.

'Terrible. I was the only immigrant in my school so you can imagine how bad the bullying was. Even my history teacher once told me to go back where I had come from.'

'God.'

'It was a bad time. I missed Azad Kashmir. The other boys and the teachers had been nice to me there. Of course, I was still mourning my parents too. It was a bad time. But I studied a lot and I learned English properly. After finishing school, I went to work in a textile mill, where there were more of us. That was better. The manager bullied us. But it was still better.'

'Yeah?'

'This was once a very intolerant country. It has become more tolerant now . . . Saying that, I started reading the *Ilford Recorder* online recently and some of the news stories were upsetting.'

'What sort of news stories?'

'Just local incidents. But they were upsetting.'

SINCE HE RECEIVED AN AAB OFFER from Goldsmiths, Hassan has been revising, revising, revising. His bedroom brims with ring binders, highlighters, index cards, plastic wallets, sticky notes.

He spends Good Friday meticulously editing photographs for his art and design coursework portfolio and Saturday reading critical interpretations of *A Streetcar Named Desire* online. By Easter Sunday he feels frazzled and only a few hours in slumps over his sociology textbook. Having slid it away, he takes his phone and opens TikTok. Any content would be more interesting than Becker's 1970s research into aggressive interview styles, even clips of American creators talking politics with bunny-ears filters. With a Sticky Toffee Pudding Hobnob treat, he scrolls.

Next, Twitter. @TheGuardian: 'Either I make it or my life is over: refugees say Channel crossing is the only option they have.' @WestHam: 'The boss speaks to the media at 12:00 ahead of our trip to Norwich. Click below for the live blog.' @DilwarManzoor: 'There looks to have been a terror attack at the #Chappe Gallery in Paris. Devastating. Praying for everyone in the City of Light.' He swears. Another one? A search for the hashtag returns hundreds of tweets from the last minute. @scoredearth: 'Islam strikes at #Chappe. Giveaway: Muslim urge to scream Allahu Akbar before every terror attack lol.' @theboogiebeagle: 'Dozens of casualties likely after an attack at #Chappe in Paris. The attacker shouted Allahu Akbar. But repeat after me: Terror Has No Religion (rolls eyes).'

He shudders, wishing a horrific photo from the scene hadn't popped up. These lunatics pretending to be Muslims – he hates them, fucking hates them. What's their problem? @DrRuth-Wright: 'What happened at #chappe today is scary af but please don't use this as an opportunity to spread your ignorant agenda. The guy was NOT a Muslim. He was a terrorist. Have some respect.' Hassan 'likes' the tweet. What will happen now is miserably predictable. Determined not to think too much about it, he returns to his work.

Item A: Investigating social class and educational achievement. Sociologists have studied the extent to which there is a link between social class and standards of achievement in education . . . Unstructured interviews have the advantage of allowing students to elaborate on their views, but they do take considerable time so . . .

This will be a long Sunday. At least the youth centre is hosting another FIFA tournament on Tuesday, giving him something to look forward to. He is on a roll, having won the previous two. A spider web glistens outside his window. The curiously large TV aerial on the house opposite casts a chunky shadow in the sunlight. He is waiting until twelve to go for a Coke Zero.

Right. Concentrate.

Unrestricted interviews take the form of a free-flowing conversation between the researcher and the subject, providing qualitative data through a range . . .

FRISKED BY THE WIND, Hassan makes his way home, his hands in the pockets of his West Ham track top. Three tournaments in a row. A FIFA legend. Officially.

In the first half of the final, Waleed held his own, carving out some clear-cut chances and edging possession. In the second, it was one-way traffic; Hassan bossed him, and it ended three–nil. The pavement is scattered with wood splinters, an empty WKD bottle lying among them. He side-foots it towards a bin with 'youve got sad trainers' graffiti, the trophy rattling in his backpack.

A gust lays waste to his new fringe. In an effort to hide his monobrow, he told his barber to leave some length on top and only cut the back and sides short. Turning into Oak Lane, he attempts to restyle it. Magpies pick at an exercise loop band in a box with 'free' scrawled on it. In the window of Just News & Convenience, the numbers 11.6 shine in red on a digital Lotto sign, 18.4 on a Euro Millions one. He entertains the possibility of relaxing tonight, returning to revision tomorrow.

The blue-and-pink Cinderella wardrobe by the communal bins of the Mendip Road council flats looks comically out of place. A van with lemon eyes fusses past.

Albert Drive. At the edge of a house to his left, on a low, crumbling step, lounges a white girl, cross-ankled, sporting a fluorescent Adidas cap and AirPods, bopping her head. The 'for sale' sign is gone. He wonders whether she and her family have moved in there. Albert Drive used to be entirely Muslim. Ibrahim once lived at number sixty.

For a moment, Hassan considers retreating. But this is a girl, and a tween at that.

'Heya.' A smile through closed lips.

He nods, slides his right hand into his jeans pocket, where he carries the iPhone he got for his birthday, and presses on.

She springs on to the pavement, blocking his way, and pinches her AirPods. 'Heya.'

The front door swings open. Two guys in their early twenties leave the house.

'How many we buying then?' one says. He has Phil Foden-esque cheekbones and is wearing a black bucket hat, a black sweatshirt and Dr Martens with red laces.

'Hang on,' the other says, zipping up a Hoodrich utility vest. He jerks his chin. 'Would you believe it, Alex? Another one.'

'Jesus,' Alex says, holding a beer bottle. 'They're fucking everywhere!'

'Paki,' the girl says. 'Paki, Paki, Paki.'

Hassan forces his way past her and continues up Albert Drive.

'Hey,' Hoodrich says. 'Paki.'

The shriek of a gate. Keeping his eyes on the pavement, Hassan walks faster. His iPhone no longer seems significant. He just wants to get out of this situation.

'Hey!'

They catch up. Alex and Hoodrich flank him; the girl follows just behind.

'You were trying it on with our sister. Weren't you?' Alex says. 'You Paki paedo.'

'Paki paedo,' the girl echoes with a giddy zing. 'Paki paedo.'

'No,' Hassan says.

'It sure looked like it to me,' Hoodrich says.

Alex takes a swig and then shakes the bottle.

'Please,' Hassan says, stopping. 'I . . . I . . .'

Sniggers. 'You what?' Alex says. 'You no speak English?'

'I swear no one here can speak a single word of it,' Hoodrich says. 'Read my lips. Eng-lish. Eng-lish . . . Fuck me, how could Mum move us to this shithole?'

'Look,' Hassan says. 'You can have my phone, my wallet, whatever.'

Alex spits. 'You think we want to steal from you?'

'No.'

'You think that?'

'No. I—'

'How *dare* you think that.'

'Please.' And tears seethe up his throat.

Alex prods Hassan on the chest. 'You're the ones stealing from us, pal.' Hassan attempts to edge away. Hoodrich grabs him by the arm. He struggles to get free but Hoodrich is too strong. 'You're the ones stealing from us, pal. You fucking Paki perv.' Alex raises the bottle.

'Look at him,' Alex says.

Hassan is curled up on the pavement, crying, a bloody mess. They stand over him.

'Pathetic.'

'Like a little baby.'

'You know what I think?'

'What?'

'He's probably worried that some of the beer from the bottle touched him.'

'Ohhhhhh. *Haram! Haram!*'

The girl screeches: '*Haram! Haram! Haram! Haram! Haram!*'

Hassan is covering his eyes. He can feel the blood trickling out from his forehead and merging with his tears, can taste the salty, buttery brew. He wonders how bad the cut is.

'Don't worry,' Alex says. 'The bottle was empty.'

'Praise Allah! Praise Allah!'

'No bad scary beer this time!'

There is a strange ringing sound in his ears. As a blob of warm, icky spit lands on his cheek, he screws up his face, a movement that hurts him so much he lets out a silly, embarrassing whimper.

'Did you hear that?'

'I heard it.'

Someone kneels beside Hassan, leans in close.

'Right,' Alex says. 'Shall we leave it there?'

'. . .'

'Shall we leave it there, Paki?'

'Yes.'

A long pause. The tears are coming faster and faster.

'Sure. Just a friendly hello. Nothing more. Do us a favour, though, will you? Tell your raghead friends in this London shithole to fucking learn the language and learn to show some respect. You all have big engineering brains, right? Use them. Eng-lish. Eng-lish. Oh, and I swear to God, if you involve the cops I will find you and I will slit your throat.'

'. . .'

'Oi. Got it? You fucking—'

'Yes.'

Another blob of spit.

'Go on, then,' Alex says, returning to his feet. 'Go on. Go.'

'HASSAN—'

'Let me be.'

'Just tell me the truth,' Mum says. 'I am begging you. Please.'

'I have.' Even to him, his voice sounds hollow.

'You expect me to believe that you were hit with a glass bottle and needed six stitches, six stitches, only because you were wearing a West Ham top?'

He rolls on to his side and closes his eyes, head spinning. The pain comes in waves, and one is currently splashing over him. King George Hospital released him in the morning; Mum and Dad insisted on staying through the night, even though that meant sleeping in a bleak, overcrowded waiting room without even a working vending machine. He repeated to the police officer what he told them, that the attackers were passing him on Oak Lane, wearing Millwall shirts, and targeted him because he's a West Ham fan. Should he have told the truth? Maybe, but it's too late now.

After coming home, he glanced in the mirror and saw the stitches above his right eyebrow and felt like throwing up. He wants only to rest.

'Do you realise how lucky you were not to suffer skull damage or—'

'Yes.'

He hears her walk over to the window. When he opens his eyes a few minutes later, she is still there. A strawy afternoon light needles the room. He asks her to turn on his lava lamp, as seeing it lifeless at this time of day is odd. She gropes about behind his desk for the switch. A click, and it snaps on, the glass vessel shading a soft purple. She stands back up and taps his Chromebook. 'Do you know how many messages Muslim Voices has received since the terror attack in Paris?'

'No.'

'Dozens.'

'Oh.'

'There have been Islamophobic hate crimes everywhere. I have heard about people being threatened, harassed, intimidated, assaulted and all the rest because of that terror attack. An old shop owner, seventy-two, told me that before locking up for the night he now checks that his CCTV is still working so that when his shop is broken into or firebombed he will have evidence for the insurance company – not if, when. This happens each time there is a terror attack anywhere in Europe. It is so predictable. And you know where the blame—'

'Mum—'

'It is with the media, with those stupid tabloid newspapers for running ridiculous, scaremongering pieces and whipping people up into a frenzy.'

'Mum.'

She is breathing heavily and glazed with sweat, as much as him.

'Mum.'

'Sorry. I see that you are in pain and the last thing you want is . . . But I still find it hard to believe that what happened was not . . . and I need to know because . . . Hassan, I am your mother and someone attacked you, they attacked you. Meaning, I failed, I failed to protect you and . . . sitting in the waiting room . . . that was the worst night of my life. I need to know so—'

He mechanically, listlessly, repeats his story.

'And you cannot remember what they looked like?'

'They were wearing Millwall shirts.'

'Nothing else?'

'No.'

'Hassan.'

'Just let me rest.'

LEAVING THE HOUSE proves to be a miserable experience. The stares from strangers come as no surprise. But the tightness in his chest – that does. It is so intense that at points he thinks he might pass out. After a few hundred metres, he turns round, returns. The rest of the week is spent in his bedroom scrolling: scrolling, scrolling, scrolling.

One evening, Dad appears with a thermometer. 'Better safe than sorry.'

Hassan puts the tip under his tongue, wraps his lips around it and waits. In the meantime, Dad sits, places his palms on his suit trousers and examines the ring binder on the desk. The lacklustre attempts Hassan made at revising also came to nothing, ending with him reading sentences again and again and again without taking anything in. A bleep. He checks the display.

'It's fine.'

'Thirty-six point nine?'

'Mm.'

'Okay. We can be confident that the cut hasn't become infected then. I'm sure the GP will double-check on Wednesday anyway, though, when you see him to have the stitches removed.' The bin is chock-full of sweet wrappers. They sit in silence, until Dad says: 'You know, I'm not sure I've told you this before. But I had a similar experience once.' Just after the factory in Bradford had closed and he'd moved to London to set up the restaurant, he went to see the Regent Street Christmas lights, as he'd heard they were pretty and wanted to take a photo for his parents. 'On the way I encountered some, well, back then they called themselves Paki-bashers, and I received the worst beating I have ever received. I broke two ribs and was bleeding like crazy. One of them had a hammer and kept pointing it at me while the others were kicking. Luckily, he was too cowardly to use it or I might not be here today.'

'Dad.'

'Anyway, the broken ribs were bad. But . . . well . . .' He signals his brain. 'The impact it had up here was worse. In the months afterwards, I kept having flashbacks. Out of nowhere, I would—'

'Dad.'

'Mm?'

'I'll be fine. Seriously, I'll be fine.'

'Of course.' Dad rubs his knees. 'Of course. I want you to know, though, that if at any point you do find yourself feeling anxious, you can talk to Mum or me. We'll be there for you.'

'All right.'

'Yes?'

'All right.'

'. . . Well. Good about the temperature. I'll let you continue with your work then.'

WHY IS IT SO HARD to concentrate?

Despite reading page sixty multiple times, nothing has sunk in, and that is making him tense, irritable, nervous. He was on top of his revision, but now he is losing time, too much time. He needs at least a B in sociology. As he rocks his elbows against his desk, the tea in his mug quivers. It's likely that the lack of sleep last night is contributing to his miserable mood. At 3 a.m. he woke up in a sweat and spent hours cycling through Facebook, Instagram, Twitter and TikTok before accepting that he might as well start the day. He urges himself to get a grip and gives it another go.

Many sociologists say that society is actually determined by the behaviour and interaction of individuals. Theories like this are called action theories because they emphasise the action of individuals, as opposed to—

Impossible. He shoves the book away. The lava lamp bathes pages sixty and sixty-one in a bottom-of-the-ocean glow. On top of everything else, he still feels dizzy from the stroll Mum made him take with her around Newbury Park. The instant he stepped outside, his chest tightened up, and it stayed that way throughout. While she bought them smoothies in a café, he waited outside and secretly, desperately, gulped air. Tomorrow he will need to go to school – the Easter holidays are over.

The GP removed his stitches without issue, confirmed that the site hadn't become infected and pronounced that he should now be fine. So what's wrong with him? There is no medical issue.

Many sociologists say that society is actually determined by the behaviour and interaction of individuals. Theories like this are called action theories because—

He flings the book at his West Ham mural.

IV

David

'IS EVERYONE READY?' Supreme Commander RitterKreuz asks.

'Yes,' David replies, in chorus with other WOTAN members. There are seventy-five in the #operations voice chat.

'Excellent. I will be posting the YouTube link imminently. You will see it on the left, in the bulletins channel. Most of you have participated in dozens of raids and know the drill. But a few of you are participating in a raid for the first time. Generals DarkSunRising and LordofKek will now share some tips for your benefit.'

David still marvels at Supreme Commander RitterKreuz's eloquence. The accent is hard to pinpoint. It sounds sort-of Canadian, but with British, German and Irish influences too. Familiar with the tips, he stretches his cramped legs under his desk.

'Thank you, Supreme Commander,' General DarkSunRising says. 'So. Some tips for you first-timers. One: Make sure that all your YouTube sock accounts have profile pictures. That is an absolute must. And the profile pictures should not just be grabbed from Google Images. They should come from real Instagram accounts. Your YouTube sock accounts need to look genuine. Two: Save your best comments for the accounts with foreign-sounding names. SJW YouTubers fear nothing more than being critiqued by foreigners – nothing. Obviously, post some comments from accounts with Western-sounding names too – the comments section needs to look realistic – but save the best comments for IbrahimSocialist33 and Jahandar4love etc. SJW YouTubers attach great weight to the opinions of foreigners. They lose their minds when they see foreigners disagreeing with them. They freak out. The comments we leave could be really demotivating for them.'

'Agreed,' General LordofKek says. 'What's more, as well as denting a YouTuber's confidence and instilling doubt in them, we can draw away potential viewers. There are many people – I know because I was like them once – who will open a YouTube video, see it has more downvotes than upvotes, and lots of negative, critical comments and, on that basis, decide not to watch it.'

'The other tip I would share is to use a laptop rather than a phone,' General DarkSunRising says. 'If you are on a phone now, move to a laptop. You can switch between accounts on the YouTube mobile app but it's fiddlier than in a browser.'

'Thank you,' Supreme Commander RitterKreuz says. 'Everyone ready?'

'Yes.'

'Yes.'

'Yes.'

'In that case, I will post the link now. Let us commence.'

David slugs Red Bull, in serious need of caffeine. It's 3.30 a.m. in England. He's exhausted, with sagging eyes. But it's imperative that he thinks creatively, that he's at his sharpest. As he opens the link, blue light glints eerily out from the slits around the keys under his fingertips.

The title of the video is 'Some facts about Islam to combat racists' and the YouTuber is Emma Donnelly. Despite only being up for a few hours, it has amassed 6,000 views. David checks out her recent uploads – 'Editing my neck on Instagram for a week', 'Reacting to people reacting to me', 'My dog is an idiot', 'Recreating outfits from Shake It Up Warning: Train Wreck', 'Why it's wrong to say All Lives Matter' – and smirks. The customary left-wing mishmash of content: beauty, fashion, cute pets and good-vibes virtue-signalling. He plays a random video.

She is about sixteen and stunning: long strawberry-blonde hair, big soft blue eyes, bright-red lipstick, flawless teeth, flawless white skin. What is she doing lecturing people on Islam?

He returns to the relevant video and advances the cursor to the halfway mark. 'There are two kinds of people in this world during times of trouble, people who come together as one and—'

Pause. There is no need to hear more. Using his Ameer el-Shehata 2001 sock account, he clicks 'I dislike this' and 'add a public comment'. The caffeine is taking effect. He sweeps his tongue across the jagged edges of his upper teeth, left to right, right to left, thinking. Then writes:

> Disgraceful. You should be ASHAMED, Emma. I left Pakistan to come to Britain so that I could taste freedom and secular life. I wanted to leave Islam and violence against women and organised marriages and blasphemy behind. And now you want to bring all that here? Why can't you let me enjoy my freedom?

He finishes his Red Bull and switches to his Princess Fahmida sock account.

> I was forced to undergo fgm at six. How dare you tell me these 'facts' about Islam? You know NOTHING about Islam. You are perpetrating hate. But as long as that gives you more views, I guess that's fine. Enjoy all the £££ skincare products this video will let you buy.

As recommended, he sourced the profile picture for the sock account from Instagram – an Asian girl with chunky transparent-frame glasses reading a Penguin Modern Classics book – and applied a rainbow filter to it. He even went to the trouble of adding a cover photo and playlists to 'her' profile page. His sock accounts appear genuine. Supreme Commander RitterKreuz has praised him on just how genuine. Over the next hour, David leaves comments from nearly fifty.

‘Right,’ Supreme Commander RitterKreuz says. ‘I’m calling time on the raid.’

‘Good work, everyone,’ General DarkSunRising says. ‘The video now has one thousand five hundred downvotes and only eight hundred upvotes. No one will trust it now.’

‘Plus a fair amount of constructive criticism,’ General LordofKek says, laughing.

‘I have been through the comments,’ Supreme Commander RitterKreuz says. ‘And I have selected ten for everyone to upvote. They are from the following sock accounts: Sauban Fallah, TheMarijaCloudburst, Princess Fahmida, Akuma4u, Adzahan Saad03, warfaaraza, thosebrowneyestho, Morning of Teenx, Holliexo, Dr Talha Malik, and alhabu hu alhabu 06. I will post the names as a bulletin. Locate their comments and upvote them. I want to see those comments at the top of the feed. Thank you to the soldiers who own these accounts. Your intelligence, creativity and commitment will be rewarded. You are a credit to the cause.’

David sits back, fizzing with pride. Princess Fahmida.

He is a credit to the cause.

DAVID KNOCKS, A THIRD TIME. 'Hey, I made us pasta.' Still nothing. 'Dad, I'm coming in.' The room is dark. A delivery driver stands outside the house opposite, holding a Subway bag and expressively knocking. Who orders a Subway online? How lazy are the neighbours? Muslims. He switches on the lights, closes the curtains and palms an apple core from the bedside table into the bin.

'Mm?' Dad blinks into the honey light.

David turns on the bedside lamp too. 'I made us pasta.'

'Dinner?'

'Yeah.'

As Dad slogs into a sitting position, David says that he can bring it here.

'What's in it?'

'Erm. I made it with spinach and tinned tomatoes.'

'And the spicy-chilli Dolmio sauce?'

'Not this time.'

'I like that Dolmio sauce.'

'It should be okay with spinach and tinned tomatoes too.'

'Bang Bang?'

'Let's try it first.'

Dad inspects his sweatshirt, streaked with blunt knives of light from the bedside lamp, wets his finger and scratches away at a spot. In the kitchen, David slops pasta on to two plates. He is not looking forward to eating it either – the spinach has a horrible texture, soft and mushy – but at least it is healthy and, since Dad had rice snaps with blackberry jam for breakfast and they will be having Pringles later, healthy is required. In summer at King George the doctor discharging Dad declared that if he didn't stop smoking and drinking and start taking regular exercise and eating a balanced diet he would be seeing him again soon, and then it would be after a real stroke, not a mini-stroke. Since Dad still smokes and drinks and spends all day in his room, a lot is resting on the balanced diet. David read that spinach prevents strokes, and tinned tomatoes must be healthier than Dolmio.

He slaps a plate on the bedside table and takes a seat with the other in his lap.

'I think it'll be nice.'

An Apple Watch lies unopened on the desk. Stephen made a big thing of buying it for Dad – he could use it to measure his heart rate, and the goal of closing his activity rings would motivate him to stand up once an hour. For her part, Mum did warn Stephen that there was no point, that Dad would never use it. But Stephen insisted, presumably seeing it as a golden opportunity to show how caring and gracious he is. Having poked the pasta about for a minute, Dad takes a listless bite.

'Is it okay?'

'Shall we put some Bang Bang on top?'

'Erm.'

'Actually. You're right. It's fine as it is.' Diligently skirting the spinach, he asks David what time he's going to the Jobcentre tomorrow.

'I need to be there at nine.'

'Just another appointment?'

'Yeah.'

David hates his work coach and their pointless weekly appointments. How is somebody who was fired from Sainsbury's going to 'stand out' and 'make a great impression' in an interview? With the economy as shit as it is, there's a slew of applicants for every job. He has zero chance of finding one. It's humiliating, a waste of time. He wishes they would send him his allowance and let him be.

'Good luck.'

'Cheers.'

He doesn't want a job anyway. Having one would make it

near-impossible to perform his WOTAN duties. The only downside to unemployment has been Mum and Stephen stepping in with financial support. He knows how much Dad would like to tell them where to stick that.

'How's *Call of Duty*?'

'Great.'

'I read something in the news earlier – esports.'

'Yeah?'

'Apparently there was a tournament in London, and a sixteen-year-old won five hundred thousand pounds. Can you believe that? It would be fun if you won that playing *Call of Duty*.'

David laughs. 'I wish I had the talent to compete with the pros. They have ridiculous skills. You can see it in the Call of Duty League streams. The map awareness and spawn knowledge and reaction times they have. Insane. They're on a different level, a totally different level.'

Disappointment slopes into Dad's voice. 'That's a shame.' He sounds as if he seriously thought David could win a *Call of Duty* tournament. 'Five hundred thousand pounds is a lot of money.'

'. . . Yeah.'

An uncomfortable, puddly silence.

'Food okay?' David asks.

'Let's put some Bang Bang on top.'

HAVING SPENT TWENTY MINUTES scrolling through German Romanticism paintings, David settles on *Wanderer above the Sea of Fog*. The way the figure in it, wrapped in a dark-green overcoat and gripping a walking stick in his right hand, gazes out over a grey landscape, his back to the viewer – he looks like a poet, a nineteenth-century Karl.

David opens the image in Photoshop, adds a black border and applies the vaporwave filter Supreme Commander RitterKreuz shared in the #resources channel. It gives the painting a glitchy eighties feel, bathing it with neon colours: light blue, pink, purple. The *Stranger Things* vibe. Next, he adds a black sun wheel to the horizon of the painting, and plays with the editing tools until the sun wheel appears to be rising over the mountains in the distance. Finally, he adds a text box, selects a stocky chrome font and gives thought to the text.

Supreme Commander RitterKreuz likes memes with 'we' and 'us' and 'ours' best. David writes 'WE WILL HAVE TOMORROW' then changes it to 'TOMORROW IS OURS' then changes it to 'THE FUTURE IS OURS' and considers. The vaporwave filter fits the painting well. The future is ours. Yeah, it is. He opens Discord and shares it in WOTAN's #memelibrary.

A spider crawls across the windowsill, rain cackling on the glass. All corners of his room glitter with cobwebs. He looks up and remembers that he has glow-in-the-dark stars, which no longer work and simply cling to the ceiling, snot-coloured. They came free with a cereal. He has no idea how to get rid of them. Once the spider has gone, he blows at the windowsill, sending dust snaggling up.

He opens the Xx Darius 1 KING OF KINGS Fan Club xX

server, exclusively for Iranian and Indian Aryans. A while back, he came across a link to it on the r/IndoEuropean subreddit. He never posts, but he enjoys lurking now and then, as there is some good content. Today, users are discussing a YouTube video with the title 'Persian beauty the Real ARYAN (ARYAN RACE)' and a thumbnail of a beautiful blonde woman with blue eyes. 'Proud to be ARYAN. PERSIAN the true ARYANS,' someone wrote. 'Iranians is dna (R1A M420) and race white. These are real women,' someone else wrote, with black heart emojis. The girls are really hot. After watching the entire video, he clicks over to Dark Fury.

Corey(515) Today at 15:05
Anyone fancy some Battlezone?

Corey(515) Today at 15:05
Cheeky pre-breakfast session

Corey(515) Today at 15:05
Watched a yt video last night and want to try out some of the tips haha

Runningngunning Today at 15:09
Yeah sure

David replies, saying he's in. Given that there are no WOTAN raids or search-and-destroy or sniper missions planned before six, he can play a couple of hours of *Call of Duty*.

'Like that meme you made,' Runningngunning says, when he joins the voice chat.

'Hang on, I'll check it out now,' Corey says. 'Ooh. Yeah. Digging that. The future is ours. Too fucking right it is. I should have the time to make a couple memes today too.'

'More NPC ones?'

'You know it.'

'Fair play. They are funny as hell.'

Last week Corey took the grey cartoon Wojak avatar with the blank, serious face and added the words 'I AM PREPARED TO DIE FIGHTING' above him and 'FOR WHAT I WAS TOLD TO

THINK' underneath him. Simple but effective. It will have triggered many an SJW.

Runningngunning is more into cartoon remixes: memes that combine characters from comic books and Disney films with hard truths. David isn't witty enough to make memes like that. But his memes do also seem to go down well with the Generals and Supreme Commander RitterKreuz.

'I ordered white laces from the Dr Martens website this morning,' David says.

'Awesome,' Runningngunning says.

'Got them on three pairs of shoes now,' Corey says.

'Reckon many people have red laces?' David says. 'Or is that a joke?'

'Fuck knows.'

All WOTAN members are entitled to wear white laces. Those who have 'shed blood' – whatever that means – are entitled to switch to red laces.

'Dunno,' Runningngunning says. 'I've never seen a photo of red laces in the server.'

'Right,' Corey says. 'Battlezone.' He shares the tips.

'Got it,' Runningngunning says.

'Just making the changes now,' David says. '. . . All right. Done.'

'Weapon?' Runningngunning says. 'Grau?'

'Go for it,' Corey says. 'I'll use the M4.'

'I'll stick with my MP5,' David says.

After weeks tinkering with his MP5, he is content. Barrel: Monolithic Integral Suppressor. Optic: Solozero NVG Enhanced (with thermal sight). Underbarrel: Merc Foregrip. Stock: FTAC Collapsible. Ammunition: 45 Round Mags. Good recoil control, range and fire rate.

'Joining a lobby,' Corey says. 'Come on, Matchmaking. Sort us out.'

While they wait, Runningngunning asks whether Corey or David read about the Antifa thugs who tore down the statue in Louisville last night.

'Scumbags,' Corey says. 'Scared of a statue.'

'If they want to tear down statues of slave owners,' David says, 'why not tear down statues of Muhammad? He bought, sold, captured and owned slaves.'

'Do they have statues of Muhammad?' Runningngunning says.

'They must do somewhere,' Corey says. 'At a mosque?'

'I seem to remember reading that images and statues of Muhammad are prohibited in Islam?' Runningngunning says. 'Like, he shouldn't be pictured or something?'

'What?' Corey says. 'Not even in Islamabad?'

'I dunno?' Runningngunning says. 'Anyway, he was a slave owner. I know that. Maybe everyone who is named after him should be made to change their name instead.'

'That would be hilarious,' David says.

'I'm willing to give up our statues to see that happen,' Corey says, before crunching something.

'What are you snacking on?' Runningngunning says.

'Fuego Takis. Got used to this ethical vegan shit now. We can still have most chips.'

'Yeah, I'm down with it,' Runningngunning says. 'Always hated chicken joints anyway, to be honest. The lowlifes that go there. I felt dirty around them.'

'The ones in London are the worst,' David says.

It was seeing Supreme Commander RitterKreuz's posts in the #bloodandsoil channel that made up David's mind: WOTAN *is* everything. Supreme Commander RitterKreuz advocates ethical veganism – a mark of empathy – for all Aryans, as a means of demonstrating racial superiority. He has been an ethical vegan for a decade. Now the Dark Fury guys are too.

'You guys in for the raid tonight then?' Runningngunning says.

'Not a hundred per cent I can make it. But I'll see,' Corey says.

'I'll be there,' David says.

'Knew you would be. You never miss one. How many YouTube and Twitter sock accounts do you have? Hundreds? You're a soldier, man.'

'Thanks.'

'You'll be promoted to General in no time.'

'We'll see.'

'Seriously. You were promoted to Gefreiter in, what, a month? And Offizier in three months? I was a Rekrut for six months. Ritter and the Generals like you.'

'You think?'

'Runningngunning's right,' Corey says. 'Everyone in WOTAN loves you. I'm not surprised. Fair play. You put the hours in.'

'Thanks.'

'Right. Game's ready.'

THE BLACK-AND-RED BODYWORKS SIGN GLEAMS in the autumn drizzle. A last drag, and David stubs out his cigarette and enters the building. He had reservations about taking out a three-month membership as the top comments on Google were ominous – from 'old school gym' through 'total dump' and 'aggressive environment, way too crowded, long waits to get on the equipment' to 'real torture chamber vibes' – but it was the only gym in walking distance he could afford.

A Muslim-looking employee in a Bodyworks tank top glances up. David has little choice but to interact with him. 'Hey, I have, erm, an induction now.'

The Muslim asks his name.

'David.'

'Hang on.' He swipes at an iPad. 'Got you. Hmm. Mikel is supposed to be taking your induction, but I'm not sure where he is right now . . . Never mind, I'll fill in for him . . . Faaiz.'

Having regrettably accepted a handshake, David sits on a red armchair, as directed, and rests his backpack – in which he has a water bottle and a small white towel – on the ground. To save the faff of using the changing rooms, he decided to come in his workout wear: New Balance.

Faaiz asks whether he's been a member of a gym or used an exercise app before and whether he has any health issues or past injuries. David answers no on all counts.

'All right. And what motivated you to join Bodyworks? Are you looking to improve your strength? To get more endurance? To just generally improve your all-round fitness? To socialise?'

'I need to be stronger.'

Supreme Commander RitterKreuz urges everyone to stay

physically fit, because well-toned, muscular bodies reflect moral virtues like bravery, courage and willpower and when the movement moves offline it will be imperative that everyone has not only the mental but also the physical capacity to play their part. David intends to play his part.

'Sure,' Faaiz says. 'Do you want to come with me then? I'll show you round.'

A song with heavy bass squelches out from the speakers. Lucozade bottles glow in the vending machines. Display stands promote Grenade Carb Killa bars. Exercise bikes whirr away upstairs. An Aryan studies her reflection in a wall-length mirror, a pair of dumbbells at her feet, while a black guy with a bandana lies on a flat weight bench, his face pressed into the padding, a lifting belt strapped around his waist, clawing metal handles, back muscles bulging.

Faaiz stops at the chest press and asks the Aryan using it how many sets he has left: only one. 'Perfect. So. David, I think this is a suitable starting point for you. It targets the main muscles of the chest, the pectorals. It will also help to build your biceps and the muscles in your shoulders and back.' Done, the Aryan takes his fluorescent water bottle and sharks away. David wonders whether he supports the movement. This is the first time in months he has left the house for something other than shopping or a Haggerston trip. He clambers on to the machine, hunches his shoulders.

'Is the seat height fine for you?' Faaiz asks. David nods. 'On the right is where you adjust the weight. Pull that out. Yep. Bring it down to fifteen kilograms. Now. Grasp the handles with a full grip. Yep. Circle the handles with your thumbs. Yep. Now push the bars.'

David feels patronised. Sure, he's new to this, but he's eighteen, not eight. He tries pushing.

'Really push,' Faaiz says. 'Keep your head steady against the pad too.'

Impossible. The machine is broken.

'Don't worry,' Faaiz says. 'We might need to lighten the load a little. That's all. Let's drop it down to twelve point five.' He edges round the machine. 'Actually, let's say ten.' He changes the weight and steps back. 'This is only an induction after all. Okay. Try now.'

This time David manages to raise the bars. His face clenches up with the effort, but he manages. He keeps pushing until the bars are fully extended and then lets them clatter back.

'Great. So. That's one rep. Between eight and twelve reps makes a set.'

'. . . Okay.'

'On the chest press, I would aim for three sets of eight reps, with thirty-second rests between sets. Once you can comfortably do that at ten kilograms, put the weight up to twelve point five.'

'Okay.'

'Do you want to try a full set now or shall we move on to the next machine?'

'Let's move on.'

'WELL?' MUM SAYS, standing in the doorway.

'Well what?'

David hates these visits – the same shit time every time – but they are a condition of the 'arrangements' Mum and Stephen have made with Dad. If he neglects to spend at least two days a week with them, they will stop sending Dad money. Because they are arseholes.

She asks what happened when he met his work coach on Wednesday.

'Nothing.'

'Is he not supposed to help you find a new job?'

'Guess so.'

'But you haven't had a single interview. What's the point if he can't even—'

'There is no point.'

'You need to be more forward. Ask for CV help. He will have better tips than us. Or for recommendations on courses you can take to improve your employability. We'll pay for them.'

'I meet with him for ten minutes. He can't work miracles in ten minutes.'

'Why is it only ten minutes?'

'Because it is.'

Glaring at him, she says that something has to change, that this can't continue endlessly, that it was bad enough for his CV that he spent so long at Sainsbury's.

'What exactly do you suggest? Want to get Stephen to swoop in and save the day by landing me an internship at Amnesty? He seems to have no problem with nepotism.'

'Zoe has a first in English Literature. She could have got an internship anywhere.'

'But she just happened to get one at Amnesty?'

'David, we're talking about you – not Zoe.'

'Ah.'

Right now, Corey, Dysruptz and Runningngunning are playing *Call of Duty*. His Companion app shows that Corey achieved ten defends and nine captures in the last game of Domination and Runningngunning twenty-six kills in the last game of Grind. He could be playing with them. But, no, he's here, submitting to a tedious lecture; Mum better hurry up because a WOTAN sniper mission is scheduled for nine, and he is not turning up late for that. Unfortunately, he will need to be mindful about what he says on the voice chat, in case she or Stephen eavesdrops. They have before.

'I'm being serious,' she says. 'This is not continuing. We are not sending money to support you sitting around at home doing whatever it is you do online all day and . . . to support your father doing whatever it is he does all day – and drinking himself to death.'

David sits up. 'Leave Dad out of this.'

'I know it's hard for you to hear that. You're only eighteen. You shouldn't be dealing with something like this. But I don't want it on my conscience either. I don't want to know that I played a part in . . . He had a transient ischaemic attack, and the way he's going he will have a stroke in the next few weeks. He will. You have to understand that.'

'Shut up!'

'Because if it happens . . . Does he exercise? Does he eat healthily?'

'Don't send your money then!'

'David.'

He snatches a pillow and threatens to throw it. 'Fuck you! Just leave us alone.'

'And what? Let you starve? This is the real world—'

'We'll be fine!'

She considers him. '. . . What do you do online all day?'

David meets her eyes. 'What?'

'You heard me. What do you do online all day?'

'More than you do at Action Aid and Stephen does at Amnesty, that's for sure.'

DAVID RUBS HIS BICEPS, berating himself for not completing a single set. In his defence, he was alert to all the Muslims swarming about, waiting to use the machines, and that made it hard to concentrate. Rolling his shoulders, he plugs in his earphones and joins the WOTAN voice chat, on which there are already sixty people. A special-ops sabotage mission is scheduled to start in ten minutes. 'Welcome, BGMP5R1A,' General LordofKek says.

'Hey.'

Runningngunning and a few other members salute him too.

'Right,' General LordofKek says. 'It's nine twenty-five. At nine thirty Supreme Commander RitterKreuz will fill us in on the mission details. Until then, silence please.'

David remembers the black bin. Having forgotten last time, he needs to take it out tonight. It is bulging with so much shit it can no longer be closed. Straight after the mission, he will see to it.

At precisely nine thirty, Supreme Commander RitterKreuz enters the voice chat and expresses his pleasure that so many members are here, as some serious artistry and acuity will be required.

'I trust I can count on you?'

'Yes,' David is the first to say.

'I knew I could. Tonight, Kameraden, we will be conducting a special-ops sabotage mission. With Antifa being fawned over and their pathetic protests praised by the puppets in the mainstream media, there is no better time to expose them for what they are – violent lowlife scumbags, cockroaches. As you may have seen, they recently got the hashtag SmackaNaziUp trending. We can use that to our advantage. We can sabotage the hashtag. Do we want to sabotage it?'

'Yes.'

'Yes.'

'Fuck them,' General LordofKek says. 'Fucking SJW cucks.'

'That is what I was hoping I would hear,' Supreme Commander RitterKreuz says. 'Yes. Let us proceed then. The mission will have multiple phases. In the first, now, everyone will be on meme-creation duty. We will create memes that advance Antifa's SmackaNaziUp position – that it is legitimate to respond to "racist" words with violence – and exaggerate that position ever so slightly to make Antifa appear even more radical and threatening than they really are. I and my Generals will then select the best memes. In the second phase, everyone will be required to tweet the best memes out from Antifa sock accounts with the hashtag SmackaNaziUp. In the third phase, we will retweet the Antifa sock accounts' tweets from our actual accounts along with comments like "Antifa, lovely people" and tag political commentators. The mainstream media is so stupid that they will report on the memes and spread the word even further, sowing doubt about Antifa among progressives and demeaning the SmackaNaziUp hashtag. Their reputation will be damaged. As it should be. As it deserves to be. I will give you all discretion on what to include in your memes, but one thing you must include is a black-and-red Antifa flag in the top-right corner. You will find a JPEG in the resources channel. So. An example. You could google "wounded cop" and find an image of a cop on a stretcher and write "all my heroes kill cops" and then paste in the Antifa flag, or you could google "domestic abuse white woman" and find a photo of a roughed-up white bitch and write "racism must be beaten out of society" and put in the Antifa flag. Those examples would work because they do go along with the SmackaNaziUp violence-is-justified position. Just ever so slightly exaggerated. Does everyone understand?'

'Yes.'

'Yes.'

'Roger that.'

'Let us commence phase one,' Supreme Commander

RitterKreuz says. 'Get to work and post your creations in the memelibrary channel. I will be back in forty-five minutes.'

'Time's up.'

David has made three memes. While working on a fourth, Photoshop crashed, and opening it again took ages: he has a buggy hacked version. Offizier MikeOxlong managed to make six memes, and all are inventive and hilarious. He will be promoted to General before David, and rightly so.

'Thank you for your hard work, Kameraden,' Supreme Commander RitterKreuz says. 'Your artistry and acuity were duly shown. You did not disappoint. We have now made our choices. The six winning memes will be posted in the resources channel.'

Limply David clicks over to #resources – and widens his eyes. What? Supreme Commander RitterKreuz and the Generals have chosen two of his memes. He collapses back into his chair.

'Now we commence the next phase,' Supreme Commander RitterKreuz says.

At 2.30 a.m. the mission finally comes to a close, the six memes seeded into the world. He slogs to the bathroom, eyes burning, tokenistically brushes his teeth, splashes his face with water. The bin won't be taken out tonight. Having struggled back to his room, he clambers into bed, craving sleep.

'Give it a shot, Joe.'

Dad? Oh no, not now.

'Give it a shot, Joe.'

What if he wakes up the neighbours? Last time he woke them up, they were furious.

Unable to cope with the soliloquising, David slots in his earphones and scrolls through his favourite Karl-and-Salomé playlist. A Discord notification flashes up. Another one. Another one.

General LordofKek Today at 04:50
CHECK ROGER EVANS TWITTER

General LordofKek Today at 04:50
RETWEETED MEME + 'SHAME ON YOU ANTIFA'

General LordofKek Today at 04:50
BREITBART COLUMNIST^ BLUE-VERIFIED TICK

General LordofKek Today at 04:50
58.3K FOLLOWERS

General LordofKek Today at 04:50
@BGMP5R1A YOUR MEME BOY

General LordofKek Today at 04:50
!!!!!!!!!

'NEXT TIME YOU SEE YOUR MOTHER,' Dad says, 'maybe slip in something about me exercising. You know. Walking. Jogging. Those sorts of things.'

'Yeah, sure.'

'You could tell her I'm working up to running five kilometres.'

'Okay.'

'That would shut her up.'

Nodding, David switches on the DVD player. The conversation is making him uncomfortable. Mum is insufferable. But she has a point: Dad needs to exercise. 'Which episode?'

With thick, sticky pupils like barbecue sauce, Dad squints at the screen.

'"The Long Legs of the Law", "Ashes to Ashes", "A Losing Streak", "No Greater Love", "The Yellow Peril" and "It Never Rains" – those are the ones on this disc,' David says.

'Maybe "It Never Rains"?'

The credits rolling, David says, 'Great episode,' and hits the power button on the remote. Normally he would suggest another, but he has no time tonight. His promotion to General has given rise to new duties and responsibilities, such as supporting Rekruts and creating his own mission ideas.

'I better head up,' David says.

Dad turns to him, surprised. 'Oh. Sure.'

'Let's watch "The Long Legs of the Law" tomorrow night.'

'That would be fun.'

'Yeah.'

Having worked his way into an upright position, Dad asks how *Call of Duty* is.

'Great.'

'Did you think any more about the tournament? I read another news story about it – on the BBC. It takes place annually and the prize money keeps going up. This time it was five hundred thousand pounds for the winner. Next time it will be more. Who knows, maybe a million.'

'I don't really have what it takes to enter tournaments, Dad.'

Dad nods. 'Just thought I would mention it.'

'Thanks.'

'Well, I'll leave you to it then.'

'Thanks . . . Give me a shout if you need something.'

'Don't worry.'

David monitors the new content. A string of funny memes from Corey. Activity in the #boogaloohq channel too: a new Rekrut has shared a link to a dark web cryptomarket and written, 'This is the place for everything, you can get weed, coke, md, ket, hacked software shit, 3Dprinted weapons, real weapons, everything. Ive used it a couple times before and can guarantee its safe and secure, when the moment comes you'll want to have this link, trust me, live free or die dudes,' with skull-and-crossbones and kissy-face emojis. When David clicks on the link, nothing happens, suggesting a special browser might be required. He considers flagging it to Supreme Commander RitterKreuz in case it's suspicious, in case the Rekrut is an infiltrator, but decides against it. Given how little used the #boogaloohq channel is, the other Generals will see it. They will know what to do.

A rattling, scuttling sound. David spins. Gone. Over the past week, he has heard it multiple times. A mouse? or even a rat? It seems to be coming from within the wall – strange. He moves on to the other channels. In #sharingcorner, another Rekrut has written a series of impassioned messages.

Tweak Tweak Today at 22:00
fckin hell i cant take it anymore

Tweak Tweak Today at 22:01
every time i go to the dunkin donuts near my house to get a coffee these fckin black kids that hang out outside smoking weed give me shit. every time. i cant take it anymore. like my dad did some shit in this town OK and I look a bit whatever being a skinny guy who wears weird shit OK but like GET OVER IT for fucks sake every time

Tweak Tweak Today at 22:01
i would stop going there but its literally 20 minutes more to the next coffee shop and thats a starbucks so too expensive too like cant they ever just FUCK OFF

Tweak Tweak Today at 22:01
What shall I do???

Tweak Tweak Today at 22:01
SOMEONE PLEASE

Tweak Tweak Today at 22:02
sorry i just cant sometimes sorry

Tweak Tweak Today at 22:02
ignore me

David musters the courage to share a personal experience. In moments like this, Supreme Commander RitterKreuz expects his Generals to step up and emotionally support Rekruts.

General BGMP5R1A Today at 22:02
@Tweak Tweak Don't apologise. There's no need to say sorry

General BGMP5R1A Today at 22:03
I know how you feel.

General BGMP5R1A Today at 22:03
I used to get shit from some Muslims. It made me hate college and walking home and everything. I still haven't really gone back to the part of town where they hang out. I know how you feel. I got beaten up and pissed on one time. Actually pissed on. It was the worst experience of my life. So trust me I know how you feel.

Tweak Tweak Today at 22:04
wow seriously? fk me

General BGMP5R1A Today at 22:05
Those black kids are not giving you shit because of whatever your dad did or the way you look. They're giving you shit because you're Aryan and they're jealous. There's nothing you can do to stop them giving you shit, non-Aryans hate Aryans. It's as simple as that.

General BGMP5R1A Today at 22:05
It's happened to all of us

General BGMP5R1A Today at 22:05
Don't worry, we've got your back here

General BGMP5R1A Today at 22:05
& one day we will turn the tide on them

General BGMP5R1A Today at 22:05
I promise

'THIS EVENING WE WILL BE CONDUCTING a new type of mission,' Supreme Commander RitterKreuz announces. 'Let's call it an air support mission. General BGMP5R1A has played an instrumental role in masterminding it. Thank you, General BGMP5R1A.'

'Thank you, Supreme Commander,' David says.

'Is everyone ready?' Supreme Commander RitterKreuz says.

'Yes.'

'Yes.'

'Yes, Supreme Commander.'

'We will be providing support to an Aryan ally,' Supreme Commander RitterKreuz says. 'A British rock musician, Karl Williams. He is not someone who aligns with all our values or shares all our moral virtues. But he is someone who has a platform in society and is using that platform to educate on the evils of Islam, attracting the ire of the liberal media elite in the process. In providing support to him, we can show that it does pay to speak the truth, draw him closer to us and tempt other artists to follow in his footsteps. We need to widen the Overton Window, and figures like Mr Williams can help us with that. We should not let the liberal media elite destroy his career. We should not let him be thrown to the dogs. General BGMP5R1A will now say a few words.'

David is shaking with nerves, excitement, expectation. 'Yeah. So.' He clears his throat. 'Sorry. So. I think it's important that we show our appreciation for artists who break from the status quo. The arts world is so PC that when a musician commits wrongthink everyone immediately turns on them. They can put out an amazing album afterwards and it will still receive one-out-of-five reviews. That scares most musicians into keeping their mouths shut. We should provide support to those who break from the status quo. I've been following Karl for a while and, well, he's a worthy ally.'

'Thank you, General BGMP5R1A,' Supreme Commander RitterKreuz says. 'Everyone, the air support mission will proceed as follows: We will key "Karl Williams" into Google News, search out negative reviews of his new record and comment on them along the lines of "review his art, not his views, besides he has never said anything unreasonable anyway, leave your liberal elite bubble for one second and you will see that", etc. We want to make progressive reviewers think twice. Next, after we have commented on multiple reviews, and upvoted other air support comments, we will search out the reviewers on Twitter. They will have tweeted their pieces. We will leave negative replies to those tweets, savaging them. Next, from our own accounts, or right-leaning sock accounts, we will tweet a link to the album on Spotify, along with a quote from Karl Williams about Islam – General BGMP5R1A will post a selection in the resources channel. As ever, we will tag right-leaning political and cultural commentators and hope that one will retweet the recommendation or, who knows, even write a positive piece about Karl Williams. Is everyone happy with that?'

'Yes.'

'Yes.'

'Yes.'

David hears Corey's and Dysruptz's voices. They are preparing to execute his plan – his plan. Karl changed his life. Now he is returning the favour.

'Go,' Supreme Commander RitterKreuz says.

EYES WEDGED SHUT, BITING HIS LIPS, David pushes the bars up. After a few squirming, shuddering seconds, he lets them clatter back, knowing that his physical capacity has been pushed to the limit. He is making progress, slow progress, but progress: six reps on the chest press. A whole set should be possible in the near future. He reaches for his water bottle. The black ceiling in the Bodyworks creates a uniquely stuffy atmosphere. He guzzles and gets up.

Next – the shoulder press. There are no waits for the machines. He heaved out of bed at 6 a.m. and slogged straight here to avoid the swarms. That meant having only three hours of sleep, but it was worth it, especially as he feels energetic anyway, still buzzing from how many WOTAN members came together to support Karl and what a success the mission was. The control panels on the cardio equipment upstairs glint green and red through the balustrade. In front of a boxing mural, an Aryan lays into a punchbag, which hangs on a heavy-duty silver chain.

He pushes the bars. After four reps, his whole body tenses up and he surrenders.

A stabbing sensation. A tightening of his skin. What? Is that—

Hassan? It is him. It is. Entering the Bodyworks, with someone. *Hassan*. He has messy hair now, messy hair and blonde highlights. But it is him. Hassan. Their eyes meet. Hassan momentarily stops and nods to him, before mumbling to his companion and heading on to the changing room.

Wiping his mouth on the sleeve of his training top, David wonders what to do. Hassan will expect him to run away. But he has no intention of running. This is England. His country. He has Aryan teammates in here. If Hassan starts on him, they will have his back. There are Muslims too, sure, who may try to help Hassan. But David and his teammates will come out on top.

He moves on to the bicep curl, sits and changes the weight to five kilograms. A thought tunnels through him: If he were to shed blood in the fight, he would be entitled to switch to red laces: no small thing. On the wall to his right, a series of TV screens play sports and news, tracing a watery blue stripe. He shrugs his shoulders, stretches his arms, slews his head from side to side, seizes the bars and begins. This is England. It is his country. He is running nowhere.

Having managed four reps, he pauses and starts a one-minute timer on his phone, confident that he can manage a second set of four. He looks about him. The Aryan on the leg press, wearing a Slipknot tank top and black shorts, would surely be up for a fight. His phone buzzes. Come on.

He pulls the bars towards him. One . . . Two . . . Three . . . Three . . . Three . . .

No more. He opens his eyes.

Leaving the changing room, Hassan nods to David and walks over.

Fuck. This is it.

Since college, David hasn't once run into Mo, Ibrahim or Hassan. But in his imagination he has – in his imagination he has many, many times.

His palms hum with fear and rage and a strange sick excitement.

'Hey bro,' Hassan says.

David blinks, wondering whether he heard Hassan right – bro?

'Is it David?' Hassan says. 'David? Yeah? Anyway. Good to see you. I've been hoping to for a while. I wanted to . . . I wanted to say sorry for the shit that happened . . . You know.'

'What?'

'In the underpass. For what it's worth, I haven't hung out with Mo or Ibrahim for ages. They're wankers. I sort of figured that at the time. But I guess I was stupid and they were my mates.' He cracks his knuckles. 'Anyway, I'll let you get back to your workout. Just wanted to say something.'

David lowers his eyes.

'Take care, bro.' Hassan says, offering a fist-bump. '. . . Hey, if you're ever looking for a post-workout protein hit, swing into Tariq's Grill. You know it? Smith Street. Just off Ley Street. Five minutes away. I help my dad out there most days. I'll sort you some tandoori chicken on the house.'

What is happening? What snidey Muslim trick is Hassan playing on him? He knows that every word Hassan has said is bullshit, that he needs to fight back, escalate the encounter, enlist his teammates, but he is struggling to think straight, and as the silence lengthens a tear bubbles out.

'Take care, bro,' Hassan repeats. Then strolls away.

Defeat.

David seeks the exit.

IN HIS BEDROOM, DAVID SKIPS from WOTAN channel to channel to channel. Despite the most recent meme he made – a vaporwave remix of a Crusades painting, *The Battle of Montgisard* – having received scores of black hearts and lightning-bolt emojis, he feels restlessly miserable.

As a General, he should have spat at Hassan and made it clear that there will never be Sharia law in England, not while he is alive, should have hit Hassan and called his Aryan teammates over to play with him, should have . . . There are countless things he should have done. Yet he crumbled and let Hassan take control, secure victory. What happened?

He seeks solace in the Karl subreddit. 'This live version really takes a great song to the next level' is the hottest thread at the moment. 'One of my real favourites.' 'So much passion in this performance. Love it.' 'What a classic show.' He watches the embedded YouTube video: 'Setting Sun' at the Royal Albert Hall. In the final verse, Karl is no longer singing – he is howling. Another hot thread is called 'He treats his fans with such love and care' and shows him hugging a male fan in a denim jacket with a Salomé patch sewn on the back. David organises the subreddit by new posts. A minute ago: 'Update re UK shows :(:(' with an official-website link.

Karl will not be touring his new album in the UK. Negotiations with venue owners and promoters have collapsed. They are too scared of a backlash from sponsors to commit and his management are not prepared to wait any longer. It is a shame, as he was looking forward to playing to the people of the UK, who endure so much. Sadly, the elites are not prepared to let that happen.

David bawls curses.

WOTAN swamped newspaper comment sections, ripped progressive reviewers to shreds on Twitter and drove up the album's streaming figures on Spotify. And what good did it do? The BBC, the *Guardian*, Nike, O2, Pepsi, Apple, Barclaycard. Every organisation is on the side of Islam. How can they compete? It is not a fair fight. He snaps open a Heineken. A hiss, and the beer romps out. It is not a fair fight. A notification flashes up. Corey has sent him a DM in the Dark Fury server.

Corey(515) Today at 21:01
Hey man fancy some 2 v 2 close combat?

Corey(515) Today at 21:01
theres a new map out which looks cool

Corey(515) Today at 21:01
guessing youre on the raid tonight too?

Corey(515) Today at 21:01
could see off an hour or two of the new map beforehand?

Wriggling in the blue light of the laptop, David takes a long sip. It is fucked up – fucking fucked up.

David1702UK Today at 21:03
yeah sure close combat sounds good

David1702UK Today at 21:03
Ill head on in 5

David1702UK Today at 21:04
going to do the raid ofc

David1702UK Today at 21:04
but sometimes do you get the feeling that things are just hopeless

David1702UK Today at 21:04
like literally HOPELESS

Corey(515) Today at 21:05
?

David1702UK Today at 21:05
i dunno just how far can we go with yt raids and comment campaigns etc etc

David1702UK Today at 21:05
like we're killing them online and what goods it doing? where is it getting us?

David1702UK Today at 21:05
words words words words and what? they're still fucking there offline

Corey(515) Today at 21:06
?

David1702UK Today at 21:06
treating us like shit and taking our way of life away

David1702UK Today at 21:06
i guess im just getting sick of winning and it meaning nothing thats all

David1702UK Today at 21:06
theyre still there they're still fucking there you know?

David1702UK Today at 21:06
i dunno i just dunno

David1702UK Today at 21:06
theyre still there it cant continue it cant continue

David1702UK Today at 21:06
I won't let it continue

Hassan

'WHAT'RE YOU AFTER TODAY?' Hassan asks.

'I'll take the lamb chops as a starter and the karahi keema as a main,' Jay says.

'Anything else?'

'Just a Coke to drink.'

'No problem.' Having finally managed to memorise how much each item on the menu costs, Hassan calmly jabs the prices into the till. 'That will be thirteen fifty.'

A regular, Jay has the exact change ready.

'Guessing this is to have in?'

'You know it.'

'Great. Grab a Coke from the fridge and take a seat. I'll bring the rest over.'

For a Wednesday, it's surprisingly busy. Just two free tables. A drizzle of conversation. Greeting other regulars on his way through the restaurant, Jay settles for one at the back, below the TV. Hassan scribbles his order on a slip of paper, nips into the kitchen and passes it to Dad, who cocks his head, registers it and continues cooking. Deep fryers pop, sizzle, around him. All four chopping boards are out. Hassan thought Dad would be well organised, but not so well organised as to have colour-coded chopping boards and knives. Back on the till, he scans the scores on Sky Sports News, which is running silently above Jay:

in the Champions League, Napoli are beating Liverpool two–nil, Chelsea are losing one–nil to Valencia and Borussia Dortmund are drawing nil–nil with Barcelona.

A chime. Hassan straightens up and turns and tenses, recognising the customer.

It's Umar, someone who used to come to the youth centre exclusively for snooker tournaments. Dressed all in white – white Adidas hoodie, white joggers and white Superstar sneakers – he approaches the counter, assumes a quizzical expression and points. 'Hassan, right?'

'Hey.'

They shake hands.

'How long have you been working here?'

'About two months. Dad's place.'

'Ah. Yeah, I remember . . . You still hit up the centre?'

'No.'

'Too busy?'

'Something like that.'

He has no desire to tell Umar about the attack and the post-traumatic stress disorder and the therapy sessions and all the other shit that he has endured over the past six months.

'Fair play,' Umar says. 'Thought I hadn't seen you for a while. Done with sixth form?'

'Yeah.'

'Just starting, me. Biology, chemistry, maths. Going for Medicine. Imperial, hopefully.'

'Nice one.'

Umar knits his brows together. 'Didn't fancy uni?'

'Nah.' Unable to concentrate on his revision, Hassan failed to meet his Goldsmiths offer. Needing AAB, he got BBB. A lot of the other shit relates to this.

'Why?'

'Just wasn't feeling it . . . Maybe in the future.'

'Go for it.'

'Mm. What are you after today then?'

'Oh. Right. Course. Forgot I came in here for some munch.'

Chuckling, Umar places his order. Hassan lets him know that it will take ten minutes to prepare.

'No worries. I'll come back then. Good catching up, bro.'

'Yeah.'

'Like the hair by the way, the blonde highlights.'

For the first time in the exchange, Hassan brightens. 'Cheers.'

He got them done last week. Now that he is working here and going to the gym, he would like to look cool again, and they draw attention away from the grisly scar on his forehead.

AFTER CLIMBING FROM DIVISION 10 to Division 2 without breaking a sweat, Hassan registers for the EA Sports FIFA Global Series. If he reaches the Elite rank and then smashes the FGS Qualifiers and FGS Playoffs, he will be eligible to participate in the FIFAe World Cup. A long shot? Yes. Impossible? No. The Instagram trailer motivated him to try. It began with a teenager sitting in a pitch-black room playing FIFA while shocked-face-with-exploding-head emojis, jazzy GOAT stickers and other social media comments swished around him. *He's burst onto the scene and is the new superstar. This is a special player we're witnessing right here.* And it finished with glitchy scenes of him celebrating and signing autographs. *The superstar finally turns pro. A meteoric rise. What a journey. What a story. He's come from absolutely nowhere to become the greatest FIFA player on the planet. Who will be next?*

He hunkers down for a daytime session, a rare treat: Mum works on Muslim Voices from the living room but is in Brighton today, interviewing someone.

EA Sports. It's in the game. The main-menu screen appears, with a vibey, tropical-rock Glass Animals track. Hassan taps his fingertips on his knees, opens Ultimate Team, scans his recent record (W, W, W, W, D, W, W, L, D, W) and weighs up whether to make any changes to his squad.

When he embarked on Ultimate Team, his stars were Bamford, Neves and Cleverley. Now, Beckham, Van Dijk, Roberto Carlos. Thanks to his shifts at the restaurant, he can buy Packs.

Happy with his starting line-up, he searches for an opponent. As he never uses the voice chat function, he hasn't made any friends online. But he isn't playing to make friends.

Always a terrific venue to watch a football match comes the commentary. *I'm talking of the Emirates Stadium here in North London. I'm Derek Ray and alongside me is the former Arsenal and West Ham midfield player Stuart Robson, and we're featuring an Ultimate Division Rivals match.*

He is wearing his blue-and-orange Nike trainers, partly because the wooden floor is icy and partly because they provide him with an obscure, irrational sense of confidence.

An impressive start. He creates a clear-cut chance within five minutes, Antonio rattling the crossbar with a finesse shot from the edge of the box. He keeps possession well and plays nifty passes. Just a matter of time. His opponent – For Farke Sake, a Norwich fan, presumably – struggles to get his frontline on the ball. At the twenty-minute mark the breakthrough comes: Roberto Carlos whips a corner in towards the penalty spot, Moura heads it on, and Iago Aspas deftly controls it, spins away from a defender and smashes it in from a tight angle. A well-deserved lead, which Hassan takes into half-time. With some more luck, it could have been two- or three-nil. For Farke Sake is on the ropes. He checks the statistics. His dribble-success rate and pass accuracy are both over 90 per cent. For Farke Sake's are 70 and 74 per cent respectively. He has this.

The door to the living room swings open.

'You are playing FIFA at this time?' Mum says.

'Aren't you supposed to be in Brighton?' he asks defensively.

'Haafiza called and cancelled our interview at the last minute. Since I was already on my way, I thought I might as well spend a few hours in Brighton and work from a café there. But everywhere was too crowded. So I went to some shops in the Lanes and then took a train back.'

'Oh.' He curses himself for turning the volume up to the maximum level. If he hadn't, he would have heard her coming. *Game resuming in 3, 2, 1 . . .*

'So. You are playing FIFA at . . .' She checks her watch. 'Two thirty on a Wednesday.'

'Mum, I need to concentrate.'

'Hassan—

'Please. Give me five minutes.'

For Farke Sake stole the ball on the edge of the six-yard box. Had he shown some composure and sought out an extra pass, rather than panicking and shooting, they would be level.

'You are wasting too much time on this. There are better things—'

'Like what?'

'Anything. I know playing FIFA is fun, and I want you to have some fun now. You deserve it. But you have the free time to do other things too. What was the last book you read?'

'Gym.'

'Sorry?'

Hassan is unhappy with the way his team is getting pulled across the pitch. For Farke Sake is taking control of the game and making him play it at his tempo. An equaliser is coming.

'Gym.'

'Gym?'

'Gym. I spend hours there every week, hours. You, Dad, the therapist, everyone. You told me to try physical exercise. Well, I am. Where's my reward for that?'

For Farke Sake has a free kick in a promising position.

'Your reward is in how it makes you feel. I am glad it seems to be helping.' She crosses her arms. 'That is an example of a good use of your time. But you have enough to go there and—'

'Argh!'

The net is rippling, For Farke Sake having curled the ball into the top-right corner.

'Please. Please. Please. Give me five minutes.'

She tuts and leaves the living room.

Hello Hassan,

I hope you are keeping well.

Thank you once again for all the support you have provided so far in our telephone befriending scheme – Jazāk Allāhu Khayran. Zulfi Khan sent me a testimonial describing the 'inestimable' impact your conversations had on his life and expressing how much he appreciated all the time and effort you put in. I will forward the testimonial on to you – and be uploading it to the blog section of the website and on social media soon!

In the meantime, I wanted to write to you to ask whether you would be interested in taking on a new client. We have received a lot of requests recently and one client in particular matches up with your interests extremely well. He is a lifelong West Ham fan. If you would be interested, let me know and I will set everything up and send you on his details.

Kind regards,

Zafarullah Jamali
Volunteering Coordinator
Newbury Park Masjid

Hassan chews pulpy mouth tissue. In September, Zulfi at last had the operation on his knee, entered a rehabilitation clinic and withdrew from the telephone befriending scheme, confident that he would soon be able to walk around Newbury Park again without pain. Hassan remains in contact with him, but they no longer speak on the phone every week. He has completed his volunteering work.

A grey morning. The gutter is wadded with yellow leaves. BT employees are excavating the street with the intention of installing a new power cable. The letter that came through their door said it would dramatically improve internet speeds in the area. He hopes so. Because every time Mum or Dad stream something on Netflix while he is playing FIFA, he experiences lag.

He wonders whether there would be any point in performing more volunteering work. If he reapplies to Goldsmiths, he will do so with the same personal statement. There's no need to improve it; the section about Zulfi is impressive enough. The only point would be to pacify Mum and Dad. As two BT employees stiffly manoeuvre a drill out of the van, he pre-emptively puts on a 'Just Hits' playlist, which starts with Ed Sheeran. When he was calling Zulfi, his parents would routinely express how proud of him they were: Dad even bought him the new Nike Merlin ball. Do this and they might let him play FIFA in peace. Given that the past six months were the worst of his life and he is working part time at the restaurant, they should let him regardless. But he knows that won't happen – they will keep on at him. This might be his best bet. It would only be thirty minutes a week . . .

He sighs and grudgingly clicks 'reply'.

Hi Zafarullah,

Yeah, I would be up for this. Let me know his details.

Best,
Hassan

This should give a month of aggro-free gaming, enough time to reach the Elite Rank. It better.

HE NEEDS TO SHAKE THINGS UP – and shake them up now. His performance against The Jeweller's Hands was embarrassing. A one–nil loss was flattering. It easily could have been three– or four–nil. He browses the Promo Packs in the FUT Store: Premium Gold Players Pack, Prime Gold Players Pack, Rare Players Pack, Rare Mega Pack, Jumbo Rare Players Pack. He checks the probabilities for the Jumbo one: a 100 per cent chance of a Gold 75+ player, a 100 per cent chance of a Gold 82+ player, a 4 per cent chance of a Gold 90+ player, a 34 per cent chance of a TOTW Player and a 9 per cent chance of a FUT VERSUS ICE Player. It costs 1,100 FIFA Points: eight pounds fifty. A lot of money. But it might be worth it. A Gold 90+ player would make a real difference to his squad: Messi, Lewandowski, Ronaldo, Kevin De Bruyne, Mbappé, Salah, someone like that.

He clicks 'buy' and whispers, 'Please, EA. Give me Messi.'

Black screen. Gold stage, steps leading up to it. Jets of smoke. Danish flag. Goalkeeper. Leicester. Kasper Schmeichel. The best player in his Jumbo Rare Players Pack is Kasper Schmeichel. He blinks with incredulity. Kasper Schmeichel is only rated eighty-six and Hassan is content with Yashin. Goalkeeper is one position he is not worried about. What a piss-take.

Exasperated, he returns to the FUT Store and buys a second Jumbo Rare Players Pack.

Black screen. Gold stage, steps leading up to it. The spotlights at the top turn on, revealing that it will be a Walkout card. Bursts of flame. England flag. Left-winger. Manchester City. Sterling. Hassan balls his right hand up into a first. 'Get in.' Sterling has an eighty-eight rating overall, ninety-three pace and eighty-nine dribbling. He *is* a significant upgrade.

Now a serious challenge can be mounted for Division 1.

He re-reads the email the mosque has sent him.

Hello Hassan,

Hope you enjoyed reading Zulfi's testimonial.

Great to hear that – Jazāk Allāhu Khayran.

Your new client is a Mr Alex Stewart. He is 75. He is not a Muslim. However, he lives in Newbury Park a few streets away from our mosque, and, after his wife passed away, he read a leaflet with information about our telephone befriending scheme and asked whether he could sign up too. He has been feeling extremely lonely. I thought you would be a perfect match for him, as he passionately supports West Ham – he used to be a season ticket holder – and never misses an episode of *Match of the Day*. I have attached a document with notes of his other interests, but football is his primary one.

His number is 07834 282717.

Let me know when you would like the first call to be. If you want to refresh your memory on the good practice guidelines or anything else, you can do so here. If you have any other questions, you can send me an email any time.

Kind regards,
Zafarullah Jamali
Volunteering Coordinator
Newbury Park Masjid

Alex? He feels a prickle in his spine but shrugs it away. He is better, has been for a long time. This is a senior citizen who signed up for a telephone befriending scheme at a mosque, not a racist teenager; refusing to speak to someone on the basis that they are called Alex would be laughable.

He suggests a call tomorrow at ten thirty.

WHAT IS WRONG WITH HIM?

Every time he keys in the number, his chest tightens up, as it tightened up when leaving the house back in spring and summer. He thought he was better. He thought he was fucking better.

It's midday, meaning Alex has been waiting for over an hour.

Determined to try once more, he places a palm on his stomach, inhales through his nose slowly, slowly, slowly, feeling his stomach expand, fills his lungs slowly, slowly, slowly, and exhales through his mouth, feeling his stomach shrink. As his therapist recommended, he repeats the exercise ten times. Then he picks up the phone. This is manageable, easily manageable.

His chest tightens up. Dizziness smears the screen, lending it an underwater texture. Red bleeds out from the end-call icon. He feels sick. After two rings, he thumbs it.

Despite it being chilly, and the sky crackling, rain imminent, he opens the window. Leaning out, panting, he watches a bus pass, carrying an ad for McDonald's new Salted Caramel McFlurry. A string of tweens zip up the pavement on electric scooters, shrieking and forcing an elderly couple on to the street.

He considers pulling out of the scheme. But telling Zafarullah will be embarrassing – and telling Mum and Dad, that will be even worse. They will want to know why: why, why, why. If he so much as hints at what happened when he tried to call Alex, they will press him to book another appointment with his therapist and to start journalling and all the other things that were suggested in addition to physical exercise. And he can kiss goodbye to the month of aggro-free gaming . . .

Infuriated, he elbows the windowpane. His shift at the restaurant starts at one. That gives him less than an hour to get a grip. How can something as insignificant as this have made him so unwell?

Dad checks his watch. 'You're late, Hassan.'

'Sorry.'

'Fifteen minutes late.'

'Sorry.'

'Don't make a habit of it.'

Hassan slings up his hoodie. Dad instructs him to set the tables and then, after a short while, setting out vegetables in the serve-over counter, asks: 'How was the call with your new befriendee?'

A noncommittal mumble.

'Did you enjoy speaking to him as much as Zulfi Khan?"

'. . . Yeah.'

'You said he's a West Ham fan?'

'Yeah.'

Dad wipes clean the rims of the hummus tubs. 'Don't make a habit of being late, son. Okay? But let's forget it this time. Your volunteering work for the mosque is commendable.'

Hello Hassan,

I hope you are well.

I have left you a voicemail. I believe Alex Stewart failed to receive a call from you at the agreed time yesterday (10:30). Did you try to call him? Let me know if you ran into or are running into any problems. If not, please do call him as soon as possible. He should be free all day today too.

Kind regards,
Zafarullah Jamali
Volunteering Coordinator
Newbury Park Masjid

This email follows a slew of missed calls and a voicemail. He will need to tell someone something soon. But whom and what? Under the impression that he had a pleasant, serene chat with Alex, Mum and Dad let him play FIFA for five hours last night without hassle. To now backtrack and inform them that, actually, he's been talking shit, that, actually, he hasn't spoken to Alex, that, actually, he's pulling out of the scheme, and that, actually, he's still experiencing PTSD symptoms – impossible.

A wafer of blue sky creeps through the clouds. The BT employees are back, with new, more elaborate tools. There were problems installing the cable, causing the internet to become even slower.

He wakes up his phone, knowing that he has to call Alex – simply has to – regardless of how shitty it makes him feel. The consequences of not calling will be worse. He opens the window and performs his breathing exercise and keys in the number and, of course, experiences a tightening in his chest.

Despite a ripple of nausea clogging his throat he calls – calls and curses.

'Hello?'

Hassan crumbles out a response, before reeling over to the window.

'Who's calling?'

He strains to inhale. The BT employees smudge together. He closes his eyes. 'Hey, this is Hassan. I'm, erm, calling as part of the mosque's telephone befriending scheme.'

'Ah, Hassan. Great to hear from you.'

'I wanted to call yesterday. But I had some, erm, health problems.'

'Sorry to hear that. I hope you're feeling better now?'

'. . . Yeah.'

His hands are shaking so violently that even holding the phone is a challenge.

'Glad to hear that. No worries at all. Thanks for calling today.'

'Mm.'

'Really. I appreciate it. So. I should tell you a bit about myself and why I signed up for this. That's what Zafarullah suggested . . . You probably know this already and find it strange but, no, I'm not a Muslim. I live a couple of minutes away, on Southdown Crescent, and got a leaflet through my door with details about the scheme. I used to pass the mosque on my way to work in the morning and I would see people outside, chatting, and . . . the sense of community . . . I had never experienced something like that, other than maybe at Upton Park. And Muslims had always seemed all right to me. So, when I saw the leaflet, I thought, Why not? My wife had recently passed away and I've been finding life without her . . . We used to go to games and watch *Match of the Day* together. I gave up my season ticket after she passed away. It wouldn't have been the same. I still watch *Match of the Day*. But that's not really the same either . . . Sorry, Hassan, I'm jabbering now. What I mean is that without her I've been finding life a little tricky. And the scheme, I figured it might help.'

Hassan has succeeded in half-listening to Alex and is starting to feel a little less dizzy. The tightness in his chest remains. But he *is* starting to feel a little less dizzy. Will the symptoms fade? Maybe? Just thinking this helps him regain composure. 'Sorry to hear that. I will be calling every week for a thirty-minute chat. Hopefully, erm, that will help . . . How are you today?'

'Ah, not too bad. Though I am still smarting from Saturday.'

'West Ham?'

'Mm-hm.'

He is definitely less dizzy.

'We were terrible,' Hassan says. 'Did we have a shot on target?'

'I think there was one early on. Yarmolenko took a punt from long range. But that was it. I can't remember us having the ball in their box. What's happened to us?'

He is definitely, definitely less dizzy.

'Selling Arnautović was a mistake. I know he was gunning to go. And we re-invested the money. But still . . .'

'How much was Ajeti? Eight million?'

'Joke. Basel should have paid us to take him.'

Alex laughs. 'Oh well.'

'I'm not convinced by Haller either. He looked unplayable against Watford and Norwich. But against everyone else he has looked, well, pretty playable.'

'I think he has potential. But it will take some time for him to adjust to the Premier League.'

'Guess so . . . We need Antonio back.'

'He's returned to training.'

'Antonio? Really?'

'This morning.'

'Great . . . Yeah, maybe we will improve, maybe we will.'

'SHALL WE HIT THE UPPER BODY?' Kenan asks.

'Sure,' Hassan says.

After spotting the bench for each other several times, Kenan suggested they exchange numbers and become regular training partners. Hassan can't see them becoming friends – they have nothing in common – but is happy to have a training partner. He needs to improve his technique.

'Sweet. Dumbbell shoulder press?'

'Yeah.'

'I'm building up to the twenties.'

'I back you.'

'I am feeling it today. Six a.m. wake up. Granola for breakfast, a protein-boosted one, Fuel. Good shit. Espresso on the walk here.' He rolls his shoulders. 'I'm feeling it today.'

They make their way through the Bodyworks to the changing rooms.

'Pretty empty,' Hassan says.

'That's why I like coming this early.'

Just a few resistance machines are occupied. The TVs are playing sports and news. Someone performs sit-ups on a red mat. Someone else lays into a punchbag. He has noticed that everyone here seems to have Beats and is tempted to buy them too. But they are the price of seventy Premium Gold Packs. Kenan directs his attention to the shoulder press and an Instagram-hot girl.

'Bro,' he says. 'Life's not fair. You know that?'

Hassan freezes. A stabbing sensation. A tightening of his skin. What? Is that—

David? It is him. It is. He has shaved his hair. But it is unmistakably him. Hassan hasn't seen him since the incident in the underpass with Mo and Ibrahim. Their eyes meet. He lamely nods.

'What's up?' Kenan asks.

'Just recognised someone from way back.'

'Yeah? All right?'

'Mm. Never mind. Come on.'

On a bench by the lockers, Hassan laces his trainers, chewing over whether to speak to him – and if so what to say. He wishes this could have happened another time. Having stuck out the call with Alex and over the thirty minutes found his symptoms melting away and then afterwards packed Maradona and made it to Division 1, placing him in the top 2 per cent of players worldwide and within sight of the Elite rank, he went to bed feeling invincible and woke up in a buoyant mood.

He makes up his mind and nudges Kenan, who still has on cargo pants.

'I'll see you in there, man. I want to speak to that guy for a minute.'

Kenan raises an eyebrow. 'Just that guy?'

'Yeah?'

'If I find you chatting up shoulder-press girl without me, there will be hell to pay.'

'Don't worry. I'll see you in there.'

'All right.'

'What?' David seems to be looking at him through his nostrils.

Hassan explains that he no longer hangs out with Mo and Ibrahim, calls them wankers and cracks his knuckles. 'Anyway, I'll let you get back to your workout. Just wanted to say something . . . Take care, bro.' Hassan offers a fist-bump, but it's ignored. He hesitates, still waiting for a sign that they are okay, that his apology has been accepted. '. . . Hey, if you're ever looking for a post-workout protein hit, swing into Tariq's Grill. You know it? Smith Street. Just off Ley Street. Five minutes away. I help my dad out there most days. I'll sort you some tandoori chicken on the house.'

David shudders, and then Hassan thinks he sees – thinks he sees tears. The memory returns to him in all its horrible vividness: David curled up, weeping, wet with Ibrahim's piss.

Hassan shuffles his feet. It's understandable, the hostility.

He should leave David be, before the tears become blatant, embarrass him.

'Take care, bro.'

V

David

Introduction

'Do not go gentle into that good night
Rage, rage against the dying of the light'

– Dylan Thomas

An Islamo-substitution of the Aryan populations of Europe and the United States is taking place, aided by globalist elites.

Muslims CANNOT be permitted to continue eroding the culture, civilisation and identity of the West. The media may deny it, but soon there will be no more LGBTQ rights or women wearing what they want to wear. And it will be impossible for anyone to read books other than the Quran or to listen to music or to refuse to eat halal meat. Sharia Law will control our lives. And not in the distant future but soon.

The replacement is already at a late stage.

We need to wake up!

As an Aryan with pure English-Iranian heritage – Iran is the birthplace of the Aryans – I believe it is my duty to step up to the plate and do something.

I hereby commence the fightback.

It is six and getting dark. A film of water flows on the paving stones in the garden. The dead stems of the creeper plant are dimly visible. He draws the curtains. The introduction is impressive. A scroll up. The cover too. On a blue-purple gradient: 'The Future is Ours' written in chunky neon-pink type and a black sun wheel. The vaporwave aesthetic always delivers.

The packages lie on the mattress. He picks one up and paws it, provoking a pleasant crackling sound from the bubblewrap. The third and final one came this morning.

How could the process be so simple? Is it a trap?

For the umpteenth time, he replays everything. After five minutes of googling, he found a guide to accessing the Dark Web. He studied it, downloaded Tor Browser, pasted in a link a Rekrut had shared six months ago, and bingo, he entered a cryptomarket that looked exactly like eBay. *Browse Categories: Fraud, Drugs & Chemicals, Guides & Tutorials, Counterfeit Items, Digital Products, Jewels & Gold, Weapons, Carded Items, Services, Other Listings, Software & Malware, Security & Hosting*. 'Weapons' brought up reams of listings: listings for Glocks, listings for Colts, listings for Sig Sauers, listings for Berettas, listings for Ekol Voltrans, listings for Rugers, listings for Smith & Wessons. He soon found a seller who looked legit: MsDutchDynamite, 98 per cent positive feedback, no mentions in the cryptomarket's scam-reports section – where buyers can report problems with transactions and get admins to step in and adjudicate disputes – and no flags from the scam-watch team.

She was selling a Baikal IZH-79 with a hundred rounds of 9mm Czech ammo for 650 quid. 'The gun is used but never shooting at somebody.' It had formerly been a theatre prop and its serial number had been removed, making it untraceable. Having set his heart on a Renetti, his favourite *Call of Duty* pistol, he hesitated, wrestling with whether to buy a Baikal or hold out for a Renetti – and with whether MsDutchDynamite really was legit.

Eventually he took the plunge and messaged her, saying that he was interested in buying it. For two weeks, they then went back and forth, using PGP software, which provided end-to-end cryptographic privacy, at her insistence. David agreed to give his real name – using a fake one would increase the chances of the packages being intercepted – and they moved on to discussing payment.

Buying bitcoin turned out to be complex, the most complex part of the whole process. Bizarrely. But he figured it out and sent her the equivalent of 650 quid. Pressing 'transfer' was excruciating. With 650 quid, he could buy everything in the *Call of Duty* store: every operator skin, every blueprint, every tracer, every calling card.

He shrugged the thought away. The situation was too serious for such thoughts.

And now he has three packages in his possession, packages that need opening. If it transpires they contain worthless hunks of scrap metal, he will have to lodge a complaint on the crypto-market and hope the admins help him get his money back. They need opening. Yet seeing the parts of a Baikal IZH-79, not to mention a hundred rounds of 9mm Czech ammo, here, in his bedroom, and touching those parts, physically touching them – the prospect still unnerves him.

The replacement is at a late stage. He will open them soon, later tonight or tomorrow morning, tomorrow for sure. He closes his eyes. The Aryan fightback is coming. It is coming. He will make it up to everyone. Supreme Commander RitterKreuz will bestow an honorary title on him. New Rekruts will worship him. He will make it up to everyone. Saint BGMP5R1A.

HE DEVOTES SIX HOURS every day to aiming drills. Sitting cross-legged on the brown living-room carpet, he boots up *Call of Duty* and creates a Custom Game. Map: Factory. Mode: Free-for-all. Killcam: Disabled (so that bots spawn in continuously and there is no let-up). Spawn Ammo Mags: Max. Primary Weapon: X-16 pistol (his best bet, the closest option to a Baikal IZH-79).

Thanks to new performance thumbsticks, which add ten millimetres of height to the stock ones, reducing the amount of force that has to be applied and, so, hand fatigue, his controller is set up for slogs. Afternoons provide tricky conditions, as an oily spring light tends to seep in through the curtain gap and give the screen a sticky glare, but proficiency in all conditions is important.

His approach is to take laps around the map, attempt to snap on to targets within milliseconds of their appearing and score as many headshots as possible.

There remains room for improvement in his technique: a tendency to spray bullets, negligence in centring. Until he can secure headshot after headshot after headshot in *Call of Duty*, he will have no chance of carrying out the mission successfully, let alone racking up a Killstreak.

The morning after the arrival of the final package, he practises for five hours straight (still postponing the opening). His only breaks are to check whether Corey has messaged him.

Since his demotion from General to Offizier, most WOTAN members have acted differently towards him, Runningngunning a prime example. But he feels no self-pity. It *is* his fault.

Just past two, his stomach snivels. He skipped breakfast, nothing left in the fridge, the freezer or the cupboards. A trip to the newsagent's is required. The weekly trip. He loathes stepping foot in there, loathes it. The Muslim slimily welcoming him, asking how he is, how Dad is . . .

Another thirty minutes. Then he will suck it up. Another thirty minutes.

Keep the reticle in the centre of the screen. Keep the reticle in the centre of the screen. Keep the reticle in the centre of the screen. Keep the reticle in the centre of the screen.

Having registered on the *Times* for two free articles a week, he reads an exclusive interview with Karl.

The same shit.

'Yes, I have changed my mind and bitterly regret that comment. It was ill informed. Having now read more widely on the issue, I believe that Islam is, indeed, compatible with Western values. What happened outside Farfield school was shameful. I maintain that. However, the problem lay with the protestors, as people, not with Islam, as a religion. I should have realised that then. I realise it now.'

The interviewer challenges him with other comments he has made. 'No, I am passionately opposed to racism and have been my entire life. It is for morons. It belongs in the sewer.'

Nothing interesting. Karl is sticking to the stance he took in his official-website statement back in September. He is a sell-out. What is he thinking? David scrolls to the comments. 'I'm not sure he understands the word racism.' 'Not buying this.' He shakes his head in dismay. Karl has no backbone. That's the problem. He's like every other liberal elite celebrity. David thought he had courage but, no, he's a cuck, a cuck who betrayed the movement in exchange for – for what exactly? The SJWs will never forgive him. He will remain cancelled regardless. He betrayed the movement for nothing.

David closes the website. Whenever he reads something about Karl now, he experiences a creeping sensation on his skin. He will never forget the moment General LordofKek shared Karl's official-website statement and wrote: 'This is our Aryan ally? WTF?'

And Supreme Commander RitterKreuz's reaction . . .

It was right to strip David of his General rank. He was naive to think Karl was more than a cuck, pitifully naive. He should never have recommended him for air support, never.

Keen to suppress these thoughts, he opens Spotify, but no longer knows what to play. He settles on a random alt-rock playlist. The band names are unfamiliar to him. A track by Muse screeches on, fast and fuzzy. Better than nothing. He hates silence – more and more, it makes him uncomfortable.

In the sticky glow of his laptop, he opens his manifesto. The reaction of the mainstream media to the Ask Me Anything section will be priceless. What TV presenter has any experience of Reddit?

He scratches gunk out from under his fingernails and inspects his hands. The hairs on the backs are becoming longer and thicker and blacker by the day. It's infuriating. He has researched hair-removal creams on Amazon and would already have bought one were all the packages not so feminine. His order history might be leaked in an effort to embarrass him. Oh well. He focuses on the screen. Work.

Q. What makes you an authority on the Islamo-substitution of Aryan populations?

He fidgets with his Swiss Army knife.

A. Having lived in London my whole life, I've witnessed the impact of the Islamisation of Europe first hand. It's impossible to escape Islam here. On top of this, I have Iranian heritage. Iran was a world-leading Aryan civilisation of music and art and culture. Until the Islamic regime came and ruined everything. Now it is a wasteland. My mother fled Iran after the Islamic Revolution – blissfully unaware that Europe would meet the same fate.

This brings the word count up to the two thousand mark. It is shaping up to be his longest ever essay – even longer than college ones. With content like this, writing is simple.

Hassan

'HEY, WHAT'S UP, EVERYONE?' Hassan says, adjusting his headset and stiffly extending his legs under his gaming desk. 'How are you guys doing today? All good, I hope? Welcome to the stream. Let's get a roll call going.' He assumes a lively expression and scans the chat box. 'CKS, what's up? DavidtheGooner, what's up? Marcio Rodriguez, what's up? Farhaan, what's up? Ayoub Kilani, what's up? Africas Champ, thanks for the sub. Harvey, thanks for the three months. KrazyNZ, what's up? SaraJ, what's up?'

CKS **yo Hazza**

DavidtheGooner **hey mate**

Asianmoon123 **Irons! Irons! Irons!**

Marcio Rodriguez **all gd Hazza bro, love these twitch streams. I just had full acl reconstruction, metal screws and everything, so watching from bed. Just keep doing what you do. looking forward to watching you kill it in the FGS Qualifiers**

Matri XXX **Prediction for Arsenal v Newcastle?**

Gamerzz18 **we getting the new OTW FUT cards today or what?**

SkippyPeenut **What you reckon, Kane to stay or go in the summer?**

Jayback **Hey bro. I'm good, hope you are too. Reckon you'll finally pack R9 today? Hahahaha. Looking forward to some more sick skills in your games today. Your tekkers in the final game of your stream yesterday (the 4-0) – fk me respect**

Sam1911947 **Loving the new light in the background mate! Vibes!**

'Sorry to hear that, Marcio Rodriguez. Hope you make a swift recovery. I'm going to go for an Arsenal win, Matri, three–one. Just because Aubameyang has been on unstoppable form. I can see him grabbing a hat-trick. You know Newcastle will get a goal though. Yeah, three–one. What do you guys reckon? Pop your predictions in the chat. Good question, Gamerz. It says on the website they will be released today, the OTW cards. But I've seen no notifications in-game to suggest that. Classic EA, one thing on the website, another in-game. We'll just have to wait and see. Skippy, I've been saying it for weeks, Kane has to go. There's no way he is winning a major trophy at Spurs, and that has to be his ambition, the Premier League or the Champions League. Jayback, cheers, man. Appreciate the kind words. And R9? I would love that, absolutely love it. I'll open another twenty Packs today, don't worry. It has to happen soon. Right? Nice one, Sam. Glad you like them.'

Behind him: the West Ham mural and a colour-phasing light featuring PlayStation icons. Away from the eye of the webcam, his room is a jungle of empty cans and snack wrappers, but no one is any the wiser. Perversely, the installation of the webcam has made him more messy: the small area it captures is all he cares about. If it weren't for Mum's nagging, he would waste even less time tidying up and just leave it to their cleaner, who comes once a week (and is hot).

Back in January, he had fewer than a thousand followers. Now he has twelve thousand, plus 450 subscribers. That people not only enjoy watching him play FIFA but also enjoy interacting with him – have indeed created a community around him – remains hard to comprehend. If it weren't for the telephone befriending scheme, he would never even have had the confidence to try this.

'Just seen a few more of you have joined. Dayson, what's up? MasonMount4Ever, what's up? TBone, what's up? TinaTime, what's up? 1Ronaldo, thanks for the sub, bro. Salmon11, what's up?'

TBone **hey hazza lkin frward to watching another masterclass**

TinaTime **Could you talk us through your tactics please? Why you use a 3-4-1-2? etc**

Asianmoon123 **Irons! Irons! Irons!**

1Ronaldo **some more info on how to take free kicks would be good too**

Thirsty95 **^ Yh**

GeordieGold **Have you seen the Sonic film?**

'Cheers, TBone. Let's see what happens today. You never know. Getting closer to the FGS Qualifiers now, though, so I really hope I can maintain my form. Tina, sure thing. I'll make sure to set some time aside in this stream to talk you through my formation and tactics. Always happy to do that. I'll try to remember to share my thought process with the free kicks I take in games too, 1Ronaldo. Erm. Unfortunately, I haven't had the chance to watch the new Sonic film, Geordie. I've been too busy with FIFA and these streams for anything else, to be honest. But I'm sure I'll eventually get the chance. Recommend it? I enjoyed the game they released a few years ago. What was it called? Hang on. Let me check. *Sonic Mania*. That was it. *Sonic Mania*. Retro vibes. Recommend the film then? Has anyone else seen it? If so, share your thoughts in the chat, without spoilers, of course.'

On FIFA, Hassan has been mindlessly browsing the Transfer Market and FUT Store. He now navigates to Ultimate Team: Division Rivals and clicks 'play next match'. Searching for opponent.

Pack openings will come later in the stream.

'Yeah? You liked it, Geordie? You too, 1Ronaldo? I'll have to watch it then. Right. Let's get stuck in. We're playing someone called Salvatore2002. Yeah? You liked it too, Skippy? Okay, I'll have to watch it. Hey, check out his custom stadium – crazy banner. Anyone seen that before?'

David

'HERE,' DAVID SAYS.

'What is it?'

'Rice with jalfrezi sauce and bhajis.'

Dad regards the plate sceptically, suspiciously.

Having plonked it on the bedside table, beside which a toolbox redundantly hunkers, David sits, thinking he can smell, thinking he can smell – thinking he can smell piss. Is that possible?

Every night now he has to pause *Only Fools and Horses* two or three times in the opening ten minutes for Dad to pop to the toilet. His bladder is clearly . . . No, he bats these thoughts away.

This is supposed to be a nice moment. It will be a nice moment.

'I heated everything up,' David says. 'Jalfrezi sauce from the newsagent's.'

Dinner tonight may be oozing oil. But at least Dad will enjoy it. Getting him to eat healthily has proven impossible. David is throwing in the towel on that – for now.

'Jalfrezi?'

'Yeah.'

'Bhajis?'

'Yeah.'

Dad takes a long look at his clock. 'Are you eating now too?'

'Just heating my bhajis up.'

The microwave pings. 'You start eating,' David says. 'I'll be back in a second.'

'So there's no . . .'

'You start eating.'

When David returns, Dad is sitting up, slicing a bhaji, the plate in his lap. His belly bulges out from his sweatshirt and the circles under his eyes have taken on a purple hue and he has a week's worth of stubble. That he used to shave every morning without fail is unfathomable.

David tucks in as well. The meal is immeasurably better than any from the past six months. It's almost as if they are having a takeaway again. The only difference is that there are no poppadoms or pickles – and they speak less now. Dogs bark. A bus chugs past. That smell: is it piss?

'Good bhajis,' Dad says, licking his fingers.

Aside from some bubbles of sauce, his plate is empty.

'Yeah,' David says. 'They're from the newsagent's. Didn't realise the newsagent's sold bhajis. They had samosas too. We can try them next time.'

'Are we still having . . . You know, spinach and those things?'

'Let's take a break from that.'

Dad rests his head on his pillows and closes his eyes, the plate still on his lap. It is a crackling indigo outside. The windowpanes are fringed with cobwebs. Dad's breathing fills the silence: a husky, heavy whistle. David waits a minute and then asks: '*Only Fools and Horses* in a bit?'

'Sure.'

'Eight thirty?'

'Eight thirty.'

David sweeps up the leftover sauce on his plate with his second bhaji, carries the plates to the kitchen and slaps them in the sink. After his toilet breaks, Dad soon crashes out. He can no longer manage to stay awake for more than half an episode, regardless of when they start watching. David tends to stay until the first snores. Hands washed, he heads upstairs. That smell: was it piss?

Seeing Dad like this kills him. But he has to remember that

everything will soon change – everything. Once David has commenced the fightback, Dad will have something to live for: pride. And members of the movement will make him the most sought-after handyman on TaskRabbit.

Grinning, he sits on his bed. Sober, healthy and revitalised, Dad will visit him in prison every week. Mum may never visit him. But Dad will. He is a hundred per cent sure about that.

DAVID TAKES A GLASS and fills it up at the sink.

'You can use the water from the jug in the fridge,' Stephen says. 'It tastes better. Until we started using a filter jug, I never realised how hard, how dirty, the water is around here.'

'Don't worry.'

'Sure? We have Twinings Cold Infuse too.' He gestures at a red-and-white plastic jar by the kettle. 'They are meant for water bottles but work in glasses too. Just drop one in and stir it for a couple of minutes. That flavour is watermelon, strawberry and mint. It's nice.'

'Nah.'

Stephen samples a Brewdog and sets the small blue can back on the table, making sure to place it precisely back on its wet ring. 'Amira won't be long. No more than twenty minutes. She's still on the 149. There was a serious accident up by Liverpool Street in the afternoon – on the A10. All the roads were gridlocked when I was getting back too. It took me nearly an hour.'

'Okay,' David says, making to leave.

'Hey, since we're here . . . I was meaning to mention something.'

'What?'

'Well, I know you spend a lot of time on YouTube. And I know you have some strong political opinions . . . Have you heard of the YouTuber Destroyer?'

'No.'

Stephen taps his lower lip. 'No?'

'No.'

'You might like him . . . He's becoming extremely popular. He has four hundred thousand subscribers on YouTube and even more on Twitch. Someone at work mentioned him. Said he'd changed her son's life. Destroyer. He's ostensibly a professional gamer, who grew famous live-streaming *Starcraft*. But he's into politics too. He does political debates. You haven't heard of him?'

'No.'

David slouches in the doorway, waiting for Stephen to shut up, drinking his dirty water. Beside Stephen, an early-evening light silvers the leaves of an exotic plant. David has seen the plant before but not the pot, which is white with turquoise swirls and Persian writing.

Stephen continues. After his colleague's comments, he read up on Destroyer and learned a lot about him. A college dropout who grew up in the trollish quarters of the internet, he has a dark sense of humour, revels in confrontation, thinks no-platforming is counterproductive and hates PC culture. 'Disciple of Voltaire. But the interesting thing is . . . He's socially, economically, left-leaning and believes in social justice and respects Islam.' His elbow brushes the leaves.

'Mm-hm.'

'It aggravates Destroyer that the alt-right have taken control of words like "reason" and "rationality" and "science" and "facts" and "logic". Because he thinks that reason actually supports his views, not theirs, that facts actually support his views, not theirs . . . So he organises political debates with alt-right personalities and really tries to *own* them using reason and rationality and science.'

David wishes he could unhear Stephen saying 'own'.

'Anyway, so, my colleague said that her son was into some of the more, well, right-wing figures on YouTube and thought that debates were all about owning the libs. Then a Destroyer video was recommended to him and he watched it and was stunned to see a lib owning one of his favourite YouTubers, demonstrating that he was selling snake oil. It opened his eyes. He now loves Destroyer.'

'Mm-hm.'

'I really . . . Check him out. See what you think.'

'Mm-hm.'

Stephen claps his hands together. His light-blue shirt ripples. 'Great. Well. Don't want to keep you. You can head up. Oh. Actually. I forgot to ask. How's the boiler?'

David starts. 'Fine.' A few weeks ago, he sold Stephen an elaborate lie. He said that the boiler at home was bust. Dad called a heating engineer in to take a look and the heating engineer told them that a replacement pump was necessary and a powerflush of the whole system highly advisable. In total that would come to 650 quid, which he and Dad couldn't afford. Was there any way Stephen could loan them the money so they could get the work done? He agreed. Was there any way, any way at all, that Stephen could avoid mentioning the loan to Mum, as she would end up arguing with Dad about it. He reluctantly agreed to that too. On balance, David would have preferred not to have to trick Stephen into funding the mission. But saving up 650 quid for the Baikal would have been impossible, totally impossible.

'Giving you no trouble now?'

'Works perfectly.'

'Glad to hear that.'

'WELL, WHAT DO YOU KNOW?'

At the kitchen table, having high-protein granola and watching a *Call of Duty* YouTube video on his phone, David looks up: Zoe, in pink-and-white pyjamas.

'Oh. Hey.'

He hasn't seen her in months. She's put on weight, but her hair is as silly as ever, short, black and spiky with lavender tips.

'Have Amira and Dad left already?' she asks.

'Yeah. Mum and Stephen have.'

'Damn. I was planning to ask one of them to post something for me.'

'. . . Shouldn't you be at work?'

'I work from home on Thursdays and Fridays.' After her internship at Amnesty, Zoe landed a job at a PR company called Yoke, based in a WeWork building, with free Prosecco on tap.

'So . . . Shouldn't you be at home then? I mean, at your place?'

'Very funny. I was out in Shoreditch last night and couldn't bring myself to take the Overground. I got too drunk – in Jaguar Shoes. Do you know it?'

He shakes his head.

'Stumbling back here was about all I could manage. Yeah, I really need coffee.'

'Don't worry, I'm heading in a second.'

'You can stay. Jesus. There's no need to run away from me.'

She opens the fridge, takes out the filter jug, refills it at the sink and sets it by the coffee machine. A tinkling sound as water strikes the plastic base. She pivots to David. 'I know we don't hang out any more and we don't see eye to eye on everything. But that doesn't mean we can't ever talk. We're in the same room.'

'Ah. Am I un-cancelled then?'

She rolls her eyes. 'You're my stepbrother. We can talk. I'm not saying we need to go to gigs together or stay up all night chatting with wine. I'm just saying we can exchange small talk without there being this annoying awkwardness.'

'Okay.'

'*Okay?*'

'Okay.'

She sighs. 'Forget it.'

'Okay.'

She takes her mug from the cupboard, an orange-and-white porcelain fox with a bushy tail as a handle and paws on the base. Having put it on the drip plate, she evaluates the coffee capsules in the silver rotating tower rack, slots one in and presses a sequence of buttons. The machine whirrs and coffee trickles into her cup. It smells nice, actually coffee-like, fruity, earthy.

He would like a coffee but can't be bothered working out how to use the machine. He had got used to the ceramic cone and filter papers. He doesn't know why they upgraded to a machine – maybe out of pity for Zoe. It was impossible to place the cone on the fox mug, due to its raised ears. She always made her coffee in another mug and then poured it into the fox one. That she went to so much effort time and again annoyed him. A mug is a mug.

There is Kenco at home. He'll wait and have that. While she takes a seat opposite him, obnoxiously slurps her coffee and flicks at her phone, he scours the granola for more chunky cocoa clusters or chocolate pieces. They are all right. It's a shame there are so few of them.

'Hey,' she says. 'Come on. Let's talk.'

He gives up his search, scrunches up the plastic covering and pushes away the cardboard box, which was messily slashed open. The plastic makes popping sounds as it unfurls again.

'Sure.'

'How are you?'

David meets her eyes. 'Me? Good.'

'Really?'

'Yeah.'

'Dad said that you're still looking for a job?'

He smirks. 'Yeah.'

'Sorry.' She wraps her hands round her mug. 'That must be shit. Going to the Jobcentre every week to meet a work coach sounds like a nightmare too.'

'It is what it is.'

'Guessing they're super-incompetent and hopeless?'

'It is what it is.'

'You'll find something soon.'

'Mm.'

A sympathetic smile.

After a short silence, she says: 'You won't believe this, but I quit smoking.'

'What? Why?'

'Erm. I fractured a rib coughing.'

'You fractured a rib coughing?'

'I know, right? It was a crazy cough, even by my standards. I was coughing so often for so many weeks that one of my upper ribs . . . It sucked. I had to lie in bed for ages. Doing nothing. I couldn't move without my chest killing me. I was alternating between paracetamol and ibuprofen every two hours. Eleanor had to bring me water and snacks and help me up to go to the bathroom.'

'Oh.'

'Yeah, it sucked. Afterwards, I figured enough was enough.'

'You reckon it was the smoking then?'

'Probably. My GP said I have mild asthma.'

'Shit.'

'Yeah, so no more cigarettes for me. Guess that's life.'

He nods blankly and returns to his phone. The *Call of Duty* video has finished playing and a new one – 'Most Viewed Twitch Clips of All Time!' – has started. He closes YouTube and reflexively opens Twitter. A fractured rib? Bloody hell. @JustaUKPirateship: 'Islam is infiltrating UK society at every level and we are letting it happen and expecting life not to change? What is wrong with

British people? Wake up! Before it's too late!' David shifts faintly in his seat. Zoe is probably exaggerating. No one has ever fractured a rib coughing. Smoking must no longer be woke. That must be it.

She taps the table with her black nails. 'Good about Karl Williams, at least.'

'What?'

'That he's turned away from the far right and at long last condemned racism. I'm not sure I forgive him. But I'm relieved that he still has a sense of right and wrong. And at least now Universal will keep him on and there will be new music from him. I'm glad. I get how much he means to you.'

David laughs bitterly, sourly.

'What?' Zoe says. 'I'm serious. I'm happy for you.'

'He's part of the liberal Islamophilic elite. Just like every other celebrity.'

'Karl Williams?'

'His new music will be shit. He's a cuck.'

'. . . Karl Williams?'

'Yeah.'

'Are you taking the piss?'

'No.'

'. . . I can't even . . . You worshipped him. You stuck by him through everything.'

A shrug. 'I guess I've grown out of that.'

Hassan

DISBELIEVINGLY, HASSAN RE-READS THE WHISPER.

Hi Hassan,

My name is Memphis Cillessen. I work for Sirius (www.siriusxp.org) – an esports talent management and content creation company.

Great stuff on the streams. I've been monitoring your progress on Twitch over the past few months. You're building up a sizeable following and have real FIFA talent.

I would be keen to chat to you about an exciting opportunity, which I think would interest you. My number is 07592 928521. Call me.

Kind regards,
Memphis

His desk banded with sunbeams, a custard scent lingering in the air from a post-workout shake, he scans the latest blog posts on the website. 'Inter has signed a partnership with esports agency Sirius alongside announcing its new FIFA team.' 'Iconix energy drink new main sponsors of Sirius esports.' 'Sirius announces esports partnership with Club Brugge.'

Chewing his lips, he weighs up whether Sirius and Memphis Cillessen are legit. The neon-on-black colour scheme, clean pages and slick headers and footers bode well. Everything looks professional. He navigates to the teams section. *Feyenoord, Ajax, Wolves, Inter Milan – West Ham*. What? No way. West Ham? A Google search for 'West Ham Sirius' returns a result from www.whufc.com, confirming the partnership. Sirius is legit – it is legit. In a flap he fumbles for his phone.

'Ah, Hassan.'

Memphis speaks with a bright, officey voice, simultaneously hearty and hollow. He explains that he is en route to a meeting at the Johan Cruyff Arena and appreciates that Hassan also operates on a tight schedule. 'Shall I cut straight to the chase?'

'Sure.'

'Do you want a career in esports?'

'Of course.'

'Excellent. Well, I think we can make that happen.'

'Really?'

'Have you visited our website? If so, I imagine you will have seen that we work with West Ham. We handle esports recruitment, content creation and coaching and performance management for them. Ambitious club. Actually, the first in the Premier League to enter the esports domain. A forward-thinking digital and commercial director. Anyway, they are currently in the market for a new esports player and I think you could conceivably be a suitable fit.'

Hassan widens his eyes. 'Me?'

'This is by no means an offer – but I would be keen to explore the possibility.'

'Okay.'

'How are you fixed for Monday evening?'

Hassan is free. He planned to watch West Ham v Watford on Sky Sports, but that's it. Memphis chuckles. 'We have a box at the Olympic Stadium. Want to watch it from there?'

'Wow. I mean. Yeah. Obviously.'

'Right. How about I schedule a meeting for us from, say, five thirty to six thirty? Afterwards you can have a bite to eat, soak up the atmosphere and chat to a current West Ham esports player before kick-off. Does that sound okay to you? I'll message you with all the details.'

'Sure.'

'Perfect. Questions?'

Hassan hesitates. 'Would it be okay to bring someone?'

'Not a problem. When replying, let me know their details and I'll sort them out with a pass.'

'Great.'

'Right. I'm heading underground. I'll message you this evening.'

'Thanks.'

'Speak soon, Hassan. Looking forward to Monday. Take care.'

He rises, performs the robot, a celebration popularised by Peter Crouch, opens the window and shouts: 'Get in!' A passer-by smiles up in bemusement. 'Lose Yourself' then 'Shape of You' then 'Stronger' then 'Lose Yourself' a second time – then he has to share the news.

Answering the phone, Dad sounds worried. 'Is everything okay?' In the background, the clang of a knife on a chopping board, the baying of a radio presenter, and the jerky hiss and pop of oil.

'Can you close early on Monday?'

'Monday?'

'Please, Dad. It's the least busy night. Just once.'

'Why?' His voice rises. 'Is everything okay?' A grizzle of age audible. The radio melts away. Hassan waits, wanting to savour his next sentence. 'Is everything okay?' Dad repeats.

'So we can *go* to West Ham v Watford.'

'West Ham v Watford?'

'Yep.'

'At the stadium?'

'Yep.'

In the silence, he can practically hear Dad thinking.

‘Will it not be sold out? Remember, we tried to buy tickets before but—’

‘Dad, we’ve been offered the chance to watch it in a VIP box.’

‘What? How?’

While Hassan recounts the conversation, emphasising the word ‘career’ and explicitly referring to his streaming as work – not a hobby, work – Dad rustles cutlery.

‘This isn’t a scam? A lot of scams online.’

‘It’s legit. Trust me.’

‘Hmm.’

‘Trust me.’

Out of sight of the webcam, his shower towel hangs over the wardrobe door. He swings the door. In pink, green, blue and red, the PlayStation icons gleam on the bedside table.

‘Trust me.’

David

IT LIES ON THE DESK assembled, actually assembled. The instructions in the PDF were easy to follow, even semi-pissed. Aware that he could delay no longer, he necked a Heineken to settle his nerves. Four cans later, the packages were open. Sunlight pours into his room. As he tilts it, ribs of inky shadow roll over the black frame. Heavy. Heavier than expected. He strokes the frame with his thumb and points it at the poster from *Uncut* and wraps his shooting finger around the trigger. The barrel level with his nostrils, he looks fixedly over it at Karl. According to Quora, it will have some serious recoil. Luckily, taming recoil is one of his *Call of Duty* strengths, and, though there will be more kickback in real life, and no aim assist, the recoil patterns will be the same. He sets it down.

What now? He is still waiting for sirens, for police officers to descend on the house. How can obtaining a Baikal have been this easy? His chest is panting with excitement.

It is there, there, on his desk, a Baikal IZH-79 – on his desk.

The only outstanding task is to select a mission skin. He stashes it away and staggers tipsily to the living room to study Alliance and Federation operators for inspiration. Even though he won't be comparably big – his plans to put on muscle scrapped – he still intends to look the part. *Call of Duty*'s menu music plays, moody and menacing, helicopter blades crackling in. He begins with the Alliance operators – combat vests, tank tops, caps, bandanas, nothing that would suit him – before moving on to the Federation ones. Arkady stands out, wearing a black military jacket with metallic buttons and black ropes plus a necklace with a rose pendant. A style that would suit him, without being too conspicuous for the streets of London. He scoots closer to the screen. Arkady has a tattoo across his right-hand knuckles. That might suit him too. But what would his tattoo read? Just a minute later he knows: WOTAN . . . a searing final sight for the Muslim cockroaches and an Easter egg for Supreme Commander Ritter-Kreuz or the Generals to find in news reports.

Heineken number five flowing, he browses eBay and searches for a tattoo salon.

Tweak Tweak Today at 14:00
Another one for ya^

General LordofKek Today at 14:05
Sweeeeeeet

Supreme Commander RitterKreuz Today at 14:10
Good work. You are a credit to the cause @Tweak Tweak

David crosses his legs and crushes his right toes against the wall with the heel of his other foot. Tweak Tweak's meme is funny – funny, but nothing special. The meme he shared in the #meme-library earlier is equally valuable. How come no one commented on it, not Supreme Commander RitterKreuz, not a General, no one? Oh well. It's irrelevant. Because it's only a matter of time. Once the mission has been executed, he will be the cynosure of all eyes: Aryans the world over will sing his praises. Rather than on memes and raids and idle chit-chat, he is right to concentrate on his manifesto, which is now over three thousand words long. He pulls out a knot of eyebrow hairs, knuckles his forehead. There are more issues he would like to cover in the AMA.

Q. Are irl missions necessary?

A. Yes. We cannot stop the Islamisation of Europe and the United States with media guerrilla warfare alone. Don't get me wrong, YouTube raids etc are important. But they are not enough. The fight can't be won with memes and words. It can only be won with ACTION. The media is controlled by elites, who support the replacement. They hold ALL the strings online and are limiting the impact of our media guerrilla warfare. They will soon start to censor everything we say. They will establish Sharia law on Twitter and Facebook and all other platforms. We need to start taking action, REAL IRL ACTION, before it's too late. With irl missions we can stop the Islamisation of Europe and the United States. We can show Muslims already in Europe and the United States that they are unsafe – as Aryans are presently unsafe – and force them to leave. And show Muslims thinking about invading that they are unwelcome and should NOT come. The irl missions will also instil a fighting spirit in Aryans who were previously unaware of the seriousness of the situation.

Q. Can I execute an irl mission? Can anyone execute an irl mission?
A. Yes. You can and SHOULD. Answer the call of duty. Take up arms and fight NOW. As an Aryan, you belong to the brotherhood. There is no network. There is no central command. Just an Aryan brotherhood. The whole world should understand that the fight-back is underway and we Aryans are going to strike again and again and again until politicians start to listen and stop the Islamisation of Europe and the US or civil wars start and the replacement is stopped that way. Whichever way is fine. But it must be stopped.

WHILE THE BATHROOM LIGHT staggers on, David raises the toilet seat and takes a piss, fixing on the flecks of shit in the bowl. This is his way of cleaning it.

He flushes, zips up and in a hazy orange light stares in the mirror.

A twenty-first-century Aryan knight. He laughs with surprise. He looks even cooler than Arkady – him. The black military tunic is perfect for the mission. That it only cost a tenner is remarkable. Aside from a musty, smoky pang, it is in excellent condition. He loves the gold-fringed shoulder straps and gold buttons with eagle icons. The skin is completed by a silver shield-charm necklace, a black scoop-neck T-shirt, black skinny jeans and Dr Martens, with white laces of course.

Leaning in, he examines his face and is relieved to see that the Veet hair-removal cream has worked. He bought it exclusively for his hands but ended up using it on his nose and his cheeks and between his eyebrows too. It all needed to go. The press photos will not show a savage.

He removes the gun from his pocket and points it at the bubble-glass window.

The tattoo will look great on his right hand. There are two places in East London that allow walk-in appointments and use vegan ink: Last Rites and White Rabbit. On his way back from Haggerston, he will go to one of them. That will give him about a week – two scrubbed visits – in which to execute the mission. Mum or Stephen cannot see the tattoo. They would lose their shit and call Prevent. Dad seeing it will be fine. There's no chance he will google its meaning.

A sneeze. He's been sniffing since the morning. His throat is a tad sore too. He spits into the sink and wipes his mouth with the back of his hand. His heart hums, spine tingles. He is a twenty-first-century Aryan knight, a twenty-first-century Aryan knight, a twenty-first-century Aryan knight.

KNOCKS. 'I'M COMING IN.'

'Mm.'

'Okay?'

'Mm.'

He rolls on to his side, the duvet up over his shoulders, grazing his chin. On the Overground, he felt fine. Now, shit. One Christmas, Dad got him tickets to WWE Live at Wembley Arena. For the next three weeks, David spent his spare time researching wrestling – which he had no knowledge about – and reading reviews of various restaurants they could eat at afterwards. Then on the morning of the event he woke up feeling so sick that he couldn't go, that Mum wouldn't let him go. They had to throw the tickets away, and he never had the opportunity to experience a public event like that with Dad, something they might later be able to reminisce about. The memory has direly resurfaced, along with the disappointment. Why can his body not cope with excitement?

'A slice of toast with a vegan dark-chocolate spread for you,' Mum says, bringing in a tray.

'I'm fine.'

'You need to eat something.'

'I'm fine.'

'I made some *sekanjabin*, too, with agave syrup instead of honey. My mother always made that for me when I was ill. I'll leave the tray here.' She puts it on the bedside table, beside a mountain of crumpled tissues, and sits on the mattress. David pulls his knees up towards him, away from her. 'Don't worry. I won't stay long.' After a short silence he tries the *sekanjabin*. Decent. But he is too nauseous to have it. She swivels the jar of chocolate spread, on which 'Vego' is written in big chunky colourful letters. 'When you were young and you were feeling ill, you used to love Nutella. It was the only thing I could get you to eat.' He nods, longing for the two paracetamol tablets to take effect. 'Hopefully this will be nice.' An engine revs outside, tugging his attention to the window. With the curtains shut, the sole light in the room comes from a plump floor-standing rice-paper lamp, which softens the bulb's glow. Next to it, the sparsely populated white bookshelves have an orange hue. Most books are in the living room. Those up here are ones Stephen and Mum want to hide from sophisticated visitors. They share the shelves with bath towels and spare bedding.

'Can I show you something?' Mum asks.

'Mm?'

'I know you're ill, and probably not interested now – maybe not at all anyway – but Sayeeda sent more of Baba's things, including a small painting, one of the few that weren't destroyed.'

'Okay.'

'Yeah? I'll be back in a second then. Have more of the *sekanjabin*.'

She returns with an A3 painting and holds it up. In the foreground, squares and rectangles. In the background, the jagged outline of a mountain. 'It's a cityscape, of sorts. From nineteen ninety-two, when he'd eliminated colour from his work and was painting only with shades of grey.'

'Cool.'

'It is, isn't it? I'm so glad that I actually have one of his paintings here now.' She leans it against the bookshelves. 'I think . . . I think I will try to start writing that memoir.'

'Mm?'

'Yeah, I want to, I should. I'd like more people to know about him. Stephen has an old university friend who might be able to help get it published. And I have so much material. There was another notebook in the package Sayeeda sent . . . In it, Baba says that when he was twenty-five, he already felt twenty-five thousand years old. And there's a glued-in drawing he must have done when he was three or four on a page from his father's account book. Every Friday, when he was young, his father would take him to his office and let him do whatever he wanted, so he'd choose to draw in the account books . . . There are so many anecdotes. I want to make something of them.'

'Go for it.'

'You think?' A smile. 'Well . . . I should let you rest—'

'Stay.'

She checks his forehead with the back of her hand. 'Gosh. You really are burning up.'

He bats it away. 'I'm fine. Stay.'

'Sure.'

To mitigate the throbbing, he closes his eyes.

'. . . So . . . I had the idea that we could do something small to mark Nowruz this year. It used to be such a big thing when I was young, basically a two-week spring celebration, but on the actual day, we would have *sabzi polo*, a traditional dish, with *haft seen*, a mix of these seven items beginning with the letter s – *sabzeh*, *samanu*, *senjed*, *serkeh*, *seeb*, *seer* and *somāq*. I was thinking I could make vegan versions of *sabzi polo* and the *haft seen* spread and you could come . . .'

'When is it?'

'Monday, the twenty-first. I mean, not a big celebration. Just some fun in the evening.'

Impossible. He will have the tattoo. But he's too weak to fight with her now. And, well, maybe he could postpone the tattoo, postpone the mission for a week? What is a week?

'Okay.'

'You would be up for that?'

'Mm.'

'That would be lovely.'

A second sip of *sekanjabin*, so thirsty – but so nauseous.

'Oh,' Mum says. 'You might not remember her, but I bumped into Laura and her mother over the weekend on Colombia Road. They were buying plants at the flower market.'

'Who?'

'Laura Carmichael. From primary school. You liked her.'

He twitches a shoulder. '. . . Don't remember.'

‘Her mother and I used to speak at the gates. Laura is studying Medicine at UCL now and told me to pass on her best wishes.’

‘Mm.’

She swirls her bracelet. ‘David, there’s something I’ve been meaning to talk to you about for a while. Maybe this is as good a time as any. You’re usually preoccupied.’

‘What?’

‘Seeing Laura and her mother reminded me that . . . Last time I mentioned primary school to you, many months ago, you flew into a rage and I dropped the subject.’

‘Mum.’

‘This is important.’

‘Mum, I feel like crap. Please.’ He thrashes his feet. ‘Please.’

‘Just listen. I’ll think about saying this forever otherwise. I know you’re feeling ill, and I don’t want to stress you. But this doesn’t need to be stressful. Just listen.’ He groans, wondering what gash she is going to come out with. ‘Don’t worry.’ A shushing noise. ‘Just listen. Just listen. Just listen . . . Oh, David, how can I say this?’ She drags out her words. ‘I know what happened to you at primary school was horrible, and I know you want to erase it from your memory. I understand that. Trust me, I understand that. I feel terrible bringing this up. Like a torturer. But with the views—’

‘Mum—’

‘Sometimes it’s important to engage with bad things that have happened to you and learn lessons from them. Nothing in life is simple, black and white. At primary school—’

‘Mum!’

‘At primary school you were viciously bullied by the other boys, and they were English boys, white boys. So this view of the world you have adopted – it doesn’t hold up. You might not admit it, but I know that something happened in college and that whatever happened has made you . . . But I had to . . . Your primary-school headmaster called me in to see him multiple times, ten times, maybe more, and each time I would sit in his office listening to these vile things that were being done to you, and each time my heart would break. I still remember when—’

'Go away!'

'David, in the playground at lunch they would kick the ball at you and pull your trousers down and write sick things on your backpack and steal your shoes and hide them, and so much more. I used to send you to school with a purple Batman lunchbox. Do you remember it? You were so happy choosing it. And I made the mistake of giving you *tachchin* – that Iranian saffron rice cake – one day. And you got bullied so badly for that. The boys said it stank and refused to sit next to you.'

'Fuck you!' David shouts. 'I'm . . . I'm ill.'

She briefly rests her head in her hands. 'I find it so hard to think about primary school too. It should have been a happy time for you . . . You don't like hearing this and I don't like saying it. Trust me. This isn't fun. The reason I'm saying it is because I don't want you to become like them, to see things in a naive way, and I don't know how else to get you to . . . I don't know . . . I'm worried.'

'Stop it! Stop it!' He covers his ears. 'La-la-la-la-la—'

'David—'

'Stop it!'

His stomach heaves, prompting him to wrinkle shut his mouth and whimper. He has shown weakness and she is capitalising on it – brainwashing him, with made-up memories. Nothing she is saying is true. Nothing. Nothing. Nothing. 'Stop it,' he pleads. 'Stop it.'

She looks pityingly at him. 'Okay . . . Don't worry. Don't worry.' When she attempts to touch his ankles, he kicks out at her and then wriggles away. 'Okay . . . You rest. I'll leave.'

She is brainwashing him. Stephen brainwashed her. Now she is brainwashing him. The mistake he made was to show weakness. God, he feels nauseous, horribly nauseous. It is coming. Any second now he will throw up. It is coming. He closes his eyes and repeats *fuck* through his teeth.

'FIRST TATTOO?'

'Yeah.'

David is in the lobby of White Rabbit, sitting opposite a tattooist (spiky ice-blonde hair, stretched earlobes, crackling beard). The walls are coated with graffiti art – in a white speech bubble, pink spray paint reads 'vegan skin candy' – and industrial-chic balloon lamps in black metal cages hang from the ceiling. He would have preferred somewhere less hipster. But he's here now.

'And you're sure you want it on the knuckles?' the tattooist asks. 'Because that is one of the more painful locations.' He passes David a laminated sheet of paper, with an image of a human body coloured yellow, orange, red and purple. The knuckles are red, the second-highest pain category, along with the face, neck, chest, knees and feet. 'Given that this is your first tattoo, you might want to think about getting it in a yellow or orange zone. Saying that, it is up to you.' The wrists are orange, biceps yellow. David wonders how painful the knuckles will be. Metallica's 'Enter Sandman' razors out from a small Marshall speaker, bringing back his headache. He skims his fingers along his jaw. He took four paracetamol tablets on the way, but red is the second-highest category. Only the groin, nipples and inner elbow are purple. There are roses and dragons and Chinese characters on the tattooist's arms. Yet nothing on his hands or fingers. A reason for that?

'You can think it over and come back some other time. No pressure.'

This is ridiculous. He wanted to get a tattoo on his knuckles. He will get a tattoo on his knuckles. Leaving the house in the morning was a challenge. He felt better, but some way away from well. Arms floppy. Ground wobbly. Dressing took twenty minutes.

Still, he was hell bent on pressing ahead with the plan. He needs to move fast before Mum succeeds in brainwashing him.

'Don't worry. It's fine. I want it on the knuckles.'

'Sure? Okay.' The tattooist goes over to a dark wooden table on which are action figures – *Star Wars*? – and a large Starbucks cup. He takes a form from a drawer. 'I'll need you to fill this in.'

David stares in triumph at his right hand.

'You made it. Feeling okay?'

'Yeah.'

In one corner of the room, spools of retro VHS tape lamps shine red, green and blue. In another, a garden gnome stands sentry, sporting a Santa hat. Ink bottles with twist tops huddle on thin shelves. The dark walls are daubed with A4 sketches, drawings. At moments during the process it felt as if he were being clawed by a stray cat – and he did shed a tear or two. But the tattooist assured him that everyone did, and that he was brave sticking to his guns and going for the knuckles.

'Dig it?'

'Definitely.'

Etched into him: WOTAN. When he requested a blackletter font, the tattooist presented him with stacks of options: A Dark Wedding immediately stood out. It was exactly as he'd envisioned.

'So. Everything will be on the aftercare form. Some basics. Leave the cling-film wrap on for an hour. Then, in an hour, or whenever you're back home, remove it and wash the hand with warm, soapy water. Not burning hot. Just warm.' He inspects the tattoo. 'Your skin isn't looking too red, so it shouldn't be sore for long. What else? Oh. Don't use hand cream today or tomorrow. Don't swim in the next week, ideally not in the next fortnight. Apart from that . . .'

'Okay.'

'Don't scratch it, obviously. Don't pick at it.'

'Okay.'

'The rest will be on the form.'

'Okay.'

'Perfect. Follow me then.' Back in the lobby, a small black printer spits it out. He staples the pages together and passes it to David. 'You a big DC comics fan?'

'Sorry?'

'I thought I recognised Wotan from somewhere. It's the name of a DC comics character, right? The enemy of Doctor Fate?'

'Yeah. That's it. DC comics.'

'Nice one, man. Got a lot of time for a left-field choice. Do plenty of DC tattoos, but usually Batman, The Joker, Aquaman, Superman, The Flash, Green Lantern. You know?'

'Yeah.'

'Actually, a fair few Catwoman and Wonder Woman ones now too. But Wotan is a first.'

'Right.'

'Do you mind if I take a photo for our Instagram page?'

'Go for it.'

As he steps over with his iPhone, David looks away, worried he will start laughing. After the mission has been executed, the Instagram post will go viral. The tattooist will be interviewed on BBC News, on ITV News, on Sky News. Their conversation will be recounted word for word.

General LordofKek Today at 15:03
Just seen that the anniversary of Chappe Gallery is coming up

General LordofKek Today at 15:07
Didn't realise it was a YEAR ago

LobsterSins68 Today at 15:10
Fuck really?

LobsterSins68 Today at 15:10
Crazy thought it was like 6 months

Tweak Tweak Today at 15:11
And there's still been no payback :(:(

Tweak Tweak Today at 15:11
cmon boys lol

Runningngunning Today at 15:12
I know someone who's cuz was killed in the Chappe shooting

Runningngunning Today at 15:12
cool French dude. Really shit

Tweak Tweak Today at 15:12
fucking hell man that fucking sucks

David keys 'Chappe shooting' into Google and learns that it is true: the one-year anniversary *is* coming up. Monday, this Monday. His pulse surges. Of course. It took place on Easter Sunday, and Easter was in late March then. Of course. He cracks his knuckles. A blue sky, with salmon smears. Tweak Tweak is right. There has been no payback. Humiliating. A sense of certainty frolics in his spine.

He pops a can of tropical-fruits Red Bull and swirls the liquid round his palate for some time before swallowing. The normal one is nicer.

Monday. Is this the sign he was waiting for? It makes sense. Monday. Not Tuesday. Not Wednesday. Monday. It makes sense. He can execute the mission on Monday, and it will be for Nmoos, Nmoos and his cousin. 'Monday.' He vocalises it. 'Monday.'

He raises a palm to block out the sunlight. Monday. The fight-back will commence on Monday. A snicker. Nowruz. He will be celebrating Nowruz too. 'The Future is Ours' is complete. The Baikal rests in his room. His skin has been constructed. He even reconnoitred the mission location last night and saw no obvious snags. Doing so, he shivered and shuddered and even felt a little unsure. But he is confident that will not be the case on Monday. Reading up on the tricks and techniques of past Aryan warriors, he found out that prior to undertaking his mission in Bergen Knut Karlsen took an ECA stack, which allowed his brain to absorb more oxygen, settling his nerves and boosting his confidence. David intends to follow his lead. He will order ephedrine on the Dark Web, where most substances are available with next-day delivery. Caffeine tablets? Boots. Aspirin? Same.

There is nothing to prevent him from executing the mission on Monday.

He angles his right hand towards him: Mum and Stephen will see his tattoo for the first time in press photos or TV coverage. He can barely sit still now. Monday.

Forty-eight hours. Forty-eight hours. He wonders how he should spend them, aside from undertaking more aiming drills. Is there anything he will miss? Not really. Even the Dark Fury *Call of Duty* sessions are no longer fun. If he takes part, the voice chat turns frosty, Runningngunning saying nothing, except for the occasional 'kill me' or 'fuck's sake' or 'so shit' in response to a missed shot from him. Being under twenty-one, he cannot get a 'whole life' order – he will get a 'custody for life' order, meaning that after serving his 'minimum term' he will be considered for release on parole. In ten years, he will be out. The parole board will be sympathetic to the cause. What are ten years? The franchise will still be going and everyone will want to play with him then, everyone.

'SHALL WE WATCH "It's Only Rock and Roll"?'

'That one's funny,' Dad says, picking at his lips.

David studies the descriptions on the different jewel cases. 'Hmm. "The Miracle of Peckham" is funny too. And "The Longest Night".'

'Mm.'

'Which one do you like best?'

'The first one?'

'That's where Rodney joins a band and Del appoints himself their manager and books them to play the Shamrock Club on St Patrick's Day.'

'That's funny.'

'You like "The Miracle of Peckham" a lot too, though, right? That's the one where the priest sees the Virgin Mary statue weeping and Del convinces him to publicise it and cash in.'

'Mm.'

'So,' David says, stress edging into his voice. 'Which one then?' Dad sneezes, his nose red and runny, having caught whatever David had earlier in the week. 'You okay?'

'It's nothing.'

'Sure?'

Dad stares at the TV. 'They're both funny.'

Although he knows every word of every episode, David re-reads the descriptions, desperate to make the right choice. This is the last time they will watch *Only Fools and Horses* together for a decade. The episode needs to match the moment. It needs to be perfect.

'Shall we go for "The Miracle of Peckham" or . . . maybe . . . No, let's go for that.'

While Dad leans securely back, David inserts the disc. How long will Dad manage to stay awake? There is a hilarious scene approximately fifteen minutes into the episode, which it would be great to get to. Dad brings a hand to his slack mouth, as though he were holding a cigarette, jerks and reaches for the Pringles tube. David asks whether he is ready.

'Mm.'

Having spent ten minutes willing Dad to wake up, he presses 'pause'. It's not happening. Bladder empty, Dad is fiercely snoring. David ejects the disc, returns it to its jewel case and slots that into the yellow-and-red box set. Saliva has built up on Dad's lower lip. David kneels beside him. He wants to be strong, strong like Captain Garrett, strong like Dad was in the army. He swipes at a tear and takes a big, soft hand. In a decade, they will watch *Only Fools and Horses* together again, with Dad alert and awake throughout and the two of them laughing together.

'See you, Dad. Visit me.' The snores fizz on. 'Yeah, I know. You will. You will . . . Don't worry, I'll remember the lines to all the episodes. We can recite them to each other through the glass. I'll look forward to that . . . Well . . . Take care.' His voice clogs up. 'I'll make you proud, I promise.'

Hassan

'KALA, HERE,' MUM SAYS, holding out a chew stick. 'Kala.'

A cautious lick, then Kala takes it over to her corner of the kitchen, pins it between her paws and starts on it. 'A new one. Lily's Kitchen. It is better for her than the ones we used to buy. It has turkey, honey, sweet potato, broccoli . . . She seems to be enjoying it.'

'Mm,' Hassan says, filling his bowl with Frosties.

Mum leans against the kitchen counter in an earthy brown jumper. There is a faint, fading smell of melted butter from the *balushahi* she made this morning. A bleachy sunlight has swept over the prints on the wall. By the porcelain vase, a fat fly buzzes. Every now and then, a scratchy clank sounds from the washing machine, leading him to worry that he again left coins in a jeans pocket.

'I researched Sirius,' Mum says.

'And?'

'You're right. It seems fine.'

'I told you.'

'But . . .' She taps her thigh with a spoon. 'That has only made me more upset.'

'Why?'

'Because this really might happen.'

'Mum.'

'I'm sorry. I want to support you. But esports has so many problems.'

Hassan groans. 'Not again.'

'These people will make you practise more, more, more, to be able to compete with FIFA players from South Korea, Russia. First, it will be twelve hours a day. Then fourteen. Then sixteen. And that is not safe. You will develop nerve damage or carpal tunnel syndrome or arthritis. I have read about it. Many esports players do. You will end up having to retire before you're twenty-five. And then what? You will have no profession, no way of earning money. Just a lifetime of pain.'

'I'll be careful – take regular breaks, sleep eight hours, keep exercising, everything.'

She shakes her head. 'You got three Bs. Those are good grades. If you had applied to the University of West London through clearing you would have got in. And then you could have got a job in the gaming world, but it would have been a graduate one, a safe, reliable one, which you could still have been doing in your sixties – journalist, promoter, event manager.'

'I don't want to be a journalist or a promoter or an event manager. No one in their right mind would want to when they could be an esports athlete. No one. This is . . . And if I have to retire in my twenties – who cares? All it will take is a few tournament wins and I'll have a million to live on.'

'Hassan . . .'

He nudges his Frosties. 'You're worse than Dad.'

A bee knocks on the windowpane by her flowers, hoping to be let in. The letterbox flaps open with a squeak, and a takeaway menu lands on the doormat in the hallway.

'You realise that Tariq will be interrogating this Memphis man on Monday?' Mum says.

'. . .'

'And that you won't be agreeing to anything without our permission?'

'. . .'

She crosses her arms. 'Hassan?'

'Fine. Whatever. Can I now look forward to it in peace?'

He is praying that meeting the Sirius team and receiving VIP treatment in the Olympic Stadium will change Dad's mind, will convince him that esports is lucrative, prestigious.

And that he in turn will convince Mum.

She sighs. 'Okay . . . I do want you to enjoy the day regardless . . . It is incredible that Tariq has never been to a game before. He must have been supporting West Ham for thirty years. Even when I first met him and he was living in Gants Hill he had a keyring.' Her serious expression melts away and laugh lines crinkle around her eyes. 'He said that he is planning to buy this season's shirt and wear it under his blazer . . . I will need photos of that.'

David

IT'S HERE. THE MORNING: here, finally here.

His insides tingle. A barely touched Pop Tart lies cheerlessly on his plate, surrounded by pink sprinkles. He takes a last stab at it, convulses, and throws it away.

ECA stack time. With shaking hands, he reads the instructions on his phone, crushes up the ingredients, slides the various white powders into a glass, runs the tap for a few seconds, fills the glass and gives it a good swirl. That the ECA stack works is essential. If his hands continue to shake like this, he will never manage to control the recoil. He rubs his right eyebrow. There is no need to worry. There is no need to worry. Everything he has read suggests that the ECA stack will work.

He will have it a minute or two before leaving, so that the effects kick in when he is on the Overground and last for the whole mission. What now? Midday. The place will still be empty.

A sweep of Twitter. @Kermitthetoad: 'Never forget Chappe Gallery. Never forget Chappe Gallery. Never forget Chappe Gallery. Never forget Chappe Gallery. Never forget Chappe Gallery.' @LilyEngland87: 'there you go with the racist card lolol. how many times: islam is a religion not a race.' @useyournoodle555: 'Sharia law has no place in a civilised society. how it can be allowed to go on oh bcs the msm & Soros.' @katiegirl84: 'violence = islam since forever and forever. bangalore riots. delhi riots. 1993 bombay bombings. hindu genocide in kashmir. 9/11 US. 7/7 UK. taliban afghanistan. isis syria, iraq. Chappe Gallery. list is endless.' He 'likes' every tweet.

Still plenty of time. He heads to the living room to conduct a *Call of Duty* training session – the final *Call of Duty* training session – before showering and changing into his skin. Apricot light hums on the carpet. Across the street, in the sun, someone walks a German shepherd. He boots up the PlayStation, picks up the controller. Recently he has been averaging 90 to 95 per cent headshots. Today he wants more: 98, even 99 per cent. Come on.

On the Oprah Winfrey Network YouTube channel, an 'Introduction to Islam' video was uploaded this morning. He switches to his Princess Fahmida sock account, clicks 'add a public comment', enters the Dropbox link to 'The Future is Ours' and, throat tightening, stares at the screen.

Quarter past two. It will now be open. He has made the ECA stack, set a new record in his aiming drill, showered and changed into his operator skin. There's no reason to wait.

He bashes the 'enter' key. Loading circle. Loading circle. Loading circle . . .

Done. The fightback is underway. Once he has posted the link in a dozen or so more funny locations across YouTube, Facebook, Instagram and Twitter, he will set out.

It is underway. It really is underway.

David navigates to #operations and leaves a cryptic message to build expectation.

BGMP5R1A Today at 12:25
London. Soon.

Who will be the one to find 'The Future is Ours' and exuberantly share it in the server? Supreme Commander RitterKreuz? General LordofKek? Runningngunning? Dysruptz? Corey?

A text, Mum. 'Do you want to come round at 6 tonight? I'll have everything ready.' He smirks. The silly Nowruz meal. He is the one truly celebrating it. 'Sure. Happy Nowruz!'

As soon as the message shows as delivered, he turns on airplane mode, to ensure he is not distracted by a surge of notifications. WOTAN will soon be a hive of activity.

Right. 'Here goes,' he announces, to no one, and then grimaces his way through the ECA stack, which tastes god-awful, shakes his head and scrapes tongue across teeth. It had better work.

Setting the glass on the desk, he realises that this is how the police will find his room. There are clothes everywhere and three days' worth of dirty dishes. A garlic whiff too: that bloody Dolmio sauce. He jams open the window and spits out – his mouth still coiny from the ECA stack. He swallows with labour. Now the Karl posters attract his attention. The *Uncut* one. The Q one. The *Kerrang!* one. The special-edition vinyl one. He swears and shreds them from the walls.

EASTERN AVENUE CRACKLES WITH LIFE. As he troops past them, a squashed Diet Coke can, a broken plastic fork and a small whisky bottle on a window ledge all jingle a silvery white. Mr Chicken & Pizza's blue is bluer than before. Five Star Cars' red is redder. Even Celebrity Curry's black is blacker. The ECA stack has sharpened his senses. A white BT OpenReach van pulls up and parks at The Queens, a grotty pub that shows football games and hosts shit tribute acts, such as Rob-B-Williams. Outside Barber King, a Muslim surveys the street, hands clasped behind his back.

David pads his inside pocket. The Baikal is still there. He has been obsessively, irrationally, checking every few seconds. It is heavy, fucking heavy. Of course it is still there. He licks his lips, wishing he had brought a bottle of water with him. He could pop into a newsagent's and buy one, but performing such a mundane task mid-mission would feel wrong. AJ Launderette's yellow dazzles.

Never has he felt this energetic. He pads his inside pocket. It's still there.

Gah. A red light. Again. There is so much waiting – waiting, waiting, waiting. He sponges sweat from his forehead with the back of his hand. To his left, an Aryan with AirPods and a navy blue Fjällräven backpack. To his right, another Aryan kneeling and cleaning white sneakers with a wet wipe. The waiting is unendurable. Green. Finally. He proceeds up Eastern Avenue.

By now someone might have found 'The Future is Ours' and shared it in the server. His mind fizzes with imagined messages. *Is the fightback on? really on? Who is our UK hero? You heard anything @BGMP5R1A? YES HERE WE GO. It's coming for those beetles!* Supreme Commander RitterKreuz will bestow an honorary title on him. New Rekruts will worship him. Saint BGMP5R1A.

TARIQ'S GRILL.

'EAT IN TAKEAWAY HALAL'.

A4 sheets blazoning 'DRIVER WANTED' and 'STAFF WANTED' are pinned up on the glass. Below them gleam images of meals and a lime-green-and-black hygiene badge.

Across the narrow street, in front of a house separated into flats, David stares, ear canals thumping. Tariq's Grill sits below more flats – between Diamond Shisha, which only opens at five, and what used to be Terry & Co. Estate Agents but is now empty, except for a stepladder.

Smith Street is mostly residential: few passing cars, few pedestrians.

There are two customers in Tariq's Grill, teenagers, wearing hoodies and shorts, sitting in the window seats, eating their vile, vile, vile halal meat, as well as an old worker behind the counter. Hassan's father? Maybe. Hassan is nowhere to be seen. But that's fine. Three is respectable, a Killstreak. Besides, more targets and David might be overpowered – stabbed? – while executing the mission. These are filthy Muslims, after all. They probably have knives on them. He should commence soon, before someone else enters. He takes a step forward, but swiftly steps back.

This is huge, huge for him, huge for his people. Without exception, Captain Garrett has a pre-mission cigar. He should have a pre-mission cigarette. He fumbles one out of his pocket.

Lighting it, he examines his hands – shaky no more. The ECA stack is working.

A long toke. He closes his eyes. The fightback will be underway. Then, an Aryan hero, in prison he will relax: watch daytime TV, read books, play pool, savour visits from Dad. There will be a vulnerable prisoners' wing, so, should the place be crawling with Muslims, he will request to be moved to the vulnerable prisoners' wing, away from them. The Aryan guards will ensure his safety. It will be fine. And after his release he will go straight to a Dr Martens store and buy red laces.

He mouths fragments from tweets he read in the morning. *Never forget Chappe Gallery. Sharia law has no place in a civilised society.* A memorable cigarette, this. A memorable cigarette. He opens his eyes and takes a final toke. It's now or never – and never is impossible. The replacement is at a late stage.

He is ready. Will of the Aryan Nation.

Having checked the windows of the flats above the businesses and those of the parked cars and then scanned the pavement left, right, one last time – the majority of the residents should be at work – he crosses the street and marches towards Tariq's Grill. The old Muslim smiles at him.

Hassan

'HEY, WHAT'S UP, EVERYONE? Welcome to the stream. How are you all doing? Is anyone as nervous as I am? What a day. West Ham v Watford, a relegation six-pointer if ever there was one. God. Is anyone as nervous as I am? Let's get a roll call going. Silent Alarm, what's up? Alter Ego, what's up? Abir, thanks for the four months, man. CKS, what's up? Alygatyr, what's up? JaySUFC, what's up? Hope you're supporting us tonight. Salty Panda, thanks for the two months. Dakota, what's up?'

Alter Ego **gd luck tonight Hazza Im United till I die but will be watching on Sky Sports and supporting you guys tonight. Never really liked Watford anyway stupid wasp kits haha**

Alygatyr **dw you got this don't stress it**

Asianmoon123 **Im fucking bricking it already we NEED to win**

JaySUFC **Of course. Hammers are my second team. Loads of my mates have season tickets. You going tonight?**

Salty Panda **What are your thoughts on this Rainbow Laces thing?**

Silent Alarm **Who u wanna pack today?**

CKS **Hey man u know whether they've nerfed the finesse shot? cant score one for shit anymore haha**

'Cheers, Alter Ego. Appreciate it, man.' He thumps the badge on his West Ham shirt. 'Claret and blue. Claret and blue. The only colours a shirt should be. Cheers, Alygatyr. Yep, Asianmoon. Agreed. We need to win. I don't see a draw being enough for us, not with the games we have coming up. Nice one, Jay. Always had a soft spot for Southend United. I got a guided tour of Roots Hall once. Enjoyed it. Am I going tonight?' A grin. 'Yep and I'll be watching from a VIP hospitality box, for a reason I hope to be able to share soon. I wish I could say more now, but . . .' He mimes zipping his mouth shut – and then looks over to the window. Even with his headset on, it is impossible to ignore the sound of sirens. There must be five or six police cars passing. Another fucking stabbing probably. He stirs in his gaming chair. 'Apologies if you can hear the sirens in the background, guys. That's London, even early afternoon. Anyway. Nice one on bringing that up, Salty Panda. I think Rainbow Laces is a great campaign from the Premier League and Stonewall. A lot of work still needs to be done to combat homophobia in dressing rooms and stadiums, and the more awareness that can be raised the better. Plus, it's just visually cool, seeing every player wearing rainbow laces. So. Yeah. It has my support. Ah, Silent Alarm, you know the answer to that, bro. R9. Hmm. I haven't read anything about finesse shots being nerfed – there have been no new EA patch notes – but I'll see how they feel today.'

Siuuuuu **Hey hey just joined looking forward to another sick stream**

Salty Panda **Legend, Hazza. I'm a fan of the campaign too. I ordered some laces for my sunday league games haha from here: https://stonewalluk.myshopify.com/products/rainbow-laces-all**

Silent Alarm **You & R9 really hope it happens soon lol. Also VIP hospitality box tonight? Get in! Love to see it, mate.**

Aldébaran **wd u want to represent England at the FIFAe World Cup?**

'Thanks for tuning in, Siuuuuu. Good on you, Salty. I'll pick some up too. Silent, it'll happen. And cheers. As I said, I wish I could say more about the situ with the hospitality box. Hopefully soon. Of course, I'd love to represent England at the FIFAe World Cup, Aldébaran, love to. Hey, would that make me the first Muslim eLion? I think so? Anyone know? That'd be ace.' He smirks. 'I shouldn't be looking past the FGS Qualifiers and Play-offs yet though . . . And on that note let's get practising.'

He opens TikTok, intending to share some excerpts from the stream and a short 'I'm forever blowing bubbles' rendition. His next posts will be from the Olympic Stadium – the Olympic Stadium. On his For You section, a video plays of a lower-league keeper making an outstanding penalty save. Impressive. As a reflex response, he flicks up and lets more videos play: 'me waking up at 7am when I'm used to getting up at 12pm' and 'this man woke up and decided to be magic johnson' and 'everyone after opening their OTW pack' – and then one he lingers on, 'TERROR ATTACK?!?' at the top and 'be careful everyone' at the bottom. 'Guys,' the person filming remarks. 'Something has happened in London, in the UK. There's police everywhere here, everywhere. I think there might have been a terror attack or something. Look.' He shows the street behind him. Hassan goes numb – numb all over. Newbury Park. He knows the street. It's only a few minutes from the restaurant. 'Check out the police cordons. I can't get closer than this but a few hundred metres away something serious has happened.' Next video: 'This might be my last dance at Tesco'.

He scrambles to check Twitter. Fuck. #newburypark is trending. @mickallen90: 'anyone know wtf is going down in #newburypark? so many coppers everywhere.' @redbridgebenali: 'hearing news there may have been a knife attack in the Sports Direct in #newburypark keep away in case.' @yellowlantern18: 'jst me who heard gun shots in #newburypark????' @AdilParihar: 'loads and loads of police out in #newburypark but dont think anything has actually happened lol. attempted drugs raid?' Gobs of crazy, contradictory rumours.

He curses, hoping for this to be nothing more than a bomb hoax. And why today – why today? It's three thirty. He wants to be at the Olympic Stadium by five. TFL might shut the Tube station and re-route buses away from the area, so he should leave now. Dad should leave the restaurant too.

Jacket, 1865 retro scarf, backpack – check.

Having darted downstairs, he jams on his trainers. Mum is doing an interview in Euston. She said she'd be back by four to wish him luck, but waiting for her is now too risky. There is no way he is turning up late.

He leaves, calls Dad. Ringing. Ringing. Ringing.

'Come on. Pick up.'

David

'STAY AWAY' AND 'WHAT HAPPENED?' and 'stay away' and 'what—' and 'stay away', and on and on. While the clamour in the street grows David grips his gun, glaring at the old Muslim. 'Someone help' and 'fucking call them' and 'they're coming' and 'where are they?', and on and on. The soles of his boots are sticky and crunchy: blood, glass. The laces splashed with Pop Tart, lumps of vomit.

Just metres away lie the two teenagers, bleeding out.

The uncomprehending fear. The pleas. He stood there, threatening to shoot, calling them what they were, filthy Muslims, filthy fucking Muslims. But he couldn't pull the trigger.

Sensing weakness, they rushed him.

It was only as they neared that he managed to pull it.

And then, eyes closed, he pulled it again and again and again.

Gurgling sounds escape the throat of the teenager with the fuzzy black beard. A shudder of his white Adidas shoe and at long last it is over: his right hand slips into the swamp of blood he has become, and his jaw slips with it. The final moments of his life were spent holding it in place.

The other teenager spasms, a bubbling hole in his neck, pulp for palms.

'Get out of here' and 'run' and 'is he still there?' and 'I called them' and the incessant buzzing of the fridge. Merging with the odours of cabbage and onion and chilli sauce are those of piss, shit. Between retches, David reminds himself that there was no choice, that it was necessary, that the replacement must be stopped. He is a twenty-first-century Aryan knight.

'Please,' the old Muslim begs, cowering behind the serve-over counter in a West Ham shirt stained with sweat, hands raised in surrender. 'Please.'

'Shut up,' David says, a tremor in his voice, standing near the entrance, as far from his kills as possible. He is a twenty-first-century Aryan knight, a twenty-first-century Aryan knight, a twenty-first-century Aryan knight, a twenty-first-century Aryan knight.

'Please.'

'Shut up!'

The police will arrive soon, any minute, maybe any second. He keeps looking over his shoulder. He needs to hurry and complete the Killstreak. He can't miss out on a Killstreak. Dizzy, nauseous, but so close. To strengthen his resolve, he says: 'Remember Chappe Gallery?'

'What?'

'Remember Chappe Gallery?'

'Please.'

'Well?'

'Please.'

'Where's . . . Where's Allah now?'

He is a twenty-first-century Aryan knight, a twenty-first-century Aryan knight, a twenty-first-century Aryan knight, a twenty-first-century Aryan knight.

'Hey!'

Jolting, David turns.

'Hey! Oi! You! Prick.'

The first-floor flat opposite. A baseball cap. Someone is leaning out of the window. As David considers whether to respond, a bottle strikes the pavement, and shards spark his way.

'You like that?' A cockney voice. 'You like that, Paki?'

Paki? Does he think David is some scummy jihadi?

‘I’m on your team!’ he corrects him. ‘I’m Aryan!’

‘You’re bloody well not. I saw you earlier. Paki cunt.’ David seizes up. ‘Yeah! You heard me. I saw you below my flat earlier. I thought, the fuck is that Paki up to? And then I clocked everything. You little piece of shit. Killing people. Stop fucking up this country.’

Sirens. The police. The police are close.

David looks at the old Muslim.

‘Please.’

‘Don’t move,’ David commands him. ‘Don’t move.’

There is blood everywhere. The play of sunlight on shredded skin. The bearded teenager is motionless, but the other one is still spasming.

A shiver. David pivots back to the flat. ‘I’m English! I’m English-Iranian! I’m Aryan!’

Doors slamming shut.

‘That’s a good one!’

Officers in the street. ‘Drop the gun!’

Three of them. Four. Five.

‘Drop the gun!’

‘Drop the gun!’

He ignores them, wondering what is wrong with his teammate, why he doesn’t get it.

‘Listen to me! I’m not a jihadi. I’m Aryan! This is the Aryan fightback!’

‘You’re a Paki. That’s what you are!’

Swinging round to the flat, an officer screams: ‘Move away from the window!’ The others keep their weapons trained on David. ‘Drop the gun!’ ‘Drop the gun!’ ‘Drop the gun now!’

How can he not get it?

‘Drop the gun now!’

He is no longer thinking straight. The ECA stack was too strong. Nothing now matters more to him than clearing this up. He has experienced hell for his fellow Aryans.

Having used his wrist to wipe wet sick from his chin, he shouts: ‘Listen to me! I’m Aryan! I’m English-Iranian! I’m Aryan.’

'Drop the gun now!'

'Drop the gun now!'

No response from his teammate. He glances back at the old Muslim, who is still cowering behind the counter. Then advances into the street, aiming up at the window.

'Drop the gun now!' 'Drop the gun now!'

He sees his teammate clearly. His teammate sees him clearly.

'Look! I'm white. Do you understand? I'm white. I'm Aryan! We—'

'Paki!'

Unable to resist, he tightens his finger on the trigger.

Gunshots – and shockwaves in his chest. Then a burning sensation, a strange burning sensation, as if he were being poked with a needle, not stabbed, but repeatedly, mercilessly poked.

He reels backwards and sees—

There is blood streaking out. The sensation fizzes through his body. He stands, stands, stands, and then, feeling faint, collapses, his Dr Martens landing centimetres away from the teenagers' shoes. The menu signs glow blue. A ceiling fan whirrs. He is losing a lot of blood: too much blood.

He recognises how important it is to keep his eyes open, to keep them open. But, God, it is hard. A high-pitched ringing noise swells inside his head.

A fog of commands from the officers, shrieks from somewhere.

'You're wrong,' he mumbles, resting his head stickily on his right hand. 'I'm Aryan.' More commands. More shrieks. 'I'm Aryan.' He squirms. The ringing. God. The ringing. His chest is mushily open. It feels numb, numb and warm, nothing more. 'We're Aryan.' But the ringing—

He needs to stop it. He needs to stop the ringing.

He squeezes his eyes shut.

A Brighter Future @abrighterfutureforuk 5s
Terrorist attack in #newburypark. Many casualties. Thanks #islam

Jenny Knowles @JennyKnowles86 8s
EVERYONE PLS STOP SPECULATING STOP STEREOTYPING JUST STOP AND WAIT FOR MORE INFORMATION #newburypark

Me Nobody Else @menotnobodyelse 11s
Fuck me! Crazy shit happening in #newburypark rn!!!! Gunshots and everything

Mostly Harmless Loo Loo @mostlyharmless_here4thememes 13s
The UK has been struck by the religion of peace again. But just wait for the response from the msm: 'mental health issues''not jump to conclusions''motives not known''no evidence to suggest this is a terrorist attack' #newburypark

Samantha Rowe #FuckRacism @SamanthaRowe03 19s
My thoughts and prayers to all those affected by the incident in #newburypark x

Jessica Williams @tessellatewithme 21s
Disgusting for people on here to be willing the shooter to be Muslim or far right. Regardless this is an act of terror on our streets and people have died. Quit the point-scoring, Twitter. Sending lots of love to you London #newburypark #uk

Rosa Blackwell @Rosa_Blackwell 24s
Rumours coming in that the shooter shouted that he was Aryan #newburypark #farright #farright #nationalism

Left Right Behind @MrLeftRightBehind 27s
This country is so fucked up and no one is willing to address

anything. London borough of Redbridge has one of the highest Muslim populations in the UK. No surprise when this happens #newburypark #islam #diversity

Danny England @DannyEnglandDifferentOpinions 35s
My mate lives in #newburypark and heard an exchange between the shooter and a member of the public. The shooter shouted Allah Akbar several times. #islam

Gavin Bartholomew @GavinBartholomew1988 40s
Eyewitnesses say that there is 'total carnage' and a 'bloodbath' in #newburypark #uk

Well Do You? @YouWillBelieveUsSoon 49s
Enjoy your diversity London! #newburypark #islam #london #uk

Charlie Spurs @Spurs4Life_Charlie 54s
Hearing two casualties in #newburypark terror attack. Police shot shooter thank fuck

Acknowledgements

Thank you to Vesna Goldsworthy for the Ph.D. supervision that shaped this novel. Your feedback and guidance have been invaluable. I would always look forward to our Turnham Green coffees. Thank you to Thomas Karshan for challenging me to think about literature in new ways and continuing to inspire me. You are the best teacher I have ever had and I'm grateful to now count you as a friend. Thank you to my incredible agent, Holly Faulks, for believing in me and making this a reality. Thank you to my superb editor, Luke Brown, for understanding exactly what I wanted to do with this novel and teasing out its potential. Thank you to my copy editor, Sarah Day, for the incisive suggestions. Thank you to Jack Smyth and Steve Panton for the brilliant cover. Thank you to Robert Greer, Lily Evans, Emily Frisella, Mehar Anaokar, Anna-Marie Fitzgerald and everyone else at Serpent's Tail for seeing this novel into the world. Thank you to Alexis Hercules for the endlessly enjoyable conversations on the craft of writing, the thousands of workshop texts exchanged, and the R+ trips, from Berlin to Budapest. Thank you to Django Wylie for the times spent listening to The Libertines, sitting on the hill at Glastonbury, and chatting about books, whether over late-night falafel wraps in Haggerston or nut pittas in Bergen. Thank you to Vishnu Papineni and Matthew Pengilly for carrying me to Warzone Ws. Thank you to Sarah Young for the evenings at BYOBs on

Kingsland Road. Thank you to Ashley Hickson-Lovence, Ferdia Lennon, John Patrick McHugh, Helen Rye, Houman Barekat, Kielan Thompson, Mark Stacey, Sophie Donnelly and Tom Lake for the friendship and encouragement. Thank you to Rainer for taking me to see Slipknot at the London Arena in 2002 and all the hours spent practising Pro Evolution Soccer and participating in clan wars. Thank you to Elke for a lifetime of support. Thank you to Aga for transforming every day with your warmth, intelligence, enthusiasm, humour and love and for all the discussions about social media and extremism that helped me to write this novel.